Kingmaker

A P Bateman

For Clair, thank you for all your support

Also by A P Bateman

Stone Cold

DI Grant

Vice

Taken

Standalone Novel

Never Go Back

Short Stories

The Perfect Murder?

Atonement

Further details of these titles can be found at:

www.apbateman.com

Chapter One
Monaco, nineteen years ago...

I t was a warm evening with the Mediterranean sounds and smells that went with it. Crickets and cicadas hummed with an electric pulse that pierced the night, and the heady scent of jasmine, rosemary and thyme permeated through the scented pines. Ignoring all of this, standing in the welcome sanctuary of shadows from the streetlamps, King's grip tightened on the chequered walnut grips of the 9mm Browning in his hand. Hammer cocked, safety off, his finger hovering tentatively near the trigger. Exiled president Lucky Man Jonathon Mugabe was sleeping soundly in his villa. Crates of Krug and Cristal champagne and a bevy of beautiful, and rather expensive prostitutes had been delivered to the property earlier in the afternoon, all courtesy of the UK taxpayer.

King watched the three men keeping to the long shadows on the opposite side of the street. At first, they had appeared to be casually ambling up the hill from town. Three men returning from an extravagant and hedonistic night in the bars, clubs and casinos below. But as they approached the entrance to the villa, their demeanour changed. Suddenly they had purpose. "Eyes on. Three men. IC-three," King said quietly into his throat mic using the IC ethnicity code for black. He added, "Moving like they have military training."

"Have that, King. Wait out." King watched the three men scouting the front gates. There were motion sensors inside the grounds and CCTV cameras on the gates. Lucky Man Jonathon Mugabe had his own security team, but they would be too drunk, too stoned and too busy getting laid to be up to the task. The earpiece chirped into life, the brash Scotsman's voice gravelly and sharp in his ear. *"Weapons?"*

"No visual," King said quietly, the voice activated microphone relaying his hushed reply. "Wait... One of the men has drawn a short," he added, using their own term for a handgun. Short for pistols; long for rifles.

"And the others?"

"One is tampering with the gate control, the other is watching the street," King replied. "The lookout has drawn a short now, too."

"Have that, wait out..." King's heart was hammering against his chest. His right hand had started to shake. He had been here before. Another time, another place, but the sensation was the same. The seconds before he would be ordered to kill. He briefly wondered who Stewart was now talking to. Getting the i's dotted and the t's crossed. A quiet office in Whitehall. The Prime Minister's office perhaps. But more likely an office in the River House on a floor otherwise in darkness. One of MI6's mandarins working late and using a secure line. What paperwork would be kept? How many times had the mandarin made a decision that would set a man like King to work and ultimately end the life of another? The earpiece rasped into life again. *"King, we have confirmation. Operation is a go. Go, go, go...!"*

There was no time for over thinking it. He had trained for this countless times. King stepped out of the shadows and walked calmly and steadily across the road. He shot the first man in the back of the head. Work smarter, not harder. One down, two to go. The man watching the street had been looking the wrong way. Bad for him, good for King. He had barely begun to turn when King double tapped him in the left side. The man working on the gates turned around and held up his hands in hesitant and hopeful surrender, but it wasn't going down like that. King had his orders and fired twice without giving the man's actions time to consider.

"No survivors, King..." Stewart's voice came through the earpiece, urgent and fatalistic. *"Don't fucking let me down..."*

King cursed as he pulled out the earpiece and stared at two of the men, who were both groaning and moving on the ground. No survivors... It was a simple order, but never for the person holding the gun. He looked around him, knowing that he did not have much time. The police would already be on their way. He looked back at the two men, then stepped closer and did what had to be done.

Chapter Two
Two days later

Peter Stewart was used to sparse meeting rooms and basic servings of instant tea and coffee, stewed and over-brewed in stainless steel air pump flasks. This room was one of a dozen ten by ten boxes with a table for six in the centre and a projector, white screen and somewhere to plug in a laptop at one end. The ubiquitous flasks of tea and coffee were on the opposite side of the room set out on a Formica table. There weren't even any plain digestive biscuits. A stark contrast to the opulence of the oak lined director's office with twenty-year old Haig whisky and Remy Martin brandy in cut crystal decanters and a seemingly inexhaustible supply of ice. Stewart never seemed to have those meetings anymore. He ran the deniable Special Operations Wing of the Secret Intelligence Service. A department that did not officially exist. The people at the very top enjoyed the distance and deniability by lack of association.

"Your operative did a good job down there."

"Thank you," Stewart replied warily. "It was a rushed

mission, the intel on the hit only came in that morning. As you know, we were both in London at the time."

"I thought your man wasn't going to cut it at one point. The ripples can still be felt from that IRA affair in France," Felicity Willmott said acidly. "It's never good when money disappears."

"It's never good when a liaison officer proves to be bent with another agenda. King put Ian Forsyth down. Okay, the asset took off with the money, but King should still be commended for his actions," Stewart replied sharply. "He's a damned good man."

"My, you've changed your tune since Angola and the Congo," she commented sardonically.

Stewart looked at her. She was a stern forty-something with wiry greyish brown hair pulled back in a severe bun. Behind her back she was known as one of the 'Emilies'. Emily was the Soviet name given in the sixties to women of a certain age who had married the British Secret Services instead of a husband, and whom they would target with thirty-something men who could wine and dine them with flattering conversation and who mirrored Adonis in looks. They would take them to bed and use pillow talk in the comfortable time which invariably ensued after sex, in a relaxed and unguarded state of intimacy. Emily had been the chosen name because its Russian equivalent was considered boring and suited the personality of a spinster in such a job. MI6 had labelled these men 'Ivans', and before long they were feeding the 'Emilies' with false information for their Russian lovers to send back to Moscow. However, in his mind, Felicity Willmott was a little past being a credible Emily. The years had not been kind to her, and nor had her acceptance of spinsterhood.

Beside Felicity Willmott sat Armstrong. He wore a navy pinstripe suit, and his hair was flecked with grey. Somewhat greyer than when Stewart had last seen him. "No doubt that operation in Angola and the Congo shaped him up somewhat," Armstrong added. "He's on good form now?"

He's not a fucking racehorse, thought Stewart. Instead, he said a little defensively, "I have no complaints." King had more than proved himself to Stewart and he no longer considered the man to be his understudy.

"Lucky Man Jonathon Mugabe now has a team of body-guards in place, courtesy of the Special Air Service." Felicity Willmott paused. "I'll be frank, Peter. The UK government can no longer foot the bill for the man's exile, his luxury villa, his fleet of cars, his predilection for the finer things in life, and I believe, some of the more sordid. And now, he has a team of eight bodyguards costing the UK taxpayer upwards of four-thousand pounds a week."

Armstrong nodded emphatically. "Yes, we need him to come good on our investment. We need his country's mineral reserves, and we need them soon. Now, with the dictator Mustafa in Burindi cosying up to the Russians and Chinese, we not only lose stability in the Central Africa region, but a guaranteed supply of oil. We have Angola with the OPEC deal, but we lost the DRC rights and that of Nigeria as well." He paused. "And the icing on the cake? Lithium. Huge amounts of it have been discovered in Burindi," he said holding up a slim folding Motorola mobile phone. "For these things. Everyone has a mobile now, and people want to have the latest as soon as it comes out. Britain needs to get into the lithium market. And we need to do it in a big way."

Stewart shrugged. "So, you finally want Mustafa out of Burindi?"

"Yes. Yesterday wouldn't be soon enough either," Armstrong replied with his trademark sardonic smugness. "And naturally, as we have paid for Lucky Man Jonathan Mugabe's exile, we will get our return on his country's mineral reserves."

"Well, he is indeed a *Lucky Man...*"

"Don't be facetious, Stewart," Felicity Willmott said admonishingly. "It's a different culture and a viable name in that region."

"Mustafa has an army," said Stewart without acknowledging the admonishment. "What do you want done?"

"If the coup d'état is a swift and decisive one, our intelligence shows that his army will switch over to support Lucky Man Jonathon. They switched once before. They're not a brave bunch by all accounts."

Stewart smiled. "I haven't known many cowardly Africans. They may not be well-trained or experienced, but I'm not sure we can so easily discount their bravery in battle." He paused. "But I get the sentiment. If you are going to kill a king, then you do it publicly and horribly and give the subjects reason not to seek retribution."

"Well, I'm sure you can work it out. That's what you do, so go and do it." Armstrong stood up indicating that the meeting was over. "Oh, and make sure nothing sticks to SIS or Her Majesty's Government."

"That's it?" Stewart asked incredulously.

"What else were you expecting?" Felicity Willmott asked curtly. "We don't want to know the details. I'm not even happy being a part of this meeting."

"Because you'll be denying it all later no doubt," said Stewart.

"No. Not if you don't give us a reason to. Because it will be a seamless transition of power and nothing is going to stick to us," Armstrong reiterated. "You have the green light, Stewart. Unlimited budget, unlimited remit. Just get it done as soon as possible."

Chapter Three
Heathrow Airport

"Fucking hell, three whole hours to kill!"

"Can't take deodorant on the plane, either."

"Or a fucking razor..." Stewart scowled. "Or a fucking washbag. Fucking Bin Laden, fucking nine-eleven. Now we have to arrive with stinking armpits and a furry mouth."

"Have another Scotch and stop bloody moaning," King said impatiently, glancing at his watch. "Jesus, I can't believe I've got three hours here with you and another seven or eight sitting next to you on the plane. For a man who's been about a dozen times round the world, you really are a terrible traveller."

Stewart scoffed. "The joke's on you, dickhead. It's thirty-eight hours with three stops..."

"You're kidding?" King stared at him incredulously. "Thirty-eight hours? Show me the bloody ticket."

"No, not kidding. Very much not kidding." He fished through the documents and handed King's ticket to him. "Ethiopia, Central African Republic, and then Burindi."

"Oh, bloody hell, I need a drink now..."

9

Stewart laughed. "Bin Laden is going to create more revenue for airports now that check-in is three hours before boarding time. There's a bar right above us," he said. "Let's just get pissed and worry about everything later."

"Well, it's a plan, I suppose."

King followed Stewart up the steps, and they took a seat at the airport's idea of a typical London pub. It was as tragic as it sounded with polished horse brasses, photographs of London taxis and double decker buses and monochrome prints of the docklands back when they were working docks and shipyards, and not a celebration of glass and chrome and redbrick apartments for yuppies and Arab business-men. Stewart ordered two shots of Jack Daniels and two pints of lager. When the drinks arrived, he ceremoniously took a sip from his pint, dropped the shot glass into the lager and grinned. "Depth charger, my lad. It's the only way to survive air travel."

King followed suit, suddenly wishing he'd suggested a cup of tea instead. But he found himself thinking of the long flight and thought - *what the hell?* The drink was smoother than he expected, and Stewart was already ordering another round.

"What's the job?" King asked.

"Just a recce for now," replied Stewart. "We're freelance hacks and we're scouting out a story for National Geographic. You're the photographer. Hence the camera equipment in the hold."

"OK."

"It's all equipment you're previously worked with, so you will be competent talking about it or demonstrating it to curious customs officers, or anyone else for that matter."

"Who?"

"Burindi's secret police."

"Right," said King. "You're not selling it to me."

"Well, it's a good job I don't have to."

"Fair enough," King replied, reminded again that he was owned by MI6 and would be for the foreseeable future. "So, if it's for National Geographic, what's the brief? Nature photographers or reporting on political corruption?"

"That would be too controversial," Stewart scoffed. "No, it's nature."

"And the job?"

"Recon."

"Right."

"You don't sound convinced."

"We're going to Burindi. I just killed three men who were going to kill the deposed president of Burindi. So, it's a recon job ahead of a coup?"

"The boy's connecting the dots. My work here is almost done."

"Funny." King paused, dealing with half of his drink, which was becoming worryingly more often. He had no doubt it was because of the company he kept. "So, we're going to get Lucky Man Jonathon Mugabe reinstated."

"Yes."

"That certainly sounds easier said than done."

"Son, you have no idea." Stewart dropped another depth charge and downed half of his second pint. He wiped the foam from his lips with the back of his hand and stared back at King. "Mustafa has a loyal bodyguard team around him called the Republican Guard."

"Original."

"Dictators aren't the most imaginative of people." Stewart paused. "To take down the man, we must take down the team. Like dominoes. If we hit hard and fast, then hopefully..." Stewart scoffed at the daunting task ahead of them, then swiftly finished his pint. "… hopefully, his soldiers will see the bigger picture and live long enough to serve another despot."

"What are we doing our cover story on?"

"Birds."

"Birds?"

Stewart reached into his carry-on and fished out a book. "Some light reading for you on the flight." He handed the book to King and smiled. "I read that there is a new subspecies of grey parrot, often called the Congo parrot, that has started hunting small birds. I thought it would be a good cover to investigate this." He paused. "You'd better get reading up on the subject."

"What do parrots normally eat?"

"Berries, seeds and nuts."

King nodded. "Vegan diets are frustrating, even for parrots…"

Stewart smiled. "You're the photographer," he said. "It's better you know your way around the equipment, and it's nothing you haven't used on surveillance jobs before but go through the kit, so you know the makes and models. Get some background reading in on the birds, the area and other flora and fauna. Leave the detailed ornithology, the Latin names and subspecies to me. I've been working on this cover for months now."

King frowned. "But I thought you only got the order yesterday?"

Stewart grinned, making no effort to hide his smugness. "This was always on the cards, so I started putting things in place months ago. I even have an asset in the region who is making his way to Burindi as we speak."

Chapter Four
Casino de Monte-Carlo, Monaco

Lucky Man Jonathon Mugabe put down his cutlery and smiled. The cutlery was gold-plated with ornate handles that mirrored the swirls and flowers in the ceiling. "You like the lamb, my friend? The herb crust is not too spicy, no?"

"It is delicious."

Lucky Man nodded approvingly. He had chosen the filet mignon with sauce bordelaise. One of the constant dishes at *Le Train Bleu*, the art deco carriage restaurant overlooking the famed Casino Square, where every year crowds flocked on balconies to watch the Formula 1 and where people won or lost fortunes every day in the casino. They had earlier ordered the caviar, but whereas Lucky Man Jonathon had ordered his caviar with the ubiquitous blinis, the Russian had chosen a fluffy baked potato and sour cream to accompany his €150 starter. The Russian had explained that was how people from his region in the Urals ate their caviar, and that caviar had not been considered a luxury in his childhood, but a staple commodity as plentiful as pork belly. He had seemed most impressed that the chef had known this and had made the baked potato one of the options, along with toast for the British and crackers for their American diners.

"Are you in the mood to win some money?"

The Russian smiled. "Always."

"Ah! We shall lose some as well, I have no doubt!" Mugabe smiled. "But losing can be fun, too. It all depends upon whose money you play with!"

The Russian nodded knowingly. "The British have been good to you?"

Lucky Man Jonathon nodded emphatically and spoke through his mouthful. "Yes, yes. Very good. But they put many stipulations on our relationship. You do not do that with friends."

"Like what, exactly?"

"Trade, of course," the big African replied. "I am an exiled leader. A democratically elected leader." He paused, and the Russian tried hard not to betray himself through his expression. If there was one thing for certain with the exiled leader, it was that his election had been far from a democratic process. It had been blatantly fixed, and voters had been intimidated relentlessly and denied a recount. He had stolen the election from Desmond Lambadi, the former teacher who had the support of his fellow Burindis and whose promises looked the most credible and substantial on the entire African continent since Nelson Mandela had won his landslide election. Desmond Lambadi was rumoured to be imprisoned in Burindi, and his situation had not changed since Mustafa's far left government had forced out Lucky Man Jonathon Mugabe after an eight-year dictatorship. Far from a bloodless coup, Mugabe had fled with much of the nation's wealth and spent time in Italy, Switzerland and the South of France before settling in the principality of Monaco a year ago. "When I return to Burindi as leader, it will be ordained by God as much as the British. It is fate. I am the rightful leader, and I will not be beholden to the British and simply hand over my country's mineral rights. They will have to bid for them like anybody else. Like your government, for instance. Or the Americans."

The Russian smiled, knowing that a deal with the British was in place and that reneging on that would not be so easy as the mad man opposite him believed. "The Americans do not concern themselves with Africa," he said condemnably. "They cosy up to the camel fuckers in the Middle East. Africa is too volatile for them. And it's true, the British will give you what they want, but they will take much in return. That is the British way. Programmed over centuries in imperialistic colonisation. Once you give them what they want, you will be under their control forever."

"And Russia will take less?" Lucky Man Jonathon asked incredulously.

"Russia wants friends and allies on the African continent." He paused. "And our current leader doesn't concern himself with the niceties of diplomacy. When he wants something, he takes it. Like Chechnya, for instance. He has, as does his inner circle, eyes on the Ukraine. He will make his move when the world suspects he has given up on the idea. That is Russia's way. The world is a complex game of chess that other world leaders were not invited to. Instead, they play checkers."

"But Mustafa is your friend," Lucky Man Jonathon ventured.

The Russian shrugged benignly. "Mustafa courts the Chinese. He wants roads and infrastructure and cheap vehicles and all the substandard crap that China floods the market with and has been doing in Africa and Cuba for years. Before he knows what is happening, China will have another province under its thumb."

"And you will help get me back in power?"

The Russian smiled sagely. "We'll let the British do that. They can risk the backlash of the world's media and charities if it goes wrong. However, once you have gained power, we will supply you with weapons, equipment and training to make sure that a coup will not happen again in your lifetime. We will build your roads and we will help with your country's infrastructure, for a fifty-percent share in your lithium, cobalt and oil."

"And the other fifty-percent will be mine?"

"It will belong to your country," the Russian corrected him. "How you divide it is up to you."

"Mine, or my country's?" Lucky Man Jonathon beamed a broad smile baring a full set of brilliant white, oversized teeth. "It is the same thing, my friend. It is the same thing..."

Chapter Five
London

"Who was the SAS officer?"

"A lieutenant Peter Redwood."

"Good man?"

"Clean as a whistle. As you know army officers serve only a four-year detachment in the Special Air Service. Occasionally an officer is invited back. He's already been earmarked to return once he is promoted to captain. After that, an officer can serve out the rest of their career in the regiment."

"Alright, alright, I didn't want chapter and verse," Armstrong said testily. "I just wanted to know if the intel would be reliable."

"He's the team leader on the eight-man protection detail shadowing that shit Mugabe after the failed assassination attempt. Should have let them pass, I reckon."

Armstrong looked at head of the Western Europe desk. "That *shit* Mugabe is set to make the country a hell of a lot wealthier. And you gather and analyse intelligence, your reckoning on this matter is not required."

Unperturbed, the desk chief smirked. "It will make a few people wealthier. Some politicians, some executives, some hedge fund managers. But not the British public."

"Oh, grow up, Simmons. Britain will benefit from any deal we broker with Lucky Man Jonathon Mugabe." He paused, flicking through the transcript of Bob Simmons' and Lieutenant Peter Redwood's telephone conversation. "Which will make this revelation all the more worrying to the powers that be."

"Lucky Man Jonathon Mugabe must be either an idiot or unbelievably arrogant. To not factor in that his new security detail, supplied by us I may add, might become suspicious."

Armstrong shrugged. "He's cut from a different cloth, I suppose. His bodyguards were hired muscle. They did what they were told and when the man dined with company, they waited outside, or left just one of them in the bar. He did not assume for one moment that we provided him with the best bodyguards in the business, but in doing so, we also put spies in his camp." He paused. "And this Redwood fellow is certain that his dinner guest was Russian?"

"Absolutely. He said they were talking conspiratorially, and the dinner had an air of celebration to it."

"The treacherous bastard." Armstrong shook his head. "And wining and dining the opposition on our expense account to boot. Outrageous!"

"We knew that he was an election cheat when we got in bed with him," Simmons countered. "He's a dictator. And when you lie down with dogs, you expect to catch fleas."

Armstrong stood up, the expansive desk still between them, but the gesture wasn't lost on Simmons, who nodded and headed for the door. He watched the section chief as he left, making certain the man had closed the door behind him. "Shit," he said to himself quietly. "What a bloody mess..."

Chapter Six
Burindi, Central Africa

The air was thick with humidity, the heat enveloping them like an open furnace door. King's shirt was already soaked, and Stewart had been right about his armpits and furry mouth. They had cleared customs, but not without an 'airport tax' on their camera equipment which was paid in cash and went in the official's top pocket with no offer of a receipt. Welcome to Africa.

"Stay alert, King," Stewart said as they entered the throng of people outside the airport. Taxi drivers and baggage handlers touted loudly for work, while little boys no older than eight slipped their hands into empty pockets hoping for a score. King had stashed his cash in a money belt and his passport and documents were in the thigh pocket of his cargoes with a zipper. Even so, the boys made a three-pronged attack, the first two taking turns to pull open the zipper as they walked past and the third reaching inside. Stewart clipped a child around the ear with the back of his hand and told him in no uncertain terms what would happen if they hung around.

"Gotta be tough on these little street urchins, King. All smiles and laughter, but they'd rob you soon as look at you." King nodded, but he also remembered what it had been like to be hungry as a child, and as they made their way to the car-hire company offices, King fished out a few hundred Burindi pounds totalling no more than five US dollars, but more than an adult's daily wage, and dropped them at their feet, where the children rugby scrummed and fought for the notes, all their Christmases coming at once.

"I wonder where the girls are?" King mused.

"Over there," Stewart said, pointing to a quieter corner, where a man was talking to a girl no older than eleven. He looked around nervously, then followed the girl down an alleyway. "Childhood ends all too young out here."

King could still hear Stewart commenting on the state of Africa when he crossed the road and followed the man down the alley. He heard Stewart call his name but ignored him and jogged to speed up. The man had his trousers around his ankles and was still looking around nervously when he saw King and bent to pull them back up. The girl was on her knees. King lunged and punched the man in his right kidney, and he howled as he fell to his knees, his trousers still around his ankles. King kicked the man in his ribs repeatedly, blind rage taking hold of him, but it was his sister's face he saw as he did it. In a cold, damp basement beside stinking wheelie bins, surrounded by roadmen in filthy tracksuits, their private parts exposed and in a state of arousal, with two of the youths' holding knives should his sister stop, threatening to 'cut her tits off'. King had never felt so helpless, pinned to the floor by a half dozen roadmen and forced to watch. He had never felt more vulnerable or ashamed, and afterwards, while his sister had sobbed in the corner, each of them had piled in and kicked and beaten King to a pulp.

"King! Stop!" Stewart hollered at him as he caught up with him and tried to drag him off. King managed a few more kicks, then staggered and Stewart pushed him up against a concrete wall emblazoned with anti-government graffiti. "For fuck's sake man!" King looked down at the man, who was groaning and clutching his shattered ribcage. The girl was squatting on the ground, her arms linked around her knees sobbing. "Fucking hell, King. What were you thinking?"

"I was saving her from a nonce..."

"You've cost her a fucking meal, more like," Stewart said coldly. "This is Africa, my friend. This shit goes on and people don't go hungry because of it."

King knew it went on. And not just in Africa. He looked at the girl as he took out a substantial wad of notes and dropped them in her lap. He said nothing as he turned and walked back down the alleyway.

"Sorry," he said quietly.

"That was bloody hardcore," Stewart commented, walking beside him and adjusting the bag so that it rested squarely on his shoulder. "You lost control."

"I know," he replied. He wasn't proud. It was a loss of control that had put him prison. Since his training, he had felt in control of his emotions, but he supposed it was down to a trigger point. Seeing the young girl with the pervert had triggered memories from his youth. The gangbang of his sister, his mother on the game to feed her drug habit. There was still so much buried within, and sometimes it scared him that it could manifest its way into a violent release. Like a pressure valve. "It won't happen again," he assured him.

"Fuck it," Stewart said.

"What?"

"That guy I thought was watching us earlier in the airport. He's back again." Stewart scowled. "Fucking hell, King. If anyone gets wind of that assault..."

"He was a filthy pervert, Stewart. Even in Burindi sex with a minor may be ignored, but it will certainly still be illegal and morally reprehensible. That sick bastard isn't coming forward to report that anytime soon."

"Well, you'd better hope so."

They had spotted their tail as they had left the stiflingly hot building which had been devoid of air conditioning. Instead, it had merely offered three slow-spinning ceiling fans to circulate the hot air. King could not have imagined anywhere hotter, until he had stepped out into the fierce sun. Burindi was in its dry season, and he knew from experience in the region that the wet season was only just around the corner, where it would rain seemingly endlessly for all but a few hours a day. The highlands of Burindi fed many rivers, that eventually flowed into Lake Victoria.

"Tall and thin, wearing gold rimmed glasses," Stewart said quietly to King as they walked.

"Yeah, I've got him."

"There'll be two of them. They always work in pairs."

"I haven't spotted the other one yet."

"Which is worrying..."

"There's plenty of time, Boss. Let's see what happens when we pick up the car."

The car hire company was a local outfit that supplied lower end South Korean hatchbacks and older Jeep Cherokees. The intel had shown that outside Umfasu, the nation's capital, the towns were shanty-like, and the roads were poor. King knew that there were two types of poor when it came to roads. Africa, and then the rest of the world. For this reason, after an hour of showing passports, driving licences, international driving licences and a last-minute cash 'vehicle tax', for which there was no receipt, they found themselves behind the wheel of a six-year-old four-wheel-drive Jeep with a four-litre petrol engine. With their rucksacks and the camera equipment in the back, they headed out of Umfasu International Airport giving their tail plenty of time to follow in a ten-year-old white Toyota Corolla.

"Well, at least we now know what the other guy looks like," Stewart commented flatly. "And these blokes look like secret police to me. Mustafa has brought in a Soviet style orchestration of police, secret police – the equivalent of the Stasi or KGB – and the military. The secret police seem to run the show, while the civil police force have little tasks to perform other than traffic violations, thefts and applying their cash *tax* to various offences."

"What's the name of the secret police outfit?" asked King, keeping his eye on the mirror and the white Toyota Corolla three cars back.

"The Department of Burindi Legal Services." Stewart paused. "Quite a mouthful. But what do you expect from a nation where *Lucky Man* is an actual name given to baby boys?"

"Sounds more like a bunch of compensation lawyers," King chuckled. "So, what's the plan for losing these dickheads?"

"Burindi itself," Stewart replied somewhat cryptically. "We head north to where these fucking parrot things have been discovered and let the mountain roads and bush increase the gap between a capable off-roader and a cheap saloon most likely with bald tyres and ten years without servicing."

"Sounds like a plan," King replied, looking forward to putting the Jeep through its paces with two-foot-deep potholes and steep inclines as they headed into the highlands, which was also the location of the main garrison of Burindi troops. "Where do we meet our contact?"

Stewart shrugged. "Pierre will meet us in a small town called Casu. There's a hotel with a bar, a corner shop and the rest of the town is just corrugated iron rooves and mud huts, apparently. That's where we'll be staying the night before checking out the parrots."

"And by parrots, you mean army garrison."

"Exactly."

They drove through the city, Umfasu not disappointing them in their expectations of a Central African city in a country that bordered on being part of the Third World, but for its oil and mineral reserves, and the wealth of the Burindi government and the inevitable businessmen who had government contacts. Downtown the business and economic sector played host to suited workers and a good selection of bars, cafés and restaurants. The streets were clean, the grass areas well-tended and the roundabouts and intersections were decorated with flowers in the nation's flag colours of blue, green and yellow. There were statues, too. However, they had largely been torn down by the new government and its supporters. Lucky Man Jonathon Mugabe's image had also been painted out on the side of buildings. He certainly wasn't going to go down in history like Che Guevara.

"There's very little evidence left of Mugabe's time as president," King commented flatly. "Makes you wonder what sort of support he'll have if he gets back in."

Stewart nodded. "The people will bend with the breeze. That's how they survive in Burindi. Hell, that's how they survive in Central Africa full stop." He paused as a woman carrying two crates of bananas on her head without the use of her hands crossed in front of them. "Would you look at that? She's a strong lass, that lot must weigh sixty pounds..."

"It's like two worlds colliding," King mused. "This part of the city could be anywhere, and then there's always a reminder that you will soon be in more primitive surroundings."

"But not yet," replied Stewart. "There's the Presidential Palace up ahead. Or Government House, it depends upon who is in power at the time."

The palace looked similar in design to the White House, but altogether larger and more grandiose. Well-manicured lawns were dotted with Royal Palms at least seventy feet high and a decorative fountain stood pride of place in the centre of the lawn. Lifesize statues of the Big Five game animals appeared to drink from the fountain pool, and the fountain itself shot fifty-feet high into the air before raining down into the pool, the light beyond creating a glorious rainbow.

"Well, that's bigger than I expected," King commented flatly. "Do we have an army, or what?"

"That's what this trip is about," replied Stewart. "But right now, two full squadrons of the SAS may prove the sensible option."

"Yeah, with three battalions of the Paras giving close fire support, and the guards on armoured vehicles and artillery. But I suppose that's not an option."

"You suppose correctly. The presidential guard barracks are a mile to the north and that's where the Republican Guard are billeted. Some of the officers have trained at Sandhurst, so knowledge and professionalism has cascaded down the ranks. Or that's the thought behind it." Stewart craned his neck to down a large mouthful of beer and said, "Intel reports state at least a hundred men armed with modern NATO kit including US K-Bar knives, Glock-Nineteen pistols and French FAMAS bullpup rifles. They also have modern US-designed body armour and night-vision."

"Nice," King replied. "Let's just hope it's a case of all the gear and no idea..."

"Possibly," Stewart replied. "But safer to assume the worst. The rest of the army are equipped with surplus kit from years of cosying up to other nations. AKs from the former Soviet Union, SLRs from Britain, Lee Enfield rifles we sold them way back in the fifties... even their uniforms are a mismatched bag of old British DPMs and green shirts, and US olive fatigues from the Vietnam War. These soldiers are stationed to the north to provide border security with less than friendly neighbours. This part of Central Africa has threats from many aggressors, especially bandits from the Congo, the DRC. Now that lithium has been discovered in Burindi several nations with scores to settle may take advantage and increase their borders into the mineral reserves."

"Overall strength?"

"Ten thousand men. Plus, a logistics corps and training academy to the south which isn't our concern. Small fry to most nations, but they have a lot of equipment such as heavy machineguns, RPGs, artillery and helicopters. The terrain negates armoured equipment, so Burindi forces have become a highly mobile airborne strike force. And there's no navy, naturally. Or air force for that matter."

"Apart from officer training at Sandhurst, what training have the army had?"

"Oh, the very best, naturally. The SAS trained a bunch of them in hostage rescue, survival skills and small arms, and as I mentioned, many of the Burindi army officers went to Sandhurst. Britain PLC will never learn that today's friends are usually tomorrow's enemies. The government take the money for training packages one minute, then have those skills used against us the next." Stewart paused. "The theory being that the training is passed down, but it can be a bit like those martial arts clubs where the training gets diluted with every new club that opens and eventually the sensei thinks he's fucking Yoda or something, and five-year-olds get given a belt for lifting a leg off the ground. Sometimes the training doesn't translate too well, and the guys who learned from the best strut about on an ego trip and bad teaching techniques mean that the skills that they learnt doesn't get passed on effectively."

"So, we don't really know," King mused. "But I would think we need to see those helicopters grounded quick smart."

"All in good time, my lad. Let's get the recce down before we start to plan. But yes, with those birds still in action, we can't do a damn thing here in the capital."

Chapter Seven
The Burindi Highlands

From inside the Jeep, with its glorious air-conditioning belying the furnace outside, the Burindi Highlands looked very much like the Scottish Highlands on a fine summer's day. They had driven through Umfasu which looked like any other modern African city with fast food outlets, offices, shops and restaurants, then headed through the shanty town outskirts which again, looked like any other African shanty town with potbellied and malnourished children, plenty of dead dogs in the gutters and men sitting around smoking, chatting and blatantly doing nothing while the women carried huge loads of fruit, or water cans or bundles of cloth on their heads. When they cleared the shanty towns, they drove out through the bush, which soon gave way to jungle and as they climbed higher, after a thousand feet of elevation the jungle started to thin out and took on a moorland feel with high mountainous peaks in the distance. This far from Umfasu the road was now a simple rutted track and they had finally lost the government men in the white Toyota Corolla now that the road had become potholed and crisscrossed with gullies that would wash deep with floodwater during the rains.

"I can't believe we got a fucking puncture..." Stewart said gruffly. "Now the secret police will catch up with us again. You can't just go blasting over potholes, even in an off-roader."

King ignored the man's moaning and admonishment. He was starting to treat Stewart's constant berating and cursing at just about everything on the planet as white noise. Stewart hadn't seemed all that bothered about King's driving when they were pulling out a good lead over their watchers. He wound up the jack and the Jeep slowly lifted high on its springs until the nearside front wheel lifted off the dusty ground. He had already loosened the nuts and set about removing them with the wheel brace. The road was narrow and opposite them, a fearfully steep drop into a tree-filled valley looked ominously dangerous without the addition of a safety barrier. The Toyota Corolla came into view and both men stared out the windows as they drove past. King casually waved and continued to take off the damaged wheel. The tall man with the gold-rimmed glasses drove, and in King's experience that made him the more junior partner. The man in the passenger seat was heavily set and wore a cheap pair of mirrored aviator glasses. He notably had a gold front tooth and chewed gum incessantly. Neither man returned King's wave. The Toyota drove on, bouncing over the potholes and out of sight around the next bend.

"Looks like we're in the clear," said King, as he placed the spare wheel over the bolt spindles. He quickly spun the nuts on until they were finger-tight, then tightened them with the wheel brace. He looked up, the white Toyota reappearing around the bend. "Shit, spoke too soon..."

"Bollocks," Stewart said, watching the Toyota. "Alright,

no sudden moves. TIA. This is Africa. A handful of US dollars should do the trick."

King nodded, dropping the jack and reaming the nuts tight with the wheel brace, now that the tyre was down on the ground. "Okay, I'll follow your lead."

The Toyota pulled up opposite them, effectively blocking the road now that their Jeep was parked up close to the drainage ditch. Both men got out. The heavily set man spat out his gum and set about lighting a thick cigar, quite unhurried, while the tall man with the spectacles opened a packet of chewing tobacco. Both men had pistols tucked in their belts, barely hidden by identical white untucked shirts. As the two men drew near, King could see that the pistols were Makarovs, which pointed towards the new government's new trading ties with Russia and China. China had simply copied the Makarov and called it the Type-59. The two men stopped and stared at them.

"Hi, thanks for stopping but we're OK, we've just fixed it," Stewart said warmly. Or about as warmly as the gruff Scotsman could get.

Both men continued to stare for an uncomfortable few seconds, before the heavily set man said, "Why you in Burindi?"

"I'm a freelance journalist," Stewart replied, taking a step towards the two men. "This is my photographer. We're hoping to sell some copy to National Geographic."

"Copy?" asked the tall man chewing through his mouthful of tobacco powder.

"An article," Stewart explained. "It's on parrots in the north of the country. Grey parrots that have appeared to cross-breed with another species and have turned carnivorous." The two men continued to stare. "It's an unusual story," he added, hoping to clarify.

The heavily set man smiled and said, "I will ask you again. Why are you in Burindi? This time, you will tell me the truth." He slowly drew the small automatic and added, "In Burindi, we deal with spies as we would deal with rats in the grain store..."

King stood up, the tyre iron in his hand. He rolled the damaged wheel with its flat tyre in front of the Jeep so that he was close to the two men. "Like he said, we're on this gig to sell a story to National Geographic. I'm a photographer. My kit is in the back of the vehicle."

"A likely cover," the heavily set man said coldly. "But you are both English, and I suspect you are here to cause trouble for our leader. That running dog Lucky Man Jonathon Mugabe is telling anybody who will listen that he will once again be Burindi's rightful president soon. That whoring playboy does not belong in Government House."

Stewart nodded. There was nothing like losing the element of surprise. "I know nothing of politics," he said calmly. "I am just a journalist who specialises in nature."

The heavily set man smiled and said, "Then you will know the Latin name for this parrot?"

"Of course, it's *Psittacus Erithacus*. Often referred to as the Congo parrot. Although, if it has bred and changed the balance of the species, then there is no name yet for the sub-species."

"I think you had better come with us," the man said, raising the pistol. "For questioning."

Stewart shrugged. "Shall we follow you?"

Both men looked at each other and started to confer. Stewart slapped the pistol aside and chopped the heavily set man in the windpipe with the edge of his hand. The man dropped onto his knees clutching his throat. King reacted, his training seeming to take over and he smashed the tyre iron into the side of the tall man's head. It was a savage blow, but the man twisted and staggered and King followed up with another strike, this time to the back of the man's skull, making him drop like a stone. It was a tremendous blow and had he had a bat in his hand, it would have been a six or a home run on the respective pitches. Stewart was upon the other man and punching him repeatedly in the throat until the man ceased choking through his crushed windpipe and rested still.

"Right, grab them and get them into their fucking car!" Stewart snapped. "Quickly, before somebody comes!"

King caught hold of the man he had just killed and rolled him over. To his horror he saw that one of the man's eyes had dislodged from the impact to the back of his skull. He felt the rise in vomit but swallowed it back down to avoid losing face in front of his mentor. He dragged the body across the road and set about the task of getting him back into the driver's seat. Stewart was struggling with the heavier body, and King went to his aid and together they got the second man into position. Stewart started the engine and released the handbrake and both men pushed as King steered the vehicle through the window and to the edge of the precipice. They rocked the vehicle several times, then in a final effort they got the front wheels over the edge of the precipice and the car rolled over. Both men watched as it gained speed and bounced and weaved down the slope. Suddenly it drifted wildly to the left and rolled over. Inertia and momentum did the rest. The vehicle rolled faster and faster, and King had given up counting at ten revolutions, then one of the bodies flew out through the open window and disappeared in the thick undergrowth. The noise from the crunching metal on rocks sounded like distant thunder and echoed throughout the valley, but eventually there was nothing but an eerie silence as the vehicle was stopped by trees. There was no dramatic or satisfying explosion or roar of flame, simply a sense of quiet finality.

Stewart turned and walked back to the Jeep. He picked up both pistols and handed one to King, who took it and checked the magazine and breech, then tucked it into his cargoes pocket and set about putting the wheel and tools back inside the boot space.

"Well, that escalated quickly," Stewart said then added most resolutely, "We're in it now. Up to our bloody eyeballs."

King nodded but said nothing as he swilled the taste of bile from his mouth with a bottle of water. He spat the water on the ground then downed the remainder of the bottle in just a few swift gulps. They certainly were in it now, but King had a terrible sense of foreboding that this would not be the last of it.

Chapter Eight
Monaco

The Peugeot hire car swept into the gravelled driveway, its tyres crunching loudly on the loose surface. Underneath the gravel the driveway had been paved at great expense, but Redwood, the SAS team leader had ordered three tonnes of the chippings to be laid and raked flat. Gravel was almost impossible to walk across without making a noise, and to the SAS team leader, prevention was always better than the cure.

Armstrong parked the budget hatchback between the Mercedes S Class saloon and the Aston Martin DB7 Vantage. The sight irked him somewhat. Lucky Man Jonathon Mugabe could afford a fleet of cars, but the British government had leased the two vehicles as a sweetener, along with the one-hundred-foot Sunseeker motor yacht moored in the marina. Lucky Man Jonathon had wanted a show of commitment for granting the rights to oil, lithium and other minerals, and some movers and shakers in Whitehall had keenly obliged.

Armstrong was well outside of his comfort zone. He was not a field man and was perfectly comfortable in his top floor office with its view over the River Thames and his ever burdening in tray. He enjoyed sending officers, agents and assets into the field and he enjoyed their successes as his own. He likened himself as something of a Lord Wellington character, positioning his men on a board and checking their progress. He enjoyed his nine to five hours - more often eight to six - but he also enjoyed after work drinks to avoid the rush hour traffic and over-crowded underground, and he liked to relax watching the evening news with The Times crossword and a stiff drink as his wife made dinner and the children showed him their homework before bedtime. He did not enjoy flying on his own, hiring cars and driving on the wrong side of the road. He enjoyed staying in hotels alone even less. But Lieutenant Peter Redwood had contacted his commanding officer in Hereford and voiced his concerns, who in turn had flagged his concerns to MI6. With Mugabe meeting with the Russian, Armstrong now had little choice but to reiterate the terms of the dictator's exile and reinstatement as leader.

The SAS team knew of Armstrong's arrival and by and large remained out of sight. Armstrong could see a man near the entrance to the garden and pool terrace. He was conversing through an earpiece and throat mic. Armstrong watched the gates closing automatically and when he looked back towards the pool terrace the bodyguard had gone.

The front door was now open with Lucky Man Jonathon's private secretary, Mamadou Cilla, standing there to greet him. "Good afternoon, Mr Armstrong. I am so pleased to see you again. And so soon!" the man said warmly, through a set of whiter than white teeth. "What a pleasure! The President will see you shortly. Please, follow me."

Armstrong almost corrected the man, told him that Mugabe was not president yet, but it would not have been conducive to the meeting. Mugabe was nobody's president. He had rigged the election and subsequently been overthrown when Mustafa had swept in with overwhelming support. The only reason that Armstrong stood here now, at behest of the British Government, was because Britain PLC stood the chance of forging a better deal with Mugabe than the leftist regime of Mustafa and his courting of both the Chinese and Russian governments.

Armstrong followed Cilla into the villa. The décor was chic European meets tribal Africa. There were tribal masks and spears lining the walls, and carved animals of comically thin and tall proportions dotted around the marble floor. Two bronze-skinned blondes lounged on a sofa dressed only in skimpy bikinis, while an Asian woman wearing just knickers and an oversized T-shirt poured herself a strong-looking drink at a half-moon bar in the corner of the room. Armstrong could see white dust residue, rolled banknotes and a credit card on the shiny ebony lid of a grand piano, and slumped in a chair wearing nothing but a pair of knickers a pale redheaded girl of around eighteen or nineteen stared blankly into space, her pert breasts uncovered with some of the white residue around her nipples.

Mamadou Cilla smiled. "Good times, yes?" He laughed. "Monaco is a crazy place, my friend..."

"So, it would seem," Armstrong replied humourlessly.

"Lucky Man is a great man!" Cilla announced affectionately. "He will do many great things when he is back as the rightful leader of our country. But here? Here he needs... a muse, if you will. For all his great ideas." He swept a hand towards the girls. "These are his muse!"

"A muse from barely legal girls and cocaine?"

Armstrong paused. "We had a deal, Cilla. You as much as Mugabe. You were supposed to keep him on the straight and narrow. And now I see this, which I am willing to turn a blind eye to, but meetings with Russians? That is beyond the pale."

Mamadou frowned, unfamiliar with the term, but he seemed to get the gist of it. He held a finger to his lips and whispered. "Being around Lucky Man Jonathon is like having a pet lion. You don't rub its nose in the carpet for pissing on the floor..." He craned his neck to make sure the man was not near. "Gently, gently is the best way forward."

"A deal is a deal. We are about to commit to an overthrow. I do not expect a change in terms at this late stage."

"Leave it with me," Mamadou said quietly. "I will guide him through."

"Ten million pounds in a numbered Swiss bank account should have been motivation enough, wouldn't you say? It wouldn't be good for Lucky Man Jonathon to find out that his private secretary has also done a deal with the British government..."

"Trust me," Cilla replied, but his smile had faded. "You *will* get your deal."

"Deals! What boring talk of deals is there left to have?" Lucky Man Jonathon filled the doorway to the next room, a broad smile taking up most of his face. "Armstrong, my dear friend. Would you care for a girl? There are more upstairs to choose from, although they've been fairly, er, well-used..." He smiled wryly, holding up his hands. "More are coming tonight, if you care to stay. There is a fixer who has arranged for six Japanese women. I hear they are both noisy during climax and entirely submissive during the act."

"No," Armstrong replied firmly. "Let's find a seat that hasn't got a naked woman, semen or cocaine on it and have a little chat, shall we?" He walked past the big African and into a lounge with a view over the pool terrace. There were girls swimming, and Mugabe's original security team were laughing, drinking and joking with them. Armstrong could see two of the SAS team watching, both dressed smartly in suits and neither man looking amused at the scene in front of them.

"Mamadou! Have somebody bring champagne!"

"No, thank you," Armstrong gestured for the man to stop. "Coffee will be fine."

"You can't make deals with coffee!" Lucky Man Jonathon exclaimed.

"Our deal has been done, Mr Mugabe. We are not making a deal, merely reiterating what we already have."

"President Mugabe!" the man corrected him firmly.

"That, *Mr Mugabe*, remains to be seen. I am not in the habit of making a deal, setting the wheels in motion, and then having you meet with the opposition and force me to come out here and renegotiate terms. There will be no renegotiation."

"Business is business," Lucky Man Jonathon replied, apparently uninterested.

"The business has been done. You are living a life of luxury at extraordinary expense to the UK taxpayer. Once Mustafa and his den of thieves have been removed from power, you will get what you want. You will once again be President of Burindi." Armstrong paused. "The UK gets all of your oil and mineral rights, and Lithium is top of that list. Your government gets a sizable commission and provides a secure and stable platform for our economic interests."

Mugabe shrugged and looked up as a maid entered with a silver tray of coffee, cream and sugar, and a man dressed like a traditional butler carried a silver ice bucket with a bottle of Krug nestled inside, and a tray with a single champagne flute. "We shall see, my friend. We shall see. There is more than enough oil and minerals to go round."

Armstrong helped himself to sugar and cream and stirred his coffee distractedly. He wondered whether he would get the green light for the same SAS team protecting him to work their way through the man and his entire entourage in the dead of night. It would certainly ease the burden on the UK taxpayer. "I'm going to tell you a story, Lucky Man. I'd like you to listen to it and think about it when I leave."

"I am too old for stories," he replied tersely.

"Even so, I think it would prove helpful to our... situation."

"Very well. If you insist." Lucky Man Jonathon swilled down his glass of champagne and reached for the bottle. "I will indulge you..."

"Good. Well, it's not so much a story as a history lesson. And I suppose, a future scenario." Armstrong took a deep breath and put down his coffee. "It's all woke these days. People are aware of everyone's needs, their cultural, sexual or racial identification. We recognise the need for sensitivity, of understanding. Very different from the Victorian era, for instance. Or indeed, from the seventeenth century when Britain, Spain and Portugal rounded up your ancestors and shipped them off to build a whole new world. Later, as the dominant country, the British Empire no less, we took what we wanted from the African continent and in return we taught the savages about Christianity, gave them education, clean water and Western medicine. We built your continent. Roads, railways, shipping. And despite a cultural inability to learn, have a solid work ethic and contribute to your own society, the African people still needed us. As the

British Empire receded, every country that governed itself ended up at war, in famine or reliant on charity. Burindi is no different. One unelected tribal chief run out of the country by another. You, Mr Mugabe, are a corrupt and unrightful leader. Presently, you have no power. What some would call a limp dick. Sure, you talk a good talk, but your only way back into power is to rely upon the British Government to give you what you need." Armstrong paused, staring at Mugabe, his eyes unblinking. "And if you think that you can play games with us, then you have another think coming. We will indulge you in your whores, your cars, your champagne and caviar lifestyle. We will indulge you in your Monte Carlo villa, and your yacht. We will also remove Mustafa from power and pave the way for your return. But if for one minute you think about going back on our deal, or of changing the percentage, or God forbid, bringing another nation into the mix, then you will wake up in your presidential palace with your eyeballs and your testicles in a glass beside your bed." He paused, still staring at the big African in front of him. "Or perhaps even while you're still in Monaco, if I'm not convinced of your level of commitment or trustworthiness."

The big African smiled, not a flicker in his eyes as he nodded and said, "It is true, some of my people are not long down from the trees. In fact, much of Africa is the same. But that is not everybody. And for every man who is barely ahead in evolutionary design, there are people of genius. Thinkers, doers and like me, leaders and people of influence," Lucky Man Jonathon smiled. "But do you think that a derogative and racist history lesson will anger me, or that threats of violence will scare me, Mr Armstrong? In my country, disputes are settled with a machete. Your threats do not scare me."

"Then I am truly sorry for your country," Armstrong shrugged. "But I just want you to know where you stand, Mr Mugabe. Whether anybody calls you President Mugabe one day, well, that all relies on how seriously you take our little chat today." Armstrong stood up and adjusted his suit jacket. "I do hope we will continue as per our initial agreement, and I look forward to a long and enduring relationship between my government and your administration."

Lucky Man Jonathon stood up. He was doing his best to save face, but there was little humour in the man's eyes and his expression was subdued as he hollered for his private secretary to show Armstrong out. He did not watch the Englishman leave, merely caught hold of one of the young women by the arm and pulled her behind him as he headed upstairs.

Chapter Nine
Burindi

The scenery flashed by, neither man seeming to notice it anymore. Stewart could not get the sight of King beating the paedophile out of his head. He had always known that the man carried a great weight of emotional baggage with him, but he did not realise quite how much. He just hoped his agent could control himself from now on. King, however, had been shocked at how quickly Stewart had turned on the man, and how he had blindly followed suit and taken another man's life. The sight of the damage done by the wheel brace had stuck with him, and he knew it would for some time to come.

"You didn't see them," Stewart reiterated for the third time in as many minutes. "You didn't even know that they were following us."

"I get it."

"Deny, deny, deny..."

"Like I said, I get it." He paused. "We just killed two men; I'm hardly going to confess straight off the bat."

"They can be vicious bastards out here." Stewart paused. "Bloody animals."

King nodded, wondering who the animals really were. "They can't be any worse than those Southside Boys in the Congo."

"In this game, whenever you think you've seen it all, some bastard comes along that turns what you know on its head." Stewart paused, watching the road ahead. "Oh, shit, looks like a roadblock. Can this day get any worse?"

King frowned. "Doesn't look like police or military to me."

Stewart grunted. In his experience locals doing a bit of highway robbery could be so much worse. "No sudden moves," he told him. "Take my lead." Stewart took the Makarov out from his pocket. He never used safeties and the weapon was double action, meaning that the hammer was down but could be fired with a long trigger pull. The first round and subsequent gunshots would leave the hammer cocked and the trigger set back for a lighter trigger pull.

King nodded. He didn't need telling. Not after what the Scotsman had pulled with the two secret policemen earlier. He took out his pistol and tucked it under his right thigh, pinning it to the seat and keeping it from view.

The 'roadblock' was simply a large log and some tyres. Two boys no older than twelve stood in front of the road-block carrying old and well-worn AK-47 assault rifles. *This is Africa*, thought King. Sadly, he had been up against children in battle and still lost sleep about it. King slowed down, looking for an escape route. He reckoned that if push came to shove, then he could weave left and power through the three-foot gap between the log and the last of the tyres, and the side of the steep slope up to the jungle. With enough power, they should push through.

"Stop the car," said Stewart. "I'll handle these little bastards."

"There are three more high on the slope on the other side of the roadblock, Boss," said King.

"Cunning little sods..."

"They look like adults."

"That would be right," said Stewart opening the door. "Let the kids take all the fucking risks, while they take all the fucking money."

King watched as Stewart walked up to the two boys. He noticed that the man had left his pistol on the front seat. That was Stewart all over. He never made plans for situations such as this, simply acted on instinct alone and expected to be backed up instantly. One of the boys looked nervous and he was pointing the AK-47 right at Stewart's stomach. Stewart made a calming gesture with both hands, slowly reached into his pocket and pulled out a bundle of banknotes. He was talking to both boys and obviously hit the right note because one of them smiled. One of the adults slid his way down the slope and shouted something at the boys, then made his way over with a swagger, the muzzle of his own rifle on Stewart. King slowly pulled out the pistol. They were twenty metres from him, and he knew he could hit them all at that range, but only until they returned fire. And then it would all be over, because he would not stand a chance with just a pistol. Of course, there was an alternative. The two boys and the young man were now all standing on King's side of the barrier. With enough throttle, he could mow them down and pin them all against the roadblock while Stewart, standing to the left, would be able to get out of the way. King slipped the Jeep's automatic gearbox into "1" and pulled up the four-wheel-drive lever. For most driving conditions "D" would suffice, but for a rapid start the lower ratio would provide the best grip. He watched the man's body language, his foot hovering over the accelerator. Something inside told him that this was it, that it was now or never. He watched as Stewart stepped into the middle and cursed that he would now be in the way. Still, the Scotsman had lightning reflexes and King was sure that he would dive clear. Stewart handed over the roll of banknotes and the man smiled. He started to count the money, then barked an order at the two boys, who set about removing the barrier. Stewart walked back to the Jeep blissfully unaware that he had been less than a second from the Jeep bearing down on him, and the close quarter gun battle which would have ensued.

"Drive," Stewart ordered as he slipped into his seat. "Are you OK?"

"Sure," King replied, slipping the gearbox into "D" or Drive, and taking off smoothly on the rutted road surface.

"They are anti-government rebels," Stewart explained. "I told them that we would be making many trips and that if they wanted more money, then they had better let us through."

"So, they support Lucky Man Jonathon?"

"No," said Stewart firmly. "They support Desmond Lambadi, the man exiled after Lucky Man's successful coup d'état eight or nine years ago. Only he wasn't exactly exiled. He was detained. Indefinitely."

"That's African democracy for you..."

"You're catching on, sunshine." Stewart paused. "Desmond Lambadi was a schoolteacher. He spoke for the people, and he introduced welfare reforms and a decent education system that kept both boys and girls in school until they were thirteen. Doesn't sound like a big deal, but you want to look at the countries surrounding Burindi where girls receive no education and only half the boys get an education to around ten. He was working on a health system with free treatment for accident and emergency and to address the AIDS and HIV epidemic, he was advocating free condoms and medication. That's pretty forward thinking for Africa."

"So, where is this guy, Lambadi?"

"Nobody knows. Could have been beheaded with a machete and buried in the jungle for anyone knows." Stewart shrugged. "He was certainly a better man than Mustafa and Lucky Man Jonathon Mugabe put together. And then some."

Chapter Ten
The Palace of Westminster, London

I t was a rare thing to meet in this office. Unprecedented as far as Armstrong was concerned. The office was oak-panelled with a view over the River Thames from two narrow windows with an ornate lead pattern along the top, and a diagonal crisscross. The desk was a solid mahogany affair that had served many leaders before the man who was now seated behind it, studying the report.

"Is our friend back in his box?"

Armstrong shrugged. He had just stepped off the plane at London City Airport and been driven straight here in a taxi. "I laid it on pretty thick, Prime Minister. He's an arrogant bastard, excuse my French. And has a touch of the invincible about him. A touch of madness as well."

"Don't they all?" the Prime Minister commented somewhat distantly. "We need him on board. No more games."

Armstrong nodded. When he had been summoned, he had expected to meet the Prime Minister at Downing Street, but in reality, much of the leader's work was done here between parliamentary sessions and Prime Minister's questions. This was the office where ministers were fired during cabinet reshuffles; their successors invited to Number Ten to be given their new position. In through the grand, public office with the world's media outside, out through the working office where nobody waited outside with a camera. This was where much of the nitty gritty work was done, and it had the advantage of the world's press not being camped out on the doorstep watching who came and went and speculating wildly on the reason. "I believe he will be."

The Prime Minister rested the file on the desk and looked at him. "We have invested a great deal of money in the man's exile, and not just his playboy villa in Monaco, but in Italy and Switzerland as well. I don't want him leading us a merry dance. We are about to become a heavy hitter in the lithium business, and I'll be damned if this joker gives concessions to the Russians after everything that we've done for him." He paused. "And I'm not losing another nation to Russia and China's new brand of socialism. Not on my watch."

"Understood, Prime Minister."

"Really?"

"Really," Armstrong replied emphatically. "I'm confident that he will toe the line from now on."

The Prime Minister seemed to mull this over, then eventually said, "Perhaps a demonstration would be in order. Something to clarify the man's thoughts." He smiled wryly. "I'll leave that with your department. You'll work out what to do."

Chapter Eleven
Casu, Burindi

The hotel wasn't what either of them had expected. The rooms were a series of outside stalls made from single unrendered concrete blocks with a corrugated iron roof. Electrical wire fed to each room from a pole in the centre of what would once have been a garden, but now looked like waste ground. The electric junction box at the top of the pole buzzed as loudly as Spanish cicadas and the wires drooped inconveniently, and quite dangerously, at chest level forcing anyone passing through to duck their head underneath.

The doors were made from plywood and chipboard and had swollen and shrunk through both water ingress and temperature variations and were now left peeling and warped and barely able to close. Inside the rooms a single lightbulb suspended from the ceiling questioned the plausibility of such dangerous and elaborate wiring, which was clearly a case of ingenuity and practicality over safety and common sense. The creature comforts began and ended with a stained mattress without either pillows or bedsheets atop a single wire-framed bed. A single wooden straight-backed chair nestled in the corner and a tiled trough with a dirty plug, a single cold-water tap and a bucket provided the most basic level imaginable in washing facilities, just short of standing naked in the rain.

"Fuck me, Boss," King said quietly.

"It's a bed for the night," Stewart replied gruffly.

"I think I'll sleep in the car."

"I've slept in worse places."

King nodded. He had seen the man use a body for a pillow in the Congo, so Stewart wasn't a man easily appalled at a roof over his head and a bed under his arse for the night. "I'm not holding out much hope for room service," he replied.

"You need to find the right people to talk to," the woman's voice said behind him. It was cultured and soft, Home Counties. "Seriously, Alex, you can do much better than this..."

King turned around feeling a flutter of excitement in his chest, recognising the voice anywhere. He smiled warmly, while Stewart simply scowled. "Lucinda! What are you doing here?"

"She's a bloody hack, King. She'll be fishing for a story, mark my words."

"Thanks, Peter, I've got this," King replied without looking at him.

"Care for a rum and coke?" she asked. "I've got the barman well trained. Cuban rum, no import embargoes to a country with Russian friends and a socialist agenda. It's not all bad."

"Careful, lad," Stewart said as he walked towards his own room. He called over his shoulder, "Just like in Angola. She's only into you for the story..."

"Are you?" asked King.

"A bit," she replied. "But we had fun in Angola, didn't we?"

"Yeah. Not so good in the Congo, as I recall." He paused. "It's been, what, a year?"

"To be fair, I never said I'd write. I told you that I was married and that my husband's position made things difficult." She paused. "But I've thought about you lots, though."

"Have you?"

"Not really," she smiled.

King shrugged. "Let's get that drink."

Lucinda Davenport led the way into the hotel. It was colonial style and would once have been a magnificent place for weary travellers to stay. It probably hadn't been painted or decorated since that first coat of paint and varnish after it had been constructed, but the wood panelled bar with its slowly rotating ceiling fan had gotten away without a modern refurbishment and looked all the better for it. Black and white pictures taken a century ago lined the walls, giving a clear view of Burindi under white rule. Railways, big game hunts and scenes of the people after landmark elections painted a potted history of the country. King chose a table looking out across the valley which was partly terraced plantations and partly over-run by jungle. The sun was low in the sky over distant mountains, golden hues melting over the grassy peaks. The barman came over and took their order. King had opted for a cold beer, while Lucinda chose a rum and coke. The drinks arrived with a bowl of peanuts. King had heard stories of how many types of bacteria could be found in bowls of bar nuts, so held off and sipped his beer. To his surprise, it was smooth and cold.

"So, what are you doing here?" she asked.

"I might ask the same about you."

She smiled. "I have it on good authority that there is going to be a coup."

"And that good authority would be your politician husband, no doubt. What is he, business secretary?"

Lucinda smiled wryly. "Indeed."

"And it's no coincidence that Britain wants a share of Burindi's lithium reserves. Let me guess, Sir Hugo Truscott has lithium interests within his own private portfolio." He paused. "Oil interests in Angola, where you just happened to be writing a story about border insurgency by gangs in the Democratic Republic of the Congo, and now lithium and no doubt other mineral interests in Burindi where you just happen to be working on a story of a potential coup. If I were a better man..."

Lucinda sipped her drink, then smiled. "I'm connected. What else can I say?"

"You didn't want to take your husband's surname, and now I can see why."

"It was solely because I had spent many years making a name for myself. I neither wanted to start again, nor have doors opened for me simply because of a name."

"But you are here for a story, and once again, your husband is connected to both the region and the current political situation."

"Okay! You've got me!" she shrugged, pulling a pained expression. "So, you've seen right through me. Yes, I play to my advantages. So, how about you tell me what you're doing here. Burindi is barely on the map. I'd wager most people have never even heard of it."

"Just bird watching."

She smiled. "I've seen you at work, Alex. There's no need to bullshit me."

"Just seeing the sights."

"And how do they look?"

"Pretty good from where I'm sitting."

"Thanks."

"I meant the view of the valley..."

"How rude!" she replied, somewhat mocking him with fake indignation.

King smiled. "On reflection, it's not so bad in here, either."

"No girlfriend?" she queried.

"No," King replied. He had been on a few dates with Jane Hargreaves, the woman he met from MI5 who had been taken hostage alongside OPEC executives and British government ministers in Angola, but nothing had stuck. She had career goals and he was seldom in London these days. He had promised himself that he would give her a call soon, but his trip to Monaco had got in the way, and now he was half-way across the world again and looking into the eyes of a beautiful, vivacious woman with whom he had once fallen for. "Nothing serious," he said.

"Serious commitments don't do well in certain careers."

King sipped some more of his beer. He wasn't about to comment on the rules or state of her marriage. After all, it meant different things to different people. Lucinda's husband was a great deal older than she was, and from what he had seen and read of the cabinet minister, quite an odious individual. Certainly, from a privileged background, and undoubtedly a politician who used politics to further his business interests. Naturally Lucinda would have been attracted to the man once, or perhaps it had always been a career move. He did not know, and certainly would not ask. "Is it common speculation that Lucky Man Jonathon Mugabe is planning a coup d'état?"

"Tell me what *you* know."

"You first."

Lucinda finished her drink and nodded at the barman for a refill. She looked back at King and said, "I caught wind of it back in London."

"Your husband talked."

She held up her hands in mock surrender. "Politicians talk to their wives. What can I say?"

"I say, loose lips sink ships..."

"I've told nobody else."

"But who else is *he* telling?"

"That's nothing to do with me. Hugo moves in certain circles. He is in a trusted position, so what he decides to divulge is usually to make a situation better, not worse," she said defensively, and King noted, quite loyally.

King had been caught off guard by her loyalty and defensiveness towards her husband. The barman came with another round, and he took his beer and put the empty glass on the tray. "I'm here for a fact-finding tour."

"A reconnaissance more like," she said sharply. "Prior to a military action, no doubt." King shrugged and said nothing. He sipped his beer as he looked back at her. He was surprised that as a journalist, she fell into his trap. Uncomfortable at the silence, she filled the void. "Come on, Alex. You and that crazy Scotsman are here because Lucky Man Jonathon Mugabe is going to try an overthrow. I want to be there when it happens. Next to you, on the ground, the first journalist in."

King thought about Mugabe in his Monaco villa, courtesy of the British taxpayer. There would be no overthrow from him. No spilled blood or knowing what it was to be in the thick of it. The man was no Fidel Castro or Che Guevara, who fought on the streets and knew what it was to pull a trigger. Simply a triumphant walk back into the Presidential Palace after the blood had already been spilled and the lives had been taken. Celebrations made; champagne swilled while the bodies outside stiffened in the heat. "Another coup for your career," he said sardonically.

"Undoubtedly," she replied, a breezy honesty to her response. "A few more coups and a news desk anchor could be mine." She paused. "And no more God forsaken hell holes like this..."

"Tell me about it, I'm not looking forward to a night in that room."

"You and your boss struck out," she teased. "You're in the rooms for lorry drivers with next to no budget. I'm in the main hotel. It's somewhat better, to say the least."

"Nice."

"It's just above us." She paused, giving him a sideways glance, her hand brushing her hair back over her right ear. "My room. If you'd like to take a look."

"No, I'd only get room envy and want to stay all night."

"That's kind of the idea," she smiled.

Chapter Twelve

K ing left Lucinda sleeping, glancing back for a last look at her shapely body, her smooth pale skin glistening with perspiration, as he closed the door. He smiled to himself as he strode down the corridor and took the stairs lightly to the tired-looking foyer. It had been quite a night. Lucinda was a passionate woman, an air of desperation and relief manifesting in her lovemaking. King had felt swept along for the ride. It had certainly been a night to remember, with the added bonus that he didn't have to spend a night in the filthy room in the courtyard.

He found Stewart asleep in his filthy cot, fully clothed and an almost empty bottle of Scotch in his clasp. A spider the size of a tea plate was on the wall, just inches from the man's head. King took another step closer, but found the Makarov aimed at him, the Scotsman's eyes tired and sore.

"Christ, your eyes look like piss holes in the snow, Boss."

"Aye, as sore as that young journalist's cooch, I bet," he said gruffly. "Good night?"

"Yes. As it goes."

"Be careful there. For a man in your position, no good can come from fucking a journalist. And especially no good comes from fucking a politician's wife." He paused. "But I'm guessing you won't be told."

"I'm here to do a job, Boss."

"Good Lad."

"Breakfast?"

Stewart shrugged. "Coffee."

"There's two types of breakfast, apparently. Did you know we're in the trucker's stop?"

The Scotsman nodded. "It's all they had available."

King nodded. "Well, for a fee breakfast is served in the hotel. It smells OK, too."

Stewart got up off the bed. "What's the other type of breakfast?"

"Posho and your fingers to eat it with. That's what the truckers were eating in a lean-to when I came down. I think I'll pass on that one. Looks like the only seasoning is what's on your hand before you dip in."

Stewart caught sight of the spider above his bed. "Fuck me, look at the size of that thing!" He paused and smiled back at King lecherously. "I bet that's what she said last night, isn't it?"

King didn't acknowledge the man's crude humour. "I'll be in the hotel having breakfast," King said, turning his back on him and heading out the doorway. He walked past the group of men eating from bowls of posho, their clothes in tatters and covered in oil. They watched him in silence as he walked past them, then continued to eat and talk when he was almost out of earshot. King climbed the wooden steps to the veranda and stepped into the hotel foyer. He found the manager at the desk. "Those rooms out there are a joke," he said. "I want two rooms in the hotel for tonight and for the next week."

"But we are full," the man replied earnestly. He was a tall, thin man in his early thirties and his suit was three sizes too big for him. King wondered whether it had once belonged to a previous manager. He placed a fold of notes on the desk and said, "This is for you. I will pay for the rooms later. Move someone." He paused, thinking about Lucinda and the night they had spent together in her sparsely furnished, but adequately comfortable and clean room. "Anyone except for Ms Lucinda Davenport." He couldn't see a repeat performance of last night if she found out he had turfed her out of her room.

"But Sir, I cannot evict people from their rooms!"

King dropped another fold of notes beside the first. They were into the realms of two-month's salary for the manager, and both men knew it. "Obviously we'll pay for the rooms separately. This is just your commission." He paused, pushing the two folds of notes towards him. "Make it happen..." King left for the dining room, which had been set out with a buffet table consisting mainly of fruit and bread rolls with a selection of jams and chutneys. A hotplate kept bacon and scrambled eggs warm in two dishes, and a pungent-smelling soup that looked like a meat and vegetable broth. King found a plate and piled it high with bacon and eggs and took a couple of bread rolls. He found the coffee and tea and poured himself a cup of tea, spooned in a sugar and topped it up with what looked like sour milk. When he sat down at a table, he stirred the tea well, hoping it would taste better than it looked. From his previous experience in Africa, even the water would ruin the taste of a cup of tea. He watched Stewart walk in and head for the coffee. The

Scotsman poured himself two cups of black coffee and spooned in a lot of sugar. When he sat down at King's table he grunted and started to sip his first cup of coffee.

"I've sorted the rooms," said King.

"Really?"

"As good as. The man has had his *commission*, it's up to him to get it done."

"Or fuck off with your money."

"That won't do him any good," replied King. "Anyway, what's on the slate for today?"

"We meet with Pierre. He's been doing a recon on the barracks."

"And who *is* he?"

"A Swiss mercenary. He served in the French Foreign Legion."

"So, he's a criminal then. Can we trust him?"

"My, we do have a short memory don't we, Mark?"

King almost jolted at the sound of his real name. He had tried his best to forget his past life. For a moment he had felt superior to this Pierre character. So much for living a lie. When you were ashamed of your past, it did not take much to bring you back to reality with a sudden bump. King looked away and saw Lucinda walking into the dining room. She smiled at him, a little red-faced, then helped herself to mystery fruit juice and some bread rolls and jam. Behind her, a rugged-looking man walked in, his clothes dirty with marks of sweat all over his shirt. He poured a glass of water and drank it down quickly, followed by another two, before heading for the coffee. King recognised him and gave Stewart a nod. "Your Russian friend is here."

Stewart turned and caught the man's eye. The Russian came over with a coffee in hand and sat down beside them. "Dimitri. An unexpected pleasure."

"What a coincidence." The Russian paused. "Here we all are again."

"You're working?"

"Always."

Stewart nodded. "Acting as a guide for that journalist woman?"

"She requested my help a week ago."

King stared at him and said, "She got taken hostage in the Congo on your watch. Hardly a glowing reference."

"I seem to remember getting her back, though," the Russian replied coldly. "And helping you all to get away, too."

King shrugged, feeling a little churlish. He wasn't given to bouts of jealousy, but Lucinda obviously liked the man and it had surprised him that she had hired his services once more. The reality that he was suddenly jealous over a woman he had slept with only a handful of times, a married woman at that, and someone who clearly would never leave her husband seemed ridiculous. Dimitri had proved to be a brave and fearsome fighter, and since the man's allegiances had been changed having been let down by his government in both Afghanistan and Chechnya, Stewart had used the man for intel over the years with resounding success. "Of course," replied King. "I didn't mean anything by it."

The Russian smiled. "You are worried that there are too many dogs sniffing around the bitch," he replied. "But don't worry. You have no competition. I am professional. Business only. Besides, you have already staked your claim, right?" He paused. "I am her guide, but I am also paid to protect. I know where she spends her nights, and with whom..."

King shrugged, tackling his mountainous breakfast. He felt a little foolish. There was no future with Lucinda Davenport, so why did he feel this way?

"Ah, isn't this nice," Lucinda commented, her fruit juice in hand. "Mind if I join you?" she asked, sitting down without waiting for a response. "Here we all are again. Hopefully no kidnapping and rescue this time."

"Lassie, you'll know by now that I don't like the fucking press," Stewart told her. "The only things lower in my opinion are politicians and child molesters. And considering your husband is a career politician, then I don't think you and I will ever be friends."

"Wow. Say it like it is."

"That's how I do things." Stewart looked at her, then at King. "But the lad here seems to like you, and I have a great deal of respect for his opinion. I don't think telling you to fuck off is going to work, because you're a tenacious one, I'll give you that. And even I'm not going to twist your neck and toss you in a ditch because of your annoying little habit of getting in the way of things. Not yet at least. So, tell me now, what do you want?"

King stared at Stewart, a mix of emotions running through him. He had no idea that his mentor felt that way about him and he felt some foolish pride at hearing the comment, but he also found it difficult hearing the man talk to her like that. And now, the fact the tough Scotsman was appearing to make a concession to Lucinda didn't make sense, either. Lucinda seemed shaken by the casual way Stewart had inferred such violence with casual indifference.

In the end, it was the Russian who defused the situation. "Well, she's my principal, so I guess you'd have to go through me first, old man."

"Just sizing up the pieces on the board," Stewart replied with a wry smile.

"OK," Lucinda said eventually. "I get that you're wary of me. But I'm here on the ground and I want an exclusive. I won't file a story until you are clear of any reprisals. How's that?"

"It sounds workable."

"I know that something is afoot. I know that Lucky Man Jonathon Mugabe has done a deal with the British government, and that means that he will become President again. I also know, and I must admit to having an interest by proxy through my husband's business dealings, that the deal involves UK rights to oil, cobalt and lithium."

"And what aspects of this will appear in your story?" Stewart asked. "Naturally, a coup d'état and a President reclaiming his power. But will your story focus on the dealings of politicians benefiting from insider knowledge?" He watched her as she struggled to answer. "I didn't think so. Because you have a conflict of interest."

"I'm here, and I will write a good piece for my paper." She paused. "Will you let me shadow you?"

"No," replied Stewart. "You'll compromise our safety. But I don't see why we can't throw you a few crumbs now and again. But let me make myself clear. While we are doing our *fact-finding tour*, you stay well clear of us."

She nodded gratefully. "I can live with that."

Stewart smiled. "Well, until Kate Adie arrives on the scene, that is. She did great work in Rwanda and Sierra Leone. Burindi should be right up her street."

"You're all heart," she replied acidly.

"Got your eye on a nice TV slot, I bet." He paused, sipping some coffee, then said, "Far better for a pretty little ambitious thing like you to be in a studio with make-up artists and a convenient autocue script. You'll be on *Celebrity Big Brother* next."

Lucinda stood up. "You may come out with a lot of crap about me, but I don't have to sit here and listen to it." She paused, looking at Dimitri. "And you can come, too. I'm paying you as a guide and bodyguard, and I want to go and look at the Desmond Lambadi angle. His home village is only twenty miles away, near the border." King frowned and got up, following Lucinda and the Russian out of the restaurant. She turned around when she realised that he was following them. Dimitri kept walking another ten paces, discreetly giving them room to talk. "How you can work for that fucking ogre is beyond me."

King shrugged. "He's my Boss," he replied. "I don't get to choose who I work with. But his heart is in the right place, mostly. What were you saying about Desmond Lambadi?"

She shrugged. "Desmond Lambadi was the closest Africa came to electing a good man. A sort of Nelson Mandela character but without the controversial background that doesn't sit right with some people. He was overthrown by Lucky Man Jonathon Mugabe before he could get into his stride. He was a teacher, a philosopher and poet. He had many ideas on health and education, and a welfare system that looked as if it could have worked. Lucky Man Jonathon Mugabe has always denied knowing the man's whereabouts, but there's no smoke without fire. This is Africa, after all."

"And Mustafa doesn't know the man's whereabouts either?"

"No. Allegedly."

King nodded. "And you said that you have an *angle* on him here?"

"Rumours, mainly. But when rumours all say the same thing, time after time, then one has to look further to see if there is a shred of truth."

King nodded. He went to kiss her but stopped himself

somewhat awkwardly. He was tempted to try again, but the moment had passed. "Well, I'll see you around, I guess."

Lucinda smiled. "You can count on it, Alex. I enjoy your... company."

King felt a lift in his chest and a lightness to his stride as he walked back into the dining room, where Stewart was draining the last of his coffee.

"You're like a giddy teenager," Stewart said gruffly. "Now, come on man. We're here to do a job, so we'd better be getting on with it."

Chapter Thirteen
Monaco

The car had been parked, locked and left in a layby popular with walkers on the mountain road overlooking Monte Carlo. There were a series of paths and ledges higher up affording wonderful views of the city and the Mediterranean and the layby was a suitable setting off point for a hike, with vehicles coming and going, and people seemingly taking no notice of the other parked cars or individuals. Redwood had watched the vehicle park, and the driver cross over the road and get into a hired Peugeot driven by another man. He did not recognise either of the men, even though he was a serving member of the Special Air Service. For the man and his driver, their job was done. Delivery only. For Peter Redwood, his task was just beginning.

He paid the taxi driver and waited until the vehicle had turned around and was heading back down the mountain switchbacks before he walked across the road and dipped under the front wheel arch to retrieve the Renault's keys. He unlocked the door, got inside and started the engine. Only a couple returning from their walk watched him drive away, and the car was so non-descript to stand out and Redwood wore a pair of Ray Ban Wayfarer sunglasses, his brown hair trimmed to short grade four all over, making him about as memorable as the vehicle.

Once down to sea level, he drove the coast road into France and after forty minutes he pulled into Port Silva Maris, a pretty marina that was frequented by boat owners who were not necessarily millionaires. The boat waiting for him on the outside mooring was a twenty-five-foot fast-fisher with a covered wheelhouse and a cuddy for day use. The vessel was powered by twin 90HP Suzuki four stroke outboards and could maintain a thirty-five-knot cruising speed while being a practical platform for both fishing and diving from. Although the SAS Lieutenant would not be casting a line today. He loaded the equipment into the cuddy, and although the craft had been procured for him by an MI6 asset embedded in the area who had been instructed how to leave the boat, he performed fuel, battery and engine checks, and even though he did not plan on using the radio, he checked that it was tuned to the emergency frequency.

Redwood checked that the throttle was in neutral and started up the engines on the one button. He cast off the ropes forward and aft, coiled them quickly as the boat started to drift, then eased the throttle forward and crawled away from the jetty and out through the craft tethered on swinging moorings and into the channel. As he cleared the red and green buoys at the head of the channel, he eased on the throttle and cruised at a steady twenty-five knots, mindful that his actions should be unmemorable. Too slow in such a craft, or indeed too fast and he may stick in somebody's mind. He motored on for twenty-minutes, the ocean clear and calm, the opposite of the busy coast road from

Monte Carlo. When he was just around the point of Fontvieille, the southernmost ward in the Principality of Monaco, he cut the engines and drifted for a while before dropping anchor and testing the rate of drift. He was in approximately a hundred feet of water. With such small tides in the Mediterranean, he allowed the rope twenty feet of drift slack before he raised the blue and white Alpha flag used throughout Europe to indicate a submerged diver in the vicinity. He hauled out the equipment that had been left for him in the car and set about first checking the hardware. Attaching limpet mines to the metal hull of a ship simply required a magnetic fixing on the back of the mine. However, modern yachts and indeed, some stealth craft were constructed from fibreglass or composite plastics. The boys from Portsmouth of the SBS, the Royal Marine equivalent of the SAS, had developed a putty that hardened when mixed with water. The putty only required pressure for around ten seconds against a plastic hull to stick securely. For safety reasons, the putty was affixed to a metal plate with a waterproof plastic covering like a sandwich bag, that needed to be removed underwater. The lightweight plastic limpet mine with magnetic strips attached could then be fastened in place. Redwood checked the two mines. He had been advised to place one two-thirds towards the prow on the port side, and the other directly opposite on the starboard side. He had also been advised that an eighty-metre exclusion zone would be needed for detonation, and by no account did that extend to being underwater when that happened.

Redwood unloaded the next bag containing all the dive equipment he would need. He would be using the SBS, and US Navy SEAL developed *Atlantis* rebreather. The two amphibious special forces had jointly developed and rigorously tested the system which produced no bubbles, a requirement for clandestine insertion and sabotage. Exhaled carbon dioxide was removed using sodium hydroxide (sofnolime) and calcium hydroxide to form calcium carbonate (solid). Small tanks of nitrogen-oxygen and helium-oxygen were released into the breathing loop and a microprocessor controlled the oxygen delivery system. The result was a longer dive time, less time decompressing at regular intervals on ascent, and most importantly of all - no trace of a diver being under the surface releasing a bubble trail. Redwood had never used the system before and a laminated 'idiot's guide' had been included in the bag of kit. He quickly read through the guide, then donned his wetsuit, weight belt, diving knife, BCD – or buoyancy control device – a lifejacket normally inflated off the dive tank, but in this instance with its own slow-release CO_2 cartridge – and stacked his fins against the side of the boat. He dropped the swim ladder for boarding, then took both mines out of the kit bag and carefully placed them in a netted bag which he attached to his weight belt. He then strapped on the dive computer, which was like an oversized digital watch which also had a GPS on it, and the only way he would reach his target covertly. He would be using a DPV (diver propulsion vehicle), in this case a hand-held propeller system that could propel him thirty feet deep and work for an hour at 3 mph. It was positively buoyant in salt-water, and he tossed it over the side and watched as it floated just under the surface, the propeller breaking the surface in the light swells from the other boats. Lastly, he strapped on his fins, put on his mask then swung the rebreather onto his back and fastened it snugly. He checked the mouthpiece, then shuffled cumbersomely to the side and rested on the edge.

The water was clear and although he could not see far enough down to make out the seabed, he could see to around twenty or thirty feet. There were pleasure craft nearby, but they all seemed to be observing the Alpha flag for now, which at least kept prying eyes away. He started to breathe, the sensation feeling a little more restrictive than breathing from a regular tank, and there was a slightly chemical taste to it that he could not identify, but he had no comparison as a point of reference and there had been no mention of it in the 'idiot's guide', so he eased himself over backwards and plunged into the sea. After he had righted himself, he caught hold of the DPV and used it to swim downwards to around twenty-five feet, taking time to equalise his ear pressure on the way every six feet or so, and then tested for neutral buoyancy. He found himself sinking a little and pressed the valve that would inflate his BCD. He stopped sinking and started to rise. He bled off some of the CO_2 and found himself suspended in the water. He took a moment to experience the sensation without a burst of bubbles on each exhale and noticed that the shoals of fish made no effort to veer clear of him. Colourful little fish swam nearby, while shoals of grey mullet enveloped him entirely. Redwood checked the GPS and started the DPV again, this time keeping a straight and steady course as he checked the GPS.

Chapter Fourteen
Burindi

The drive to Seringa had taken two hours but it could have been walked in less than three, such was the state of the roads. A deluge of rain lasting no longer than half an hour had flooded the roads and turned the dust to thick, cloying mud. The potholes were now invisible, and progress had been painfully slow, jarring and uncomfortable. When they arrived the town barely made the journey worth it, but for the fact they could both get out and stretch out their stiff legs and aching backs.

The town of Seringa was a mixture of concrete, corrugated iron and timber. The main strip had been tarmacked many years ago with concrete pavements in a state of general disrepair. Wooden stalls seemed to have sprung up randomly and without consideration for vehicles using the road and sold everything imaginable from brooms and mops to bicycle wheels and street food. Goats and chickens roamed the street pecking and foraging at weeds and litter, and the carcases of tiny unidentifiable birds and strips of spiced mystery meat roasted above charcoal-fuelled flames, and cups of thin soup with bread seemed a popular choice with many people eating on the go. As they got out of the car a group of children flocked around them trying to sell them various fruits, and plastic bottles of water with worn labels and broken seals. King got the feeling that Western visitors were few and far between.

An old, open-topped Land Rover Defender drove erratically through the melee giving the people little choice but to scatter or die. The vehicle screeched to a halt and a compact man of sparing movements hopped out and walked confidently towards them. Stewart sent the children packing with a few stern words that seemed to be universally understood. King felt bad for the kids, but he could do without a bottle of amoebic dysentery and the fruit was looking about a week past its best, but the flies seemed to be enjoying it.

"Pierre, good to see you," Stewart greeted him warmly, shaking the man's hand.

"It's never good to see you, Peter." Pierre grinned, looking at King. "And this must be King, who I've heard much about..."

King shook the man's hand. His grip was firm, but there was no effort to dominate, which King always found so tedious. He had once broken a man's hand who wouldn't give up on his alpha-male aspirations of the dominant handshake. "Hopefully you heard something good," King replied.

"Only good things," Pierre replied, then added, "Since your recent adventures in the Congo."

King nodded. He had redeemed himself there, and Stewart would not be standing here had King not carried him out for mile after bloody mile.

"Pierre is my eyes and ears in the region," Stewart explained. "He's been here on the Firm's payroll on and off for six months." The ink on their mission may still be wet, but Stewart had seen the writing on the wall some time ago and had put an asset in place. Stewart's remit was vast, and the man could virtually write his own cheques. Stewart looked back at Pierre and said, "Show us the safe house first, then we'll see what you've found out."

They followed the Land Rover closely, Pierre playing a one-sided game of 'chicken' with the people, goats and pecking fowl of Seringa. Somehow, King thought the people had all been there before, their lives meaningless to people like Pierre, their own government's troops, police or soldiers from other countries routinely probing the borders of Burindi to see if there was any reaction. He felt sorry for the people, knowing that whether Mustafa remained in power or if Lucky Man Jonathon regained his presidency, it would make little difference to them. Out here, there was no bright future, no career opportunities. Survival and perseverance were all that mattered.

The road took them high into the mountains and the terrain gave way to agricultural terraces of cassava, yams, millet, corn, and bananas with men and small boys working the fields, and the women and girls wearing brightly coloured dresses carrying tremendous loads upon their heads. Higher still and they passed cotton, coffee, and tobacco plantations. There were grand yet dilapidated colonial houses of British and European influence isolated like lone islands in a sea of green. King did not know who lived in them, nor owned the plantations, but he doubted that they would get away without heavy taxation from Mustafa's socialist government. Or, lived under the threat of people trying to take what they had by any means.

After ten tediously uncomfortable miles, Pierre pulled into a narrow track so potholed that it looked more like a steep dried-up riverbed, with great boulders sporadically creating blockades that they had to manoeuvre around slowly. The track was hemmed in by thick brush on either side and Stewart shook his head irritably and drew his pistol. "Bloody ripe for an ambush," he said. "I don't like this..."

"You don't like anything except for whisky and whores," King replied, keeping his eyes on both the road and the brush on either side.

"Aye, well, not liking things has kept me alive this long," Stewart replied, but King said nothing. He was an agnostic, but if there was a god, then only he would know why Peter Stewart was still on this earth. The man seemed to have luck on his side, but he also knew that you made your own luck. "Looks like we're here," Stewart said, then added dejectedly. "Shit, what a dive."

The house was of wooden construction and reminded King of an Indonesian long house. Built on stilts and sitting four feet above the ground, the house was approximately fifty feet by twenty and open-fronted with a longer roof which acted like a veranda over the decked porch. The roof was finished with grass thatch. The walls largely bamboo and split branches. Outside, there was a covered cooking area with an open fire and a clay oven.

"Looks like we're shitting in the woods," said Stewart, getting out of the car as Pierre walked towards them. "Hey, Pierre, this is what my money buys?"

"Inconspicuous," he replied. "But all the mod-cons, as you English say."

"Aye, well, I'm a Scot and it looks about as comfortable as a fucking prostate exam without the fucking lube."

"Come on, Boss," King interjected. "We won't be spending much time here, anyway."

"There's a shower out the back," Pierre told them.

"There is?" Stewart asked.

"Yes, well. If someone holds the bucket while the other washes," he replied. "I'm glad you're here now, it's tricky washing your back on your own," he grinned.

"Fuck off." Stewart snatched his backpack off the rear seat and strode towards the hut. Inside there was a hammock and a couple of mattresses. He slung his bag in the hammock and said, "That's me..."

King could tell that Pierre had been using the hammock, but the man did not protest. King tossed his own bag on one of the mattresses. They were back in the hotel in two nights' time, this time in the main building in the comfortable rooms. King did not care who had been thrown out, just as long as he had a nice comfy bed and clean sheets after this place. Already, he could not wait. He thought about Lucinda and wondered whether she would be staying there when they returned. For a moment he was lost in the memory of her warmth, the softness of her skin the heaviness of her hair cascading over his stomach, her scent and touch, her taste.

Stewart looked at Pierre and said, "Right, show us what intel you've got."

Chapter Fifteen
Monaco

Lucky Man Jonathon Mugabe posed for photographs with the two women, an arm around each, his hands resting on their stomachs, low enough to be inappropriate had he not been confident in their intentions. The women were scantily clad in bikini tops and cut-off denim shorts. Tanned and slender they were ten a penny in Monaco, on the hunt for celebrities, film stars or billionaires enjoying the tax haven. They most likely had no idea who the man with his hands now firmly *mons pubis* was, and nor did they care. They had found a likely candidate for their affections. Lucky Man Jonathon, for all his failures as a nation's leader, exuded power, confidence, wealth and excess. And these two women could smell it like an alpha's pheromone in the animal kingdom.

The exiled president's usual entourage surrounded him, his former security team who had little training and even less of a clue what went into keeping a principal safe. Redwood watched the men surrounding Lucky Man Jonathon, acting like they were on their way to a party. Three more women had joined the gathering, and several of the entourage were sweeping up the newcomers with compliments, joviality and promises of a good time. The girls seemed happy enough to ignore the man at the centre of everyone's attention and latch onto these men, much like women hoping to get backstage at a concert and doing what had to be done with the stage security to get near the main act.

There were three men from the SAS team forming a triangle around Lucky Man a dozen paces away from him. Like Redwood, all three men were armed with Sig Sauer P225 9mm pistols. Leaving two men back at the villa as static security, the remaining two bodyguards waited in the Range Rover for a swift evacuation if required, one armed with a G36 assault rifle for good measure. The entourage had not been so prepared, parking their Mercedes S-Class saloons at the entrance to the marina, neither vehicle being legally parked but enjoying diplomatic immunity stickers on the windscreens. The entourage wore vast amounts of garish gold rings on their fingers and heavy chains and gold medallions over white T-shirts or singlets with unbuttoned Hawaiian style shirts billowing in the breeze, enough for their pistols to be seen tucked into their waistbands. They were undisciplined and a liability to the operation. But Redwood knew that things would soon change. He watched as a well-dressed man with jet black hair slicked-back in a ponytail walked directly towards Lucky Man Jonathon. Redwood recognised him as the Russian from the casino. Lucky Man had obviously not heeded the warning from the man from MI6. Redwood took out his mobile phone and dialled a number from his call list as Lucky Man Jonathon, the Russian and the entourage made their way down the quay. The women followed, five of them in all. Redwood wondered whether they knew what they would be in for with a man like Mugabe and his entourage. Promises of champagne and cocaine and partying, but they had really signed up for a gangbang that could last for days. Mugabe and his entourage were like a depraved tag-team and being at sea offered the women no chance to change their minds and return to shore. Redwood imagined that dealing with misogyny would not be high on Lucky Man Jonathon's agenda or manifesto when he returned to power. The call was answered, and Redwood wondered whether this would be the women's lucky day. He spoke quickly, told the man from MI6 (no names had been given) about the Russian's presence, heard the man berating Lucky Man Jonathon Mugabe in a string of creative profanities, then listened to what the man from MI6 had to say next. When he ended the call, he did not know whether the fate of the women would be worse or not, but at least they had a chance. He really could not afford to worry about it. People made their own choices and even on a base level, picking up rich men on the street was never the most sensible thing to do, and going out to sea on their yacht wasn't exactly being in control of the situation.

There were two tenders. Each was a taxi service to and from shore, and both were timber craft glistening with stain and wax and powered by twin V8 motors. Piloted by experienced helmsmen in matching white shirts and tailored shorts, they performed an efficient service while Lucky Man Jonathon, his entourage and the women packed out the two classic speedboats, popping bottles of champagne and drinking like there was no tomorrow.

"We'll take it from here," Mamadou Cilla said matter-of-factly. Mugabe's personal secretary seemed to relish standing Redwood and his men down. "Besides, what you don't see, you can't be witness to later..."

"We have been tasked to protect Mugabe," Redwood countered. "We can't do it from the shore."

"That's *President* Mugabe!" Mamadou Cilla snapped, his change of both tone and mood seeming unbalanced, almost bipolar.

"Not yet, chum," Redwood replied. "And he can't take his country back if he's dead."

"Our men have weapons. The boat is a safe place."

Redwood shrugged. "I decide what is a safe place."

"Problem?" Lucky Man Jonathon asked, abandoning one of the girls and leaning over the polished timber transom. "You can't babysit me all the time. Take the day off."

"We're your protection detail. That's how it works."

"We are safe on the boat!" Mugabe snapped. "Now, leave us be!" He swept a hand around the people in the two boats. "This is a private party," he said, his tone softening. "And you are not invited. My men will keep me safe."

Mamadou Cilla smiled smugly as the two boats cast off. "We'll meet you on the dock in around eight hours. Or tomorrow, I guess we'll see how we feel." He cupped his hand to his mouth over the roar of the engines. "Enjoy the sunshine! Put your feet up, Sass man! Leave the drinking and the fucking to us!"

Redwood watched, irked that the Russian had given him a smirk before turning his eyes to the horizon, but satisfied that someone in London had done their research thoroughly.

"Problem, Boss?" Mitchell asked. He was a sergeant, and on this operation, he was second in command, or 2 I/C.

"Not at all," Redwood replied. "It's all going to plan."

"What plan?"

Redwood smiled. "Just a bit of *secret squirrel* stuff."

"That slimy shit from Six who came to the villa?"

Redwood nodded as he took a radio control unit out from his pocket. It was about the size of his own Nokia 8210 mobile phone, but with a telescopic antenna. "Make yourself scarce, mate. Take the Range Rover back to the villa with the lads and I'll meet you there later."

Mitchell had been in the regiment long enough to know when he was stumbling into a paygrade matter. He shrugged and made his way back down the marina, having a quiet word with the other men before heading for the Range Rover.

Redwood climbed down the ladder to the twenty-two-foot RIB that had been procured for him. It was equipped with two, four-stroke Evinrude 150 HP engines and he had them started and running at a virtually silent tick over and was cast off inside three minutes. He motored out from the moorings and into the channel, taking off his jacket and tie and unbuttoning his collar and rolling up his sleeves as he guided the wheel with one hand. When he cleared the red and green marker buoys of the channel, he pushed the throttles forward, the prow rising, and he used the trim and tilt to adjust the angle of the propellers and fins as the craft settled into a flat plane and full speed.

Mugabe's one-hundred-foot Sunseeker motor yacht, courtsey of the UK government, was moored on the far side of the bay. The vessel had likely seen its fair share of gratu-itous sex, and copious consumption of alcohol and cocaine, but probably not in the quantities that Lucky Man Jonathon and his entourage were accustomed to. Which made the piloting of the vessel an issue when Lucky Man Jonathon preferred not to employ a captain, but take the helm himself, cheering as he cut across sailboats and left them in his violent wake as they tacked desperately to avoid a collision, as the deposed dictator was egged on by his ever-sycophantic entourage and the naïve good time girls of the day.

Redwood had gained on the two water taxis. He was now just a hundred metres behind, and a hundred to their starboard to avoid the considerable wake made by the massive twin-propellors driving both craft. The Sunseeker was moored in splendid isolation and steadily growing in size as they approached. Redwood throttled back and crawled forwards until the wake gradually caught him up to avoid flooding over the outboards. When the craft settled, he switched off the power and drifted, the silence filling his ears. The two water taxis had slowed, too. They were greeted by two of the three crew members who always remained on board providing a security presence and making sure that the champagne was chilled, the ice buckets were full, and the fridges were stocked with food. The third crew member was the captain, who brought the vessel in for fuelling and maintenance and would soon be redundant when Lucky Man Jonathon took over the helm for another white-knuckle ride along the principality of Monaco and the French Riviera.

Redwood watched the first boat moor alongside the swim platform. Typically, Lucky Man Jonathon was first off, followed by Cilla, who helped two of the girls off the boat. Fake stumbles and lots of clutching on to steady their balance showed which women were interested in whom, and Mugabe's personal bodyguard was last off and as the boat pulled away, the second water taxi moored expertly, and the entourage and girls followed. One of the girls seemed to have a change of heart and had to be cajoled out, looking back at the shore and about to make what could be a life-changing choice. She leapt back on board the water taxi and was immediately picked up by one of Mugabe's bodyguards and forcefully dumped on her behind on the swim platform. The water taxi cast off and the man at the helm seemed unperturbed by the incident. In Monaco, money ruled, and he had seen it all before. He'd see it again tomorrow.

The mines that the engineers in Portsmouth SBS barracks had developed had been adapted in many ways, but the most significant was the waterproof receiver units, that for reasons of simple physics trailed out from the mine above the plimsol line of the boat and were held in place by the same water-initiated putty to allow detonation from radio signal. Radio signals could not be sent or received underwater. Redwood pulled out the remote-control device and extracted the telescopic antenna. He needed to time it just right, because he did not want casualties, although he had already made peace with the possibility of Lucky Man Jonathon, Cilla Mamadou and the entourage being injured or killed in the blast. However, the good time girls and the crew would be unacceptable losses. He had no idea where the captain was, but if he was going to do this, then it would have to be now. Everyone was either on the swim platform, the transom or the aft quarter of the sleek vessel. He switched on the remote-control device and held down one of two buttons with his thumb for a count of three. A red light flashed, and he pressed the second button for another count of three and watched the red light burn solid. The device was now armed. When he released the button, an almighty explosion filled the air as both mines detonated at once. Two terrific geysers plumed into the air, a hundred feet high and splashing down over the boat as if it were monsoon rain. Redwood had seen figures thrown into the air by the blast, some landing in the water and others crashing down on the deck as the shockwave enveloped them. The same people clambered unsteadily to their feet or surfaced and treaded water as the flames caught towards the prow and the front section forward of the point at which Redwood had laid the mines broke off and the main body of the craft filled with water and quickly upended, forcing the rest of the people to leap overboard. Redwood tried a head count and was satisfied that the crew and good time girls had survived. Several of Mugabe's entourage were poor swimmers, and Redwood watched, sickened as they succumbed to a factor that the SAS soldier had considered, but not given great thought about. Drowning.

He was the closest vessel by far, but he had his orders. And besides, a few less of Mugabe's entourage could only make controlling the deposed dictator a whole lot easier for MI6 and Her Majesty's Government. Redwood needed to compartmentalise his actions. Had he been in a conflict lighting up the target with a laser designator for a fast jet dropping a Paveway bomb, then he could and would do nothing for the casualties. He needed to treat what he had just done as the delivery within a chain of events. The outcome was yet to be defined; he had merely guided events towards the end objective. He tossed the remote-control unit into the sea and started up the twin engines. Turning to starboard, he did not look back as he returned along the coastline to the marina.

Chapter Sixteen
Soka, Burindi

Pierre moved quickly through the undergrowth. King had operated in jungle before in the Democratic Republic of the Congo, but this was more like a cross between jungle and the heavy brush found on the savannah. The trees and bushes were thorny, and the ground was dry underfoot, despite the recent rains. The heat was less oppressive than what he had previously experienced when he had first landed, but they had still built up a sweat traversing the slope on the northeast side of the mountain. Pierre was clearly used to the terrain and King could see that he had a lot to learn from the mercenary, his Legionnaire training operating in hostile environments was truly evident by his lightness of foot and the way he contorted himself past thorny fronds, where Stewart stubbornly hacked his way through with a machete. Pierre's mantra was clearly – work smarter, not harder. King followed Pierre's lead, and although he was considerably taller and broader than the man leading the way, he found himself snagged less and less, until he eventually sheathed the machete and moved more quickly, with Stewart – an experienced ex-para and SAS trooper – becoming snagged on the swathes of thorns that he swiped at with the blade.

Pierre stopped in his tracks and held up his right fist. King instinctively squatted on his haunches, aiming the Makarov at something unseen beyond the Swiss mercenary. "Rock python," Pierre whispered eventually. "Five metres long and about ninety kilos. They have a nasty bite and latch on with backward facing teeth, then coil around you quickly and squeeze harder every time you breathe in. A snake like that would be five times stronger than any of us. He's a real big boy..."

"It couldn't take us on though, surely?" King stated tentatively.

"We'd be alright, lad. But a little runt like Pierre could be its breakfast," Stewart chided. King stood up slowly to get a better look as Stewart brushed past him. He crept closer and studied the creature, which was coiled and looking straight at them, its head at least three feet off the ground. Indeed, it was the largest snake King had ever seen. Stewart continued onwards unperturbed, and the snake somewhat predictably lunged at him. The Scotsman swung the machete, and the snake finished its strike with its head rolling off into the brush. The animal's headless body thrashed and twisted and coiled on the ground in its death throes as Stewart stepped over it and took over point. He turned around and said, "If the wee beastie is still there on the way back, then we can have it for supper." He looked at King and said, "Get your machete out, lad. The next snake we see may be a Black Mamba, and you'll wish you had it in your hand then. They attack and chase you down on sight."

King stared at the animal's head; the size of both his fists clasped together. Its lifeless eyes 'blinking' in that unnerving reptilian way of just a clear membrane washing over from the side, and its mouth gasping for air that would never come.

Pierre smiled. "Better to walk around a snake than to get in its way."

"But at least we have something for dinner later." Stewart paused. "How much further?"

"Three clicks, same heading," Pierre replied.

"Chances of a roving patrol?"

"Almost nil."

"Almost?" Stewart asked incredulously. "I hate almost."

"Our cover is intact," said King. "If we run into anyone, then we use it. Photographer, journalist and guide."

"Fucking parrots!" Pierre laughed.

"You got a better idea?" Stewart barked and pushed past him into the brush.

Pierre looked at King and said, "You'll get used to him."

"I bloody hope not," King grinned back at him.

Pierre laughed, but then his eyes flickered for a moment, and he shouted, "Contact!" as gunfire erupted and the brush around them splintered and was torn down and all three men fled through the bush as all hell broke loose behind them.

Chapter Seventeen
The Savoy Hotel, London

The waiting staff were smartly attired in black and white and carried themselves with poise and purpose. The wooden tables and panelling shone with a rich lustre, polished and waxed for decades. Linen tablecloths were washed and starched and brilliant white. Ironed on the table to render them devoid of a single crease. Glassware caught the light like diamonds under a jeweller's lamp and the silverware glistered like treasure. The music was low, and the conversation was high. The room seemed to breathe with the atmosphere, lungs filled by the ambiance of good times, anticipation and decadence. To eat here was a culinary experience to be savoured.

"I do enjoy it here," Armstrong said, spooning caviar onto a blini and topping it with sour cream. "The head chef has returned after a ten-year absence. I understand he came here from Green's Restaurant and Oyster Bar."

Sir Hugo Truscott smiled. "Which is why I invited you here. You can't go wrong at the Savoy Grill. Tell me, how is the sevruga? Overfishing has driven up the price and will likely affect supply before long."

"It's divine," Armstrong replied without any apparent concern for the dwindling numbers of Black Sea sturgeon.

Truscott had opted for the steamed scallops with lemon and samphire velouté. He finished his final mouthful and placed his knife and fork deliberately on the plate until he had found the exact position. A stippler for tradition, he had placed the tines of the fork at twelve o'clock with the handle naturally at six. His knife was placed directly across from three to nine with the blade at the nine o'clock position indicating that he was ready for his next course. He watched as Armstrong simply placed his knife and fork together with the handles nearest him and he smiled at the man's lower middleclass pretentions. Ignorant in the formalities of fine dining. The waiter took Truscott's plate and asked Armstrong if he was indeed ready for his next course. He smiled at Armstrong's bemusement. Another waiter brought Truscott his steak knife on a folded linen napkin on a silver salver, as he had ordered the sirloin steak. There was no knife for Armstrong as he had ordered the lobster thermidor.

"How goes the Burindi situation?" Truscott asked casually, but with a little more enthusiasm than he had hoped for. "All well for Lucky Man Jonathon's... *re-election?*"

"That's quite a way of putting it," Armstrong replied, marvelling at the politician's almost blatant diplomacy. "Reinstatement would be closer to the truth."

"And..." Truscott paused awkwardly. "Is there a hope of the coup being a bloodless one?"

"Yes," Armstrong replied, pausing as the waiting staff produced his lobster and buttered asparagus. He watched as Sir Hugo's steak and side dish of pommes dauphinoise was placed before him. They declined offers of anything else and once left alone, Armstrong said. "The only hope is none

whatsoever. Lucky Man Jonathon Mugabe will be reinstated once Mustafa has been deposed." He paused. "There
will be blood. And a great deal of it..."

"Regrettable."

"Indeed. But sadly, unavoidable."

"But you have deemed it possible."

"You've been in the meetings with the PM."

"I have. But I want your take on it."

Armstrong smiled. "You have personal interests?"

"You know I have."

"Lithium."

"There's no point denying it. Not to a man like you."

Armstrong knew all about Sir Hugo Truscott's business
interests. Or at least most of them. He also knew that the
cabinet member had advocated giving Lucky Man Jonathon
Mugabe aid in his exile, removing Mustafa from power and
reinstating the former leader. He had been extremely vocal
in his support. "I know all about your metallurgical interests
in the region, as well as your oil interests in Angola. It rather
seems you are heavily committed, or at least *invested* in the
stability in western and central Africa."

"I cannot afford for there to be any hiccups in regime
change."

Armstrong shrugged as he ate some of the delicious
lobster then washed it down with a mouthful of the
chardonnay which had been expertly paired with the dish
for its oaky, buttery and fruity overtones. "My department
are instigating the overthrow at the behest of the Prime
Minister, *not* the minister for business. Your business interests are not the concern of SIS. You seem to be lacking that
ministerial quality of being an unbiased conduit for the
public's best interest." He paused, smirking. Even though
he would not be picking up the bill for the meal, he did not

hide his bemusement at the situation and the blatant conflict of interest that the man seated opposite him had in Burindi. "But then, I suppose all members of parliament start with the best of intentions..."

Sir Hugo Truscott raised an eyebrow as he smeared the quenelle of glistening bone marrow butter over his steak. The knife was a sharpened affair with a polished rosewood handle, more like a chef would use than a patron. The meat gave way willingly and he ate the mouthful savouring both taste and texture with equal enjoyment. "You knew what this conversation would regard," he said measuredly. "*When* you accepted my invitation to lunch."

"I was curious," Armstrong replied. "And the chance of lunch at The Savoy isn't something I would turn down without good reason."

"So, you would be open to an incentive?"

"I serve my country, Sir Hugo. That has always been enough for me."

"As do I." Truscott paused. "But you already accepted a free lunch. And that will be at least a few hundred pounds, so what's the difference with accepting more? One needs to live, and one needs a nest egg to retire on. It is extremely difficult to get a foothold in the financial market these days."

"I understand your keenness to control what seems left to fate," Armstrong said before taking another mouthful of succulent lobster. He chewed unhurriedly, then drained his twenty-pound glass of chardonnay. A waiter glided past, taking the bottle from the ice bucket and topping up his glass before seeming to glide to another table. The bottle was empty, and his glass was full. Three glasses from a sixty-pound bottle, but Armstrong wasn't going to be taking out his own wallet today. "I have always wanted to invest, but I am a little naïve in the subject of shares and stock portfolios," he ventured. "I assume you have people who could take care of that for me?"

"Certainly."

"And as a mere civil servant, I have little in the way of capital to invest."

Sir Hugo nodded and smiled wryly. "I understand entirely."

"I think lithium, cobalt, uranium and oil would be most interesting to me."

"That is sound practice," Truscott replied. "Staples like uranium and oil are bankable, and speculative minerals like lithium make sense in the new and evolving technology and electronic market." He paused. "Like my grandmother used to say – the farmer who grows his own vegetables and potatoes doesn't have to spend his money when he slaughters a lamb for his Sunday roast."

"She sounds like a lovely old girl."

"Couldn't stand her, personally. But I get what the old crab meant. Cover all the bases, and you can't go wrong."

"I'll leave the investment to you, Hugo. Whatever you think it's worth..." He studied the man opposite him. Red-faced, working towards portly and the wrong side of fifty. Lord only knew how he had hooked a woman like Lucinda Davenport, the foreign correspondent for the Telegraph and infrequent, though well-liked special correspondent for Sky News. But then he thought about Sir Hugo's millions and his political career. It certainly hadn't harmed the woman's journalistic career, although he suspected she would have made it on her own. The woman had looks, talent and tenaciousness in abundance. "I mean, it would be a relief for you to know you had the inside track and that your interests would be supported because of my own."

"It certainly would."

The two men made their way through the delicious meal. Armstrong had set his cutlery down like most people would, but Sir Hugo made great deliberation spacing his knife and fork like an 'equals' sign, the tines of the fork and tip of the blade pointing to the three o'clock position, indicating that the meal was indeed excellent. Desserts, cheese and port followed and after an hour and a half from finishing their main courses, Sir Hugo and Armstrong shook hands in the foyer of The Savoy and both men were picked up on the only anti-clockwise roundabout in London by their cars and respective drivers.

Armstrong lost sight of Sir Hugo Truscott's Jaguar XJ6 around Covent Garden. His driver headed down to the river and past New Scotland Yard, where he pulled in and picked up their passenger. They both rode in the back, the driver taking no notice of them as he drove a circular route that would once again, take them past The Savoy and on towards Westminster and the River House.

"Have we got him?" Felicity Willmott asked.

"Absolutely."

"You are sure?"

Armstrong smiled. "Hook, line and bloody sinker..."

Chapter Eighteen
The Burindi Highlands

Stewart's heart was pounding. He had broken left on the contact and fought his way through thick cover, the bullets deflecting off trees and branches behind him as he ran. King had gone right because the direction and ferocity of the gunfire had given him little choice in the matter. Pierre had started to follow Stewart but had gone down after a volley of gunfire, crying out in shock and pain. The last Stewart had seen of Pierre, the man had been scrabbling on his belly and elbows into the brush.

The Scotsman held the Makarov in his left hand, his trusty sheath knife in his right. In the confines of the heavy brush, he would use the knife as effectively as a gun, and he could fire most weapons ambidextrously, but wanted the dominant strength and dexterity of his right hand to wield the blade. He had not gone back for Pierre. There were times when you could, and times when you couldn't and knowing the difference had kept Stewart alive for twenty years in his profession. The gunfire had been sustained and heavy and they had avoided being pincered by what he could only have supposed to be a negligent discharge by one of the Burindi soldiers. It had given them vital seconds to move before the rest of the troops had opened fire. He took out his button compass and checked the sun for a directional prompt. He had not fired the Makarov, so had eight rounds at his disposal. Good that he was armed, but far from ideal up against automatic weapons. He was seriously under gunned and estimated the gunfire to have come from a force of at least thirty troops. Stewart headed west - his pace rapid and his breathing steady for the brief rest - and could only hope that King was still alive.

Chapter Nineteen

King had found himself separated from the others, the gunfire erupting to his left, and sporadically from his right. He had chosen the path of least resistance and while he fled to avoid the overwhelming gunfire, he had slipped and fallen down a steep incline, his fall slowed by saplings that snapped as he ploughed through them, and his fall was only broken after a hundred metres of travel by thicker trees and snagging thorns. Above him, gunfire bore down around him, and he pushed his way through the thick thorns, the barbs tearing at his flesh and ripping his clothes.

He had lost the Makarov and machete in the fall, and now had only his Leatherman multitool in his pocket. It had a folding, locking blade that was honed to a razor-sharp edge, but at slightly less than three inches in length, it was a tool first and foremost and only turned to a weapon in a pinch. Behind him branches shattered with the gunfire, but he was out of their line of sight, and more or less out of range. Even bullets from the most powerful guns, capable of penetrating half an inch of steel plate, could be deflected by flimsy branches. He limped on, feeling a twinge from his ankle which must have been sustained during the fall, his adrenalin levels too high at the time to feel the pain.

The gunfire died down, then somewhat eerily, ceased altogether. King reflected how nature had seemed to hold its breath. Not a sound. No monkeys chattering, no birds calling and no ground animals rustling in the undergrowth. King had never felt so alone. He checked the dials of his watch against the sun to find west, lining up the hour hand on the sun and bisecting the angle from north to south. He had to visually place Burindi on the atlas, determining whether it was in the Northern Hemisphere, which indeed it was, but only just. He also had to make allowances for daylight saving, but his training was still fresh in his mind, and he had excelled at orienteering and survival practices taken on the Brecon Beacons and in the New Forest. He had experience in the jungle from his recent operation in Angola and the Democratic Republic of the Congo, and the terrain in the Burindi Highlands was far less dense, far cooler and a lot easier going for his escape. However, without a machete for the thicker brush, a weapon to use against his pursuers or dangerous animals, he had never felt more exposed nor vulnerable.

Chapter Twenty
Monaco

Despite the warmth of the sun Lucky Man Jonathon Mugabe sat with a silver emergency blanket pulled tightly around his shoulders and a forlorn expression quite at odds with the exiled dictator's usual arrogance. Paramedics had given him a clean bill of health, but some of his entourage had not been so lucky. Four men had drowned, one body not yet recovered. The good time girls and the crew had made it, as had Lucky Man Jonathon's private secretary, Mamadou Cilla. However, the experience had knocked the arrogance out of him also, and he huddled underneath his own survival blanket, a cup of strong coffee cradled attentively between his shaking hands. The warm Mediterranean shallows crowded at the shore with topless women and pot-bellied men was quite a different experience a mile out to sea with nothing to latch onto.

Redwood watched from the street. Private ambulances in the form of black Mercedes Vito vans had taken away the bodies, while four ambulances had taken the injured to hospital. Police had done their best to question both

Mugabe and Cilla and had met a brick wall of diplomatic immunity. A senior detective was talking to someone who looked like a civil servant and shaking his head despairingly. The detective shared a few short words with Cilla, left his calling card and stalked off towards a beaten-up Fiat Panda that did not have a single panel of its powder blue paint-work left unscathed. Redwood walked calmly up to Mugabe, the few men remaining from his entourage acting as a cordon around the exiled dictator, bedraggled and soaked and exhausted from their time treading water or swimming towards the shore for their lives.

"You were supposed to protect us!" Cilla snapped as Redwood drew near.

"Then you should listen to your head of security and not dismiss both the team and him as you would domestic help on minimum wage," Redwood replied unperturbed. He pushed past the largest of Mugabe's entourage, glaring at the man, daring him to make something of it. The man, all six-four and twenty-stone of him, backed down and returned to the others who were slowing drying in the Monaco sunshine. Redwood ignored Cilla and stared at Lucky Man Jonathon. "That was your wake-up call," he said coldly. "I've spoken to London and if you don't stop this shit, don't listen to your security..." He thumbed his own chest, his eyes hard and unafraid. "That's me, by the way, dickhead... then the deal is off. A crisis team are assembling to hash out a trade deal with Mustafa, or whoever the hell is in power in Burindi next month, and you will be cut-off both financially and politically. You won't afford the Monaco lifestyle after Interpol have seized your assets and you will likely end up in Malaga on the Costa-del-Crime with fat, tattooed wannabe gangster cockneys and their orange, plastic wives as your social circle."

"My men are dead..." Mugabe said somewhat meekly, and Redwood recognised shock when he saw it. The exiled dictator looked to be a shadow of his former self.

Redwood squatted on his haunches, his eyes level with the man's own, then said quietly, "Your Russian friend didn't make it, did he?" Mugabe shook his head despondently, the realisation that he had been playing both sides and was now back at square one with no other options available suddenly hitting him with as much force as the bombs that had shaken his world just two hours previously. "So, all side deals are off. The people you are dealing with do their research. They don't take kindly to being shafted once a deal has been made." He smiled as Mugabe frowned, his shaken mind starting to connect the dots. "That's right, big man. Your Russian friend couldn't swim. He was, of course known to the British intelligence services. It's frightening what information is in those files, deep in the basements of MI6 and MI5. A person's blood group, their predilections and vices, their family and known associates. And then there's the unusual stuff, the information that may come in handy one day. Like whether they're diabetic, have a heart condition or a food allergy... or just matters like whether or not they can swim." He reached out and patted the man's cheek. "Welcome back, President Mugabe. Now, let's keep you safe until you return to Burindi."

Chapter Twenty-One
The Burindi Highlands

Stewart had been around the block enough to trust his instincts and he had operated in enough of the world's hotspots and warzones to know when he was being followed. Confident that he had evaded the main force, he found a rock crevice behind a fallen tree and hastily tucked himself inside. He had sheathed the knife and now held the Makarov firmly in his right hand, the sights trained on the path he had taken among a myriad of animal trails, and he closed his eyes, breathing steadily before holding his breath and concentrating on nothing but sound. Tiny creatures scuttled on the forest floor, birds called on the wing – still too spooked to return to roost – but above all these things, he heard footsteps. Stewart opened his eyes his breathing shallow and his chest shook slightly as he tried to control it and make as little noise as possible with each exhalation. His hand shook minutely, but not enough to affect his aim at this distance. Besides, after the first shot, the first contact, he knew that his body would cooperate, and the shakes would only come again afterwards when the adrenalin started to subside. And sometimes in the middle of the night, but a good slug of whisky would take care of that.

The footsteps stopped and Stewart steadied his aim. Slowly, they started again, easing forwards. Stewart suspected just one man, but that did not mean that others had not held back to provide covering fire. He was confident that he had not been heard, and he was sure that he had left little sign since bugging out, at least taking more care not to break branches or twigs or kick over stones or step in soil that was still damp in the permanent shade under the canopy of trees.

"Stewart..." Pierre called out nervously, but as attuned to his surroundings as the Scotsman.

Stewart kept his aim but did not reply. He wasn't about to trigger a trap set with a gun held to the Swiss mercenary's head.

"I've got an SLR and will shoot up the area in three seconds if you don't show yourself."

That changed matters somewhat.

"Alright, pal. Step through, nice and slowly like." Stewart heard five footsteps before he could see Pierre through the brush. As Pierre cleared the trees, he could see that the man was bleeding from his right arm and shoulder. He held the massive rifle in his left-hand pistol style. Whether the man could handle the massive recoil of the 7.62mm L1A1 SLR one-handed would remain to be seen. "Shit, you've been shot!"

"Fucking tell me about it..."

"I just did," Stewart stepped forwards and inspected the man's wounds. Two bullets, thankfully 9mm. As well as ex-Soviet stock AK-47 and AK-74 assault rifles and British

SLR battle rifles, the Burindi military armed their soldiers with Israeli Uzi 9mm machine pistols, as well as British supplied 9mm Browning pistols. Pierre had been lucky, if being hit by two 9mm bullets could be classified as such. "At least it wasn't a round from that," he said, nodding at the rifle on the ground. The rifle, known in the British military as the L1A1 had been designed at a time when military rifles had been made to kill, not wound. Wounding tied up the enemy. Wounded soldiers needed medics and exfil or medevacs and doctors and nurses and rehabilitation. Dead soldiers required a body bag. "You'll live," he said, taking out a small medical pack and opening antiseptic wipes and handing them to him. "Give it a scrub," he told him. "As hard as you can handle. Where's King?" he asked, opening a packet of blood coagulant powder.

"No idea," Pierre replied through gritted teeth, the pain all too present now that he had stopped moving and his adrenalin was subsiding. "He went one way when we went the other..."

Stewart shook the powder over the two wounds and then applied two heavy-duty adhesive pads. He taped the pads in place with microfibre tape and handed the man a pill. "Opiate," he explained. "Chew for best results. You've got a graze on the arm and a through and through in the shoulder. Doesn't look like the collarbone was hit. I will clean them, stitch and patch them when we get back." He nodded, chewing emphatically on the opiate. "How did you get the rifle?"

Pierre shrugged. "I ran into one of them in the chaos and relieved him of it."

"I bet he didn't like that."

"I don't recall giving him much choice," Pierre said quite seriously. "What about King?"

Stewart shrugged. "He's a big boy and he knows the risks." He paused as he checked his button compass. "He also knows that he's on his own from now on."

Chapter Twenty-Two

Blood and sweat contaminated his eyes. His heart rate was off the scale. He could not breathe. He knew he was going down, and he knew that he would not be getting back up. He had only felt this way once before, but he had had a referee in the ring and people in his corner and upon his opponent's last flurry of punches he had pulled a lucky uppercut and stayed on his feet when the other man went down. But there would be no lucky punch today. There were bodies around him, but they were unconscious not dead. Cornered, exhausted, they had been set upon him by their commander like hounds on a fox. King had held them off at first, one or two punches dropping each man in a well-disciplined display of pugilism. Seven men in and seven men down. They changed their tactics and came in two or three at a time and King pulled the dirty tricks out of the bag - eye-gouges, kicks that knocked the kneecaps clean away from bone and ligament, throat strikes – he did not hold back, but he was exhausted now and the men kept coming and all at once, he found himself overwhelmed and the kicks and punches rained down upon him, and then the stamps of boots were replaced with rifle butts and as he was dragged onto his knees in front of the Sandhurst-trained officer, he felt the impact against the back of his skull which shook his brain so hard that he felt a nauseating pain at the front of his skull and then, predictably everything faded to black.

He came round an indeterminable amount of time later. Hands and feet bound and taking his weight, a thick and sturdy trimmed branch threaded through with his back grounding occasionally on rocks and thorns, two men at each end as a rich safari hunter's bearers would bring back game after a hunt. He could barely see, the blood caked at his eyes, and he knew that his nose had been broken, the metallic taste of blood at the back of his throat and in his sinuses. Every movement hurt his ribs and his limbs felt as though they were on fire taking his weight, and he could no longer feel his hands or feet, the circulation cut by the excruciatingly tight bonds. Soon, the terrain changed, and the ground levelled out. King was aware of vehicle doors opening and closing, the sound of men climbing up into flatbed lorries and sorting out their equipment. He was dropped onto the hard earth, the pole used to bear his weight was removed and his arms screamed with pain as what little blood that could get past his bonds pumped through his veins. He received a kick to the ribs and gasped as the wind was knocked from his lungs. There were voices – instructions shouted in a tribal language that he was unfamiliar with – and then some pidgin English.

The officer's face came into view, his eyes hidden by 70's mirrored aviators. His face was pock-marked and wet with perspiration, and some of it dripped into King's own face as he spoke. "Welcome to Hell," he grinned, displaying huge white teeth with the largest gap between two front teeth that King had ever seen. "Now, you will see how we treat spies in our country."

"I'm not a spy," King managed to spit out. Better to start denying straight away. "I am a photographer working with a freelance journalist!" He paused. "We're here for the flesh-eating parrots!" He heard himself say it, but it sounded ridiculous and forced the moment the words had left his lips.

"Zombie parrots!" the man roared, and his men all laughed raucously. Then he looked at King seriously as he removed the cheap sunglasses. "Nature is nature. It evolves. And this is Africa, the cradle of the world. People know less about nature than they could possibly ever know. There is no story here, white man. You will have to do better than that. But first, I think you need some time to reflect." The man's sweaty face disappeared and was replaced by the faces of three young men. King knew what was coming next, but there was nothing he could do but take their beating and hope he could stick to his cover story, but as he started to fade to unconsciousness, he did not hold out much hope.

Chapter Twenty-Three

"You *will* talk. It is as simple as that. There are many things that can be done to make this a reality. Firstly, there are psychological techniques. Lies will always reveal themselves. Eventually, you will forget what you have said and will inevitably be tripped up, because everything you say will be recorded and cross-referenced and revisited. Secondly, there is conditioning. Cold, heat, thirst, noise, light, sleep deprivation, hunger... all these things break a person down eventually. And all these things combined can do it extremely quickly. And then, of course, there is pain. Torture can take many forms from slapping and punching to waterboarding, and stress positions. These methods break a person's soul. But for the very toughest, the pain can always be increased. Cuts, burns, electric shocks, tooth removal, fingernails, digit removal... it really is endless and left best to the imagination. Although one thing is for certain... everybody talks eventually. Everybody has a limit."

King could see her now as he closed his eyes, thinking on her words back inside that cold, remote farmhouse on the

Brecon Beacons, where the SIS and MI5 trained their field recruits alongside the Special Air Service. He had been naked and shivering and she had laughed at the size of his penis and joked among the other interrogators that no woman would ever even know if he was inside them. He knew it to be far from the truth, it was classic humiliation, but by the end of the first day he would have doubted his own name and started to believe anything she said. He had been starving and thirsty, cold and exhausted. The woman from MI5 was an expert interrogator and it had been true – he had broken eventually. Sort of. He had told half his story to buy himself some time, but he had become confused and disorientated and the lies had tripped him up. Lesson learned. And all without physical violence, save for the odd slap and rough handling in and out of the cell and the inter-rogation room. But King had taken something vitally impor-tant away from the experience, and the entire physical training in the field operations division. Train hard; fight easy. Not that this would be easy, but he would bet that he knew a hell of a lot more than the man opposite him.

King slowly opened his eyes. It was a struggle because both were swelling shut and bruised terribly from the beating.

"Once again... who are you working for?" the man snarled at him from behind the desk. After a silent count of three, the blows came just as King had expected. The man smiled as the two soldiers beat him. When they had finished, he examined an imaginary spot on a fingernail and looked to have an idea. He snapped something in pidgin English and a third solider wheeled over a trolley containing an array of tools, medical implements and a boxcutter. "We shall see if you tell the truth."

King, naked and strapped to a straight-backed wooden

dining chair with sturdy arms, flinched as the man caught hold of the nail of his left little finger with a pair of pliers and started to wriggle the tool from side to side. He gritted his teeth and sucked in air as the soldier pulled and twisted and the nail was pulled clear, the strangest sensation imaginable creeping into his fingertip. There was a sadistic grin on the soldier's lips and for a moment that seemed to trouble King more than the removal of the nail, but then the pain kicked in and he shouted and cursed something inaudible, the searing agony making him forget all about the soldier, who had already secured the next fingernail and was waiting for the word from the man behind the table. There was no question, not so much as an indication of one. The man nodded and the next fingernail was torn slowly out of King's finger. King was ready this time and closed his eyes as he gritted his teeth but made no sound other than that of his raspy breathing, his broken nose making a faint whistling sound.

"Who are you?" the man asked once again. He was dressed in jeans with a white shirt that had picked up some grime along the way. King did not know the man's name, but he had heard the officer dismissed and assumed that he was a member of the Burindi secret police that Stewart had briefed him on earlier. The same secret police that were missing two of their number in a wrecked vehicle somewhere down a ravine.

"My name is Alex King..." he replied, sticking to Stewart's golden rule for field group agents. King had spent four years learning to leave Mark Jeffries behind and take on the legend of Alex King. Checks would show Mark Jeffries having a criminal record and drowning in a bog escaping prison on Dartmoor, but nothing would show for Alex King, apart from a website Stewart had commissioned with various photograph's highlighting King's supposed portfolio and a biography of who he had worked for over the years. Enough to keep the Burindi secret police busy and hopefully satisfied. "I work as a freelance photographer," he rasped. The man nodded to the soldier and another fingernail was ripped out of his finger. King screamed loudly this time, remembering Stewart's teachings. Look broken and defeated while you still had reserves and they may not take you to the brink. He did not have to fake it though, simply let down his guard and acknowledge the pain. "Please..." he begged right out of the playbook. "I am just a nature photographer!"

"You are one of Mugabe's spies!"

King stared at the Rolex Submariner on the man's wrist. There was a white tan mark on King's left wrist where it had spent the last two years. He refocused, his eyes meeting the new owner of his watch. "Who?" he said, feigning confusion.

"Lucky Man Jonathon Mugabe!"

King frowned. "But he has been exiled. President Mustafa is Burindi's leader."

The man slammed his fist down on the table. "Enough!"

King shook his head. "But I don't know what you mean!"

"Silence!" The man looked at the soldier and shouted, "Break a finger!"

The soldier did not hesitate and bent King's left index finger upwards. King tried to resist but failed dismally and the finger cracked like a dry twig and when the man released his grip, King's finger was pointing to the ceiling and immovable. King breathed sharply, the break not hurting as much as he expected, but he knew that setting it would be a different matter entirely. Straight out of the playbook he wailed and rocked, then within a minute he was no longer acting and genuinely reeling in pain. He started to try and control his breathing, then closed his eyes and slumped in the chair. He felt a slap to his head but did not react. He needed time to think and the best way to do that was to play unconscious. He doubted that it would work, but two pairs of rough hands clamped his shoulders and a third sliced through the cable ties, so he guessed he had been convincing enough. He was dragged roughly from the chair, and he kept himself a dead weight for the two men, who coped well enough with his fourteen stone frame. After around a hundred feet or so, they paused and unlocked a cell door, and he was tossed inside. He landed heavily, groaned involuntarily and lay on the cool stone floor waiting to hear his captors retreat, which they did ten minutes later after sharing a cigarette at the door. The heavy metal door closed, and their voices echoed down the corridor and eventually an ominous silence ensued.

Chapter Twenty-Four

Stewart looked up halfway through hastily packing his bag. Whoever had knocked on his door was not going away. He picked up the pistol and crept across the hotel room to the door. There was no spy hole, so he stood to one side and said brusquely, "Yes?"

"It's Lucinda Davenport."

"Fuck off lady, I'm busy."

The knock was louder this time. "Please open the door." Stewart cursed loudly and unlocked the door. He opened it cautiously, the pistol pointed at her, or anyone using her as a Trojan Horse, from behind the door. "I know something is wrong," she explained. "And considering that the jungle telegraph is saying that two members of the secret police have been found killed in the highlands and that an Englishman suspected of spying has been captured by local troops out on an exercise, then I sort of put two and two together." She looked past Stewart at the pile of clothes and the open bag on the bed. "Well, that kind of confirms it," she said emphatically.

"I have to get going," he said impatiently.

"Just like that?"

"Just like that."

"You're leaving him?"

"He'd leave me if the tables were turned."

She scoffed loudly. "When you were shot in the Congo, he carried you for miles on his bloody back!"

"This is different. In battle things are always different."

"Bullshit!"

"It is what it is."

"So, you're leaving before he succumbs to torture and gives you away? Nice."

"Everybody breaks, luv. It's just how it is. He's a tough lad, but he'll talk, and when he does, he'll tell them where I am and what we were really doing out here."

"Good to see you have faith in him," she replied sardonically. "How far did he carry you on his back?"

Stewart glared at her and said, "Look, I care about the lad. But he's finished." He paused, shaking his head. "Now, like I said earlier, fuck off and let me pack." He watched as she turned and stormed out of his room. "And you'd best forget about him too!" he shouted, but she had already slammed the door.

Chapter Twenty-Five

King had tried to get to his feet but found it difficult to stand. He slid down the stone wall exhausted, the coarse stone grazing his back. He looked at his ruined finger and took a deep breath before examining it. It was most likely broken as well - he would never know what damage had been done without an x-ray - but he could clearly see that it was severely dislocated. He caught hold of it with his right hand and took another deep breath as he pulled it out to reset it, but it simply would not budge. The pain was acute, but he knew that it was going to get a whole lot worse, because it was going to require all his strength and resolve. A couple of deep breaths, a clench of his teeth and he heaved on the finger, stretching the ligaments until the digit straightened and realigned. He gasped as the joints touched together, and with a wriggle and a twist to fine tune it, the finger was straight and seemed to be back in place. He could not bend it, but he had broken a finger once before and knew that it would be a long recovery that needed a few days taped and splinted before he would be able to attempt to bend it again. Looking around the cell, he saw a piece of broken cable tie among the dried faeces, vomit and bloodstains. As he bound his index and middle finger together with it, he wondered how it had worked out for the last person to wear the cable tie around their wrist.

King tried to stand again and leaned against the wall to steady himself. His finger throbbed, but now that the pain was somewhat less acute, he could suddenly feel where the blows had struck his face, head and ribs. He looked down at his left hand. The fingernails, or rather where the fingernails had been, were bloody and bruised and incredibly tender. They would eventually grow back, he had been told that much during his training, but it would take at least six months or most likely a year. Either way, he realised that his missing fingernails were the least of his concerns right now.

Bars on the window and a yard outside. That was for starters. King could see a double wire fence with a six-foot gap between the two wires. On top, razor wire coils on both sides made for a near-impossible obstacle. Not good. And with the fact he had no equipment and was as naked as the day he was born, it looked even worse. But he was puzzled because he had studied the military base from the reconnaissance photographs that Pierre had taken, and the buildings were all of wood construction with corrugated iron rooves and there had only been a single wire fence cordoning the area. There had also been four guard towers, and King could not see any sign of a guard tower from his cell window. Instead, a cluster of CCTV cameras looked in every direction from the top of a tall wooden telegraph pole. He had clearly been taken someplace else. He came back off his tiptoes and looked back at the door. It was metal with a hinged inspection slot and a larger flap which would be used to pass in food. Hopefully soon, because he was starving. But it never arrived. He was taken again hours later, long after it had gone dark. Just when his reserves were at their lowest and tiredness had forced him to finally succumb to sleep.

The light was bright and focused directly on his face. Blinding, intrusive. His lips were dry, and he tried licking them, but his mouth was parched and devoid of any moisture. Still squinting at the brightness, he asked for water and was met with an obnoxious laugh.

The light lowered and the man smiled at him from behind the table, the stainless-steel Rolex on his wrist glinting in the light. "First, you talk..."

"I am a British citizen," he rasped, his throat dry and constricted. "My name is Alex King, and I work as a freelance photographer specialising in the natural world."

"You are a spy, Mister King. Do not insult my intelligence."

"I would never mean to do that," King lied. There was plenty he would like to do to the man as well as insulting him.

"I see you have triaged your finger," the man grinned as King involuntarily flinched. "Please, I am not so short on ideas or repertoire as to go over old ground. There are plenty more body parts for my men to explore."

King stared at his watch, the man's words washing over him. There was nothing he could do if the man wished him harm. He just had to take it on the chin. That was one of Stewart's euphemisms. *Take it on the chin, laddie. Be a man about it...* Well, here was his chance. To last long enough for his mentor to escape capture. Stewart was never going to hang around and play the diplomat card in a country where there was no longer any British presence either by embassy, or even a lone ambassador sharing an office. No, Stewart would run for the border and cross over to a friendlier African nation before flying back to England and facing the music for a botched operation.

The man behind the table nodded to the men behind King, and he was met with a flurry of punches. He could not defend himself against the melee, but bowed his head, tucking his jaw to his chest to make it more difficult to target, and clenched his teeth to avoid biting his own tongue. The men were well-practised. They did not use all their force, but they didn't mess about, either. King felt his eyelid split open, as well as his top lip. He started to black out, but the beating stopped, and water splashed his face. One of the guards sloshed a ladle of water over him again, the rusty metal bucket in his other hand. King made the most of it, opening his mouth and licking the salty mix of blood and water from his lips. Small though the amount was, it soothed his throat and he found it easier to breathe as a result.

"We found your equipment," the man said staring at him. "A camera bag with photography equipment inside." King reflected that the man's English was excellent and that he was probably trained at the British army's officer training college at Sandhurst. The United Kingdom had a somewhat repeatedly perverse history of training allies that so quickly became enemies. But who knew, this man would probably survive the next regime and they'd all be friends again. But not if King ever saw him again. "Perhaps you wouldn't mind telling me the make of your camera?"

"Canon EOS-1V as my main SLR, or single-lens reflex," King replied shakily. "And a Canon Digital IXUS which I use on the go and for sighting shots."

The man nodded. "New technology. No film needed. The sort of equipment a spy would use."

"Or a photographer embracing the millennium. It's not even new technology, now."

"Forgive me for living in such a backward country..." the man replied acidly.

"I'm sorry, I did not mean to offend," King proffered. The last thing he wanted was to give the man more reason to hurt him, but he needed to shut down the spy avenue as quickly as possible. "But I still use thirty-five-millimetre film for my project work. The resolution is better on most film cameras, too." He nodded towards the man with the bucket. "Please, can I have some water?"

The man gestured to the guard and King got a splash of water in his face and then the guard held the ladle for King to drink from. No more than 7oz – and he did not drink all of it because it spilt on the ground and the guard did not turn the ladle to accommodate him - but it felt incredible, despite being a cloudy brown colour with a metallic taste to it.

"Water is so important, isn't it?" the man asked pointedly. "We can't live without it for more than a few days, but too much of it and we would sell our own mothers for the chance to breathe." He paused, nodding at the guards. "Do it!"

King was under no illusion where this was going. He had been waterboarded by the lovely lady from MI5, held down by her SAS henchmen during his training. He felt rough hands on him, but he knew that to fight would be a futile waste of both time and energy. He would likely be shot before he could do any serious damage, and then he still had to escape. His one saving grace was that he was a strong swimmer and swam as part of his regular fitness regimen. He could hold his breath for three and a half minutes, and these men would not be used to torturing someone who could do that. People weren't big on swimming in Central Africa. With no ocean and the rivers and lakes infested with crocodiles, it hadn't exactly caught on. A cord was placed around his neck and pulled tight, which they controlled him through - like a horse with a barbaric rope twitch around its nostrils and lips - and heaved and pushed him to the corner of the cell where a board was laid across two chairs. King knew what the men wanted from him, but during the struggle the cable tie broke and he lashed out breaking the nose of one of the men. He was beaten and harangued for his trouble, but he wanted them to know that he was resisting for all he was worth. His hands were bound again, this time with several cable ties that threatened to cut off his circulation entirely, and he was pressed down onto his back, his head hanging off the edge of the board. The bucket of water that had slaked his thirst a few minutes ago was pulled near and a cloth soaked in the water, before being folded and pressed over his mouth and nose, with both ends pulled tightly while water was poured steadily onto the cloth. King had managed two-dozen short breaths to hyperventilate and increase his lung capacity, then snatched a good breath and scrunched his nose to lessen the chances of water entering his airway, while he clamped his mouth shut and held his breath. His nose had been broken anyway, so the airway was pinched and let in less water than it otherwise would have. He struggled at around fifteen seconds, started to convulse at thirty, then went still. He knew he would be alright when he felt the cloth loosen. He kept his eyes closed and lay still while one of the men slapped his cheeks repeatedly. Spluttering apparently back to consciousness he focused his eyes on the man, who had left his desk and was looking down at him. King could see his own wretched reflection in the man's mirrored aviators. It was not a pretty sight.

"Who do you work for?" the man shouted.

King spluttered. "Freelance... nature photographer..."

"Again!"

King got a breath and repeated his performance. This time, he faked unconsciousness at forty-five seconds, but he had plenty of air in reserve. To his consternation, there was no attempt to revive him. Had they seen through his act already? Just as he was about to exhale, the slaps came savagely.

"Give me your name!"

"Alex King."

"Who do you work for?"

"I... am... a... freelance..."

"Two intelligence officers disappeared while following you. What do you know about this? Where are they?"

King hoped he hadn't shown a sign or tell as he looked up at the man. He had been sticking to his cover story so desperately that he had forgotten about the messy incident on the mountain road and the two men who had followed them from the airport to their own demise. "I didn't know that anybody was following us..."

"Us?"

"My colleague and I."

"You killed them!"

"No!"

The man nodded and King was yanked back downwards, and the water tipped over the cloth. The sensation was as close to drowning as you could get, but King kept telling himself that it was just a sensation, and that he could get through it. His large lung capacity, honed through swimming and free diving, would allow him to overcome the ordeal. When he was finally released, he spluttered and snatched lungful after lungful of precious air.

"Who was the other man?"

King frowned, making a deal of recollecting. "Our guide."

The man scoffed. "He killed a soldier and took his rifle. This man was no mere guide!"

"He was our guide. Your soldiers fired upon us, what was the man meant to do?" King replied weakly, but the thought that Pierre had killed one of the men buoyed him on, and the fact that he was being questioned so much about it meant that both Pierre and Stewart had evaded them.

"Who was he?"

King shook his head. "No idea. Someone that Peter organised from his list of contacts."

"What contacts?"

"Years of working all over the world as a journalist."

"OK," the man said, smiling wryly. "Let's start again. Who are you, and what are you doing in Burindi?"

"I told you... my name is Alex King and I'm a freelance photographer..."

"Very well," the man replied. "We can do this all night." He looked at his new watch and smiled down at King. "I've been timing you on my pretty new Rolex. Let's see if you can beat your last time..."

Chapter Twenty-Six
London

"**F**or God's sake Armstrong, we have adjoining offices! Why the cloak and dagger routine?"

"Stewart was compromised," Armstrong replied gruffly. "That's why."

"I see..." Felicity Wilmott said quietly. Despite being virtually alone in St. James' Park she looked around her, nonetheless. A few joggers and dog walkers, nothing to concern her, but she spoke in a low tone, barely moving her lips in an attempt of subterfuge. "Where does that leave us?"

"Not good." Armstrong paused. "King has been captured. Stewart says it's only a matter of time before he spills his guts. Stewart is concentrating on damage limitation."

"And what does that entail?"

"Leaving the country, I imagine."

Felicity shook her head. "No. We have too much invested in Lucky Man Jonathon. The government are all set to broker contracts for British mining concessions. We need the revenue from their uranium and lithium. The *country* needs the revenue. We're too reliant on Russian oil and we have refineries across the border in Angola that can deal with all the Burindi oil that we can get out of the ground."

"We've lost the element of surprise. Mustafa has always suspected that Mugabe is in bed with us, and now he will know for sure."

"Unless..." she stared out across the park thoughtfully.

"Unless what?"

"It's obvious, isn't it?"

Armstrong shrugged. "Nothing is bloody obvious in this game," he said sharply.

"Contact Stewart. Tell him to remain in place. Tell him to get King the hell out of there before he *spills his guts*."

"It would be a suicide mission!"

"Well, that's what these tough men are bloody well paid for!" she snapped, forgetting her efforts of subterfuge. "I don't care if it's tough. I don't care if it's impossible. He either gets King out, or he kills the man himself. Whatever is easier. Whatever is most effective. But one thing is for sure, King cannot be allowed to talk."

Chapter Twenty-Seven
Burindi

Nothing. He had no idea how he had held out, but the waterboarding had yielded nothing for the man from the secret police. After being taken to the limit, he had almost spilled and broken his cover story, but he figured that they could not continue much longer. They had refilled the bucket a dozen times, and the men were exhausted from holding him down and beating him. Just when he was about done, so were they. He was dragged off and dumped in another holding cell. He reset his finger again, not even realising that it had been twisted during the waterboarding, but certainly feeling it once they had finished. Clasping his nose with his right thumb and forefinger, he manipulated it until it cracked, and he could breathe better. The fact that it no longer hurt told him that it was realigned. In the absence of a mirror, he hoped he had gotten it straight, but also realised that it was the least of his concerns.

It was daylight outside, warmth and light searing through the window, the bars casting shadows over him, and he reflected that it looked as though it was consolidating his incarceration.

The hatch opened and two bread rolls tumbled onto the filthy floor, along with a half-litre plastic bottle of water. Clothes followed. A white T-shirt, black shorts and cheap, thin flip-flops. King squatted naked and drank thirstily. He ate the bread, his teeth, gums and lips smarting from the beatings. He was ravenous, but his stomach had shrunk through his hunger, and he had to force the last of the stale bread down, helping it on the way with the last of the water. The T-shirt was a little tight, but the shorts and flip-flops fitted well enough, and he paced around the cell, testing the view out of the high window from both acute angles, only to be disheartened that he could not see anything significant. He was not being held at the military barracks, that was for sure.

The door opened around an hour later and two guards armed with batons ushered him towards the door. He was roughly handcuffed and pushed ahead of them down the corridor. They passed the interrogation cell, King tensing and readying himself for another round, but they merely prodded him in the back, and he was taken outside into a yard with wire fencing all the way round, topped with razor wire. Again, there was around a six-foot gap and another wire fence on the other side. He felt the handcuffs being unlocked and was shoved forwards in the small of his back. He stood for a moment, the sun bathing his face in warmth. When he finally turned around the two guards had gone. He walked along the fence but could already see it was hopeless. The wire mesh was buried in the ground and there would be no way through without wire cutters. The razor wire made climbing an impossibility and at each corner, a telegraph pole anchored a cluster of CCTV cameras. Hopeless. Tunnelling? If he could get out of his cell, find a digging implement and work all through the night like an Irish navvy, then maybe. But how deep into the ground did the wire go? And it would be a safe assumption that the CCTV array would have a PIR, or passive infrared camera of some sort.

"No way out, my friend. Believe me, many have tried."

King turned around and saw a kindly-looking man of around fifty years of age. He had inquiring, intelligent eyes and scars on his face that belied his kind demeanour. The man was stick-thin, and King knew that it would not have been by choice. "Been here long?" he asked.

The man smiled. "More years than I think I have remaining."

"Great..."

"We don't get many white men in here. Come to think of it, you're the first."

"I'm here to appease political correctness. You'll get a lesbian, a ginger and some guy in a wheelchair soon," King smiled.

"Oh, we have a few wheelchair users already," the man replied. "Quite a few on crutches, too. Incidentally, do not steal. They will remove your hand as soon as look at you. And if you try to escape, then they'll take a foot. Hence the wheelchair users."

King wanted to ask the man if he was kidding, but something about the way he said it told him that he wasn't going to be that lucky. As if on cue a man wheeled himself into view struggling on a wooden dining chair with two bicycle wheels fastened on the rear and what looked like supermarket trolley wheels on the front. It wasn't the vision that King had imagined when the man had said wheelchair. The man struggling with it in the dirt had one arm and no legs. The stumps that remained had been severed way above his knees. "He tried to escape twice?"

"Three or four times," the man replied. "They took pieces off him each time, and then I think the last time they thought they'd solve the problem and left him nothing but short stumps." He paused. "A machete and a bucket of hot tar to cauterize the bleeding and stop infection, that's all they use. And that is how much that poor man wanted to go home."

"Jesus..."

"He will not help you here, my friend." The man paused. "I was a religious man when I arrived, but not anymore. Truly, if there had ever been the man we know as Jesus, if there really was a Lord God Almighty, then this place would not exist."

King watched a procession of men walk into the yard. One of them sauntered over to the man struggling in the makeshift wheelchair and helped him through the dirt. King turned back and looked at the man. "My name is Alex, by the way."

"Desmond."

King shook the man's hand. "Nice to meet you," he said, eyes on the men across the yard. "Do I have to worry about asserting my dominance in here?" he asked, familiar with prison and the rules. He figured things were the same anywhere in the world. "I don't much feel up to a fight." To be fair, it looked like he had been hit by a truck. Battered, cut and bruised, he nursed his left hand against his chest, his finger throbbing and the scabs where the nails had once been were sore and weeping pus.

Desmond smiled. "Strangely, no," he replied. "With a regime as totalitarian as this, with prisoners so poorly treated, it is us against them. We seldom fight amongst ourselves."

"That's difficult to believe," said King, eyeing up the largest of the men at the other end of the yard. "Law of the jungle. If you pardon the pun."

Desmond laughed. "The men here have not had a trial. They do not get visitors. In fact, their families do not even know where they are or if indeed, they are still alive. This isn't a typical Burindi prison. This is the place where dictators send the people who oppose them, who speak out against them, the people who dared to ask for political change."

Suddenly King realised that he wasn't just in the shit, but that he was in it right up to his nostrils. "From President Mustafa?"

"Some," Desmond replied. "But most from that running dog Lucky Man Jonathon Mugabe and his time as a brutal dictator." He spat on the dusty ground at the utterance of the man's name. "You are English?" he asked, and King nodded. "Your country is backing Lucky Man Jonathon, by all accounts. Paying for his playboy lifestyle while we rot in this living hell. They should have done something about him when he was in power. Instead, they pay for his lifestyle and back him to regain power. I wonder if in a hundred years from now the historians will look back on Britain the same way they view other axis of evil in history? Certainly, the slave trade and colonialism of the British Empire are matters of which few people would be proud."

King shrugged. "It's degrees of expansion, I suppose. Granted the slave trade was horrible. But Spain, Portugal and America certainly played their part, and let's not forget that Britain banned slavery sixty years before America fought over it in civil war." He paused. "Likewise, people enjoyed education and protection and infrastructure under the Empire. I guess when everyone was all caught up the picture had changed."

The man smiled. "That is the trouble with education," he replied. "The students become the masters very soon."

"Anyway, I don't make policy," King said pointedly. "And I certainly don't apologise for history. Ancestorial guilt is not a thing."

"But we must all learn from it. What the British do with Lucky Man Jonathon will be written in history for future generations to judge."

King couldn't argue with the man. When he had started this idiotic career, he saw himself as a vital piece on the chessboard. A knight with its precision technique of staying off colour, or being placed not for its next move, but the take in five moves time. Or a rook working in tandem to put the king in checkmate. But he knew now, more than ever, that he was just a pawn. A lowly pawn that moves one place at a time and only in one direction, and almost always sacrificed intentionally. "I am just a freelance photographer." He studied the man's eyes for a tell. There was always the chance that the regime running this prison camp would put one of their own inside to glean information. "I'm just a case of mistaken identity."

"Of course," Desmond replied wryly. "Come, let me show you around." He looked at King's left hand and said, "That looks painful. I will take you to somebody who can take care of that. He was a doctor on the outside. The last thing you want in here is for it to go septic and give a guard an opportunity to heat up the tar and sharpen a machete."

King followed the man across the yard. Several men looked up as they approached. A few of them were missing a hand, others a foot. They did not, however, look broken.

The largest man walked up to them and said to Desmond, "*S'allright*, Boss? Who's the *baturai*?"

Desmond smiled. "We do not use slurs like that, Jacob. Remember? We cannot move forward as one society with segregation, no matter how insignificant it may seem. Today's unkind word is tomorrow's barrier to freedom for all."

"Sorry, man."

"What did he call me?" King asked incredulously.

"It's a slur on whites. *Baturai*. It means *man with no skin...*"

King shrugged. "I've been called worse," he replied amiably. "Anyway, it looks like I may have plenty of time to work on my tan."

Both men smiled and Desmond said, "This is Jacob. He is a man to be trusted. Now that you have been seen with us, you will have no trouble. Not that I think you would anyway, as we seem to have risen above those dark days."

"And what days were they?"

Desmond sighed. "This place was lawless, godless and hopeless. The men fought among themselves. There were rapes, beatings and murders. There are no rapes now. There are homosexual men who have consensual sex – a crime punishable by death on the outside – but by accepting it in here, we have eliminated rape. There are few beatings now, and there hasn't been a murder in here in four years."

"Do you see yourself as in charge?" King asked.

Desmond smiled and shook his head. "No, sadly the guards are in charge. But I facilitate among the prisoners. I am open to discussion and respectful of differences in opinion. That is democracy. When people become so polarised and can no longer listen to, or accept a different opinion, then democracy is threatened, and society will fall."

"You should go into politics."

"I did."

"Desmond..." King said thoughtfully as he stared at the man, suddenly remembering the conversation with Lucinda at the hotel, and again on the drive into the highlands with Stewart. "Jesus... you're the schoolteacher," he said. "Lambadi."

"I am," he replied without any sign of ego or infamy. "They have moved me around a lot, but not for the past six years. But there has been no indication that with your arrival I shall be leaving."

"Good news for you," replied King.

Lambadi nodded. "Which is bad news for you, my new friend, because I fear they will never allow you to leave now that you know I am here."

Chapter Twenty-Eight

Stewart switched off the sat-phone and slammed his fist against the steering wheel. Ahead of him he could see Pierre watching him in his rear-view mirror. He got out of the Jeep and walked along the side of the rutted road and leaned in through the man's open window. "Change of plan," he said.

"It did not look like a good conversation, my friend," Pierre observed. "Let me guess, King is a loose end."

"Exactly."

"Rescue?"

Stewart shook his head. "Or termination."

"That is bad. I liked him."

"Indeed."

"Kind of makes me think twice about working for you..."

"We're all big boys; we all know how it works."

"Ouch."

"We can't get into that military base, not just the two of us." Pierre paused. "Only a crazy man would do that. Or two crazy men, and I'll tell you now, I'm not that crazy."

"Agreed."

Pierre shrugged. "But I have a theory," he said. "Five clicks to the east, there is a prison camp. It's not registered, so the prisoners being held there are political. Either that, or what the government would call subversives."

"Our intel has it down as a training camp for officers."

"Well, your intel is wrong," Pierre replied. "I have been there to do a reconnaissance and trust me, there are men being held there. The prisoners are let out into the yard in the morning to eat and again in the evening."

"And you think he will have been taken there?"

Pierre shrugged. "It makes sense. Especially as they will assume, quite rightly, that he is a spy."

"What is it like, this camp?"

"Low key. I have pictures hidden in a safe box buried near the house."

"Okay..." Stewart mused on this. "But less security than the barracks?"

"Yes, way less. It's basically a double wire fence with CCTV and armed guards patrolling on the outside. An admin block, a few portacabins and the main building which is made from concrete blocks."

"Still sounds a tough job for two men." Stewart frowned, gnawing tentatively at his lip. "I suppose we could go back and look at the photographs. If we can get into that camp, or whatever the hell it is, and get him out then we should try. Otherwise, King can't be allowed to talk."

"He probably has by now," Pierre replied. "They don't recognise the Geneva Convention or Amnesty International in Burindi. They chopped a mercenary friend of mine into little pieces down near the capital. He was buying guns to sell in Somalia. He was taken apart finger by finger, toe by toe. He told them everything before they eventually hacked off his legs and he bled out."

Stewart said nothing. He was damned either way. He knew he had next to no chance of rescuing King, especially with the Burindi army stationed in the neighbouring camp. He had no men, next to no resources and little time. The only alternative was to kill his boy, his protégé. And as much as he hated to admit it, his friend. Stewart never formed emotional bonds. He had suffered enough loss, especially as a young para in the Falklands War. After he had joined MI6, he preferred to keep everyone he worked with at arm's length. But King was different. King had reminded him in many ways of himself. He was certainly the toughest and most resourceful man he had ever known, but it wasn't just that. King had saved his life in the Congo. Risked his own life and chance of escape to carry Stewart on his back to safety. In that moment, King had ceased to be Stewart's colleague and become his friend. He was certainly the only person he had taken home to meet his long-suffering wife Margaret, and stay for dinner.

"Are you with me to attempt a rescue?" Stewart asked.

Pierre shrugged. "It could be suicide. He knew the risks. I suppose if we had time on our side and more men, then maybe..." He paused. "He's not my brother or anything, I just met the man. Sorry, but there it is. With just two men, I don't see it as possible."

"Well, we certainly haven't got time or men. It's just us."

"Then we're down to a long-distance rifle shot," Pierre replied. "Or mortars. Or both."

"Fuck," Stewart shook his head. "Well, let's get back to the safehouse, dig up those recon photos and get things moving."

Chapter Twenty-Nine

The 'doctor' had washed the raw scabs where King's fingernails had once been, and after a lot of pain and manipulation, King's left index finger was now set correctly and bound to his middle finger using strips of cloth. He told King that here wasn't much that could be done for his nose, but the reflection from an old saucepan the doctor had polished to a mirrored shine told him that it was about right, and he didn't know whether to be pleased or offended. The man had used homemade alcohol distilled from yams and potatoes to clean the wounds and the bandages had been fashioned from a T-shirt. Cut to size, soaked in the alcohol and dried, the man had rolls of them stacked in his windowsill and the alcohol was clear and looked somewhat innocuous in used plastic water bottles. The doctor was a real doctor, having trained in Kenya he then worked for two years in London and three years with *Médecins Sans Frontières* before returning to Burindi and working at the central hospital in the capital. When Lucky Man Jonathon Mugabe overthrew Lambadi's fledgling government, the doctor was imprisoned because of his vocal views on free contraception. Since Mustafa seized power, the doctor's release had been overlooked because Mustafa's government were behind keeping women in the home to breed and look after Burindi's menfolk.

The doctor had stitched the cut to King's right eyelid using a needle and thread, again doused in the alcohol before use. After he had finished, the doctor, King and Lambadi sat on the man's cot bed and drank some of the alcohol, which to King, tasted somewhere between rum, vodka and turpentine. However, he was glad of the mellowing effect, and the other two men didn't seem to need an excuse.

"They took it easy on you really," Lambadi said eventually.

"I'd hate to see them do a thorough job," King replied irritably.

"My friend, it means they don't believe your story about being a photographer, but also realise that you may well be of use to them as a political pawn. They know that you will not talk until they start removing things from your body, but that wouldn't make a good trade," Desmond Lambadi smiled. "I do not believe your story, either." He paused looking at King, who simply shrugged. "I have seen men like you before. Tough, muscled, intelligent, resilient... you are a foreign spy. I am right, am I not?"

King said nothing. He sipped the last of his drink, the liquid burning in a not unpleasant way down his throat. He wondered briefly if he got out of here, a bottle of the stuff might make a nice gift for Stewart. Something different for the man to swill before breakfast. "Well, I'm going for a mooch about the place," he said as he stood up.

"Mooch?"

"Yeah. Like a walk and a look, just casual, like."

Lambadi nodded, but he didn't quite understand. "You still don't trust me?" he asked, unable to feign indifference.

King held up his left hand, showing off the bandaged fingers and the raw-looking fingertips. "I've had enough of questions for a while."

Lambadi smiled. He held up his left hand also. King hadn't noticed, but the man only had four stumps remaining, the digits all amputated at the middle joints. Nothing of the thumb remained. "Twice, each finger," he explained. "First the tip, then lower still. Ten times in all. Ten chops of the machete, and each time they held another machete above my other arm, so if I did not willingly submit a finger, then they would take my whole other arm." Lambadi paused. "If you can't trust me, Alex, then you can't trust anyone in here."

"This man was our leader," the doctor interjected in faultless English. "He was the country's greatest asset. He was going to reform our health service selling a percentage of our mineral assets for bonded investment. That way, the money would always be ring fenced to prevent bad management. The same scheme would be replicated to offer free education to all children including girls, which sadly ended when they were nine. The key to equality and ending misogyny is to educate girls and women so they know that they can take on other roles. But that is not the point I am making... the point is this man is the only *true* leader, the only *honest* leader that Burindi has ever known, and he was overthrown and imprisoned without trial or sound accusation, and he was tortured and degraded, mutilated and incarcerated for more than a decade. He has helped everyone here, brought order and dignity to lost souls. If you can't trust him, then be on your way and ask nothing from any of us in return." He paused, regarding

King with contempt. "And we'll see how long you last in here."

King nodded considerately. "I'm sorry. I did not mean to offend."

"Walk with me," Desmond Lambadi said. "We can both *mooch*." He thanked the doctor and the two of them walked out of the man's cell, through the shower block and into the yard. "Your country is going to back Lucky Man Jonathon Mugabe against Mustafa."

"That's about the size of it."

Lambadi nodded. "I can see that he is the better man for your government's interests. Mustafa has never hidden his enthusiasm for forging relations with both China and Russia. I understand that lithium has been discovered. The United Kingdom already has an established telecommunications industry, whereas China is still in its infancy. And who the hell will buy a Russian cell phone?" he smiled.

King could have told the man that Russian engineer Leonid Ivanovich Kupriyanovich invented a mobile phone that went on sale exclusively in the Soviet Union in 1963. The device was smaller than modern Nokia phones and enabled the user to call phone booths and landlines. This was ten years before Motorola, credited as the first mobile phone. King had learned the fact during his in-depth radio and communications training at GCHQ in Cheltenham. Nevertheless, he did not correct Lambadi, and would have to agree that a Russian mobile phone would likely be about as desirable as the cars they made.

"I suppose choosing between the two men would be like choosing which sexually transmitted disease would be the best to catch," said King. "Neither is something you really want, but some are better than others."

Desmond Lambadi smiled thinly, but King could see

that humour was something that had been worn from him like everybody else in the camp. "I like your analogy, my friend. However, both men are butchers and megalomaniacs. They look on as their minions kill, rape and steal. There is no chance of law and order with either man in power. Only corruption at every level. No chance of health reforms, educational development or political and social stability." He paused. "I really thought that Burindi could be a beacon of light in Central Africa. I thought that if I could lead and make a difference, then we could welcome democracy and political opposition. Fair and honest voting, an opposition party like in the UK, where the party in power is held to account and elections held every four years would give the people control of their destinies." He sighed, his eyes moist as he recounted his dreams, and hopeless reality. "I long for a time when women can do more than tend the home, slave at the stove and breed endlessly. To receive an education that consolidates confidence and shows them a future. With a free birth-control prescription, women can choose when to have a child, and how many children to have. This is one of the factors that will forever keep Africa poor. Too many mouths to feed, too many children draining medical resources. If women have more choices, then they have a bright future. If families have less children, then the children they do have will have a brighter future also."

"It's a great idea," King replied. "But I grew up on a council estate in South London where it doesn't sound much different to what you just described. Even ideology doesn't work in some places where these things are a reality."

The man shrugged. "I understand this," he said heavily. "But we had a very real chance of freedom and opportunity, without corruption and avarice. How many African nations can say that?"

King nodded. They had reached the corner of the yard. Beyond the fence the brush offered if not sanctuary, then at least the chance of escape. King turned and looked at the hill on the other side of the compound. It was the ideal spot for a sniper, and he wondered why such an issue had been overlooked in locating the prison camp, but he supposed that the fact they had been compromised so quickly as they neared the camp meant that the Burindi regime were confident in the matter. Besides, who would want to kill a single prisoner? And attacking the prison camp by eliminating the guards with long-distance rifle shots would be inefficient, as after the first guard had been shot, they certainly wouldn't stand around waiting for their turn. King discounted the thought. A sniper on the hill was the least of his worries right now.

Chapter Thirty
London

Sir Hugo Truscott had bumped his eleven o'clock and was now looking at moving his lunchtime meeting with the Department for Transport minister to discuss the possibility to link London and the North by a second high speed rail link, similar to the *Eurostar*. It was an important meeting and would attract many tenders, and a lot of controversy, but Sir Hugo had an inside track and held many interests in the construction industry. Between now and the tender date, he had enough time to hide his interests and drive a successful bid forward with the chance to make millions. If he could buy properties along the proposed route, then he would also benefit from high compulsory purchase orders. Why else would he have gone into politics and worked his way into the Cabinet?

He read the email again, his chest both fluttering and tightening at once. Everything he had been working towards in Burindi could come crashing down if he did not act both decisively and swiftly. He checked his watch deciding whether it was too early for a hard drink. Of course not. He opened his drawer and took out the bottle of twenty-year-old Haig. There were two crystal tumblers in the drawer, and he took one and filled it with two fingers of the single malt Scotch. He took a large gulp, held it for long enough to mellow the burn, then swallowed. It was a great deal of money, but he could trust the source and from the brief report, if he did not move on this now then he could kiss goodbye to his investments and interests in Burindi's latest resource and the access that Lucky Man Jonathon Mugabe would give him once he regained his leadership.

Sir Hugo finished his whisky and contemplated another generous measure but decided on a single. He poured, and swilled the single malt down lavishly, then replaced the bottle and used glass back in the drawer. His secretary would wash out the glass for him before she left work for the night. She was loyal and discreet and had been with him since he won his first local election twenty-years ago. When he was in opposition as a backbencher and when he found his place in the shadow cabinet. Now, as a member of the cabinet with a prominent ministerial position, she knew all his secrets, but he paid her well and had furnished her with investment advice early on for her to make good money on the side, and her signature was on enough illicit paperwork for her to realise what fate would be bestowed upon her if she ever decided to have a crisis of loyalty or indeed, conscience.

He typed out a reply to the email and sent it on its way. He had used his own personal email account which was routed through Holland and unmonitored by the Personnel Select Committee and Standards Commission. He then logged into one of his offshore bank accounts and transferred the money. As expected, he received a text message with a six-digit code and entered it onto the screen. In under a minute, three-million pounds had left his account and with it, the very real possibility that his Burindi business interests were back on track.

Chapter Thirty-One

The mortar was a 60mm and originally issued to the US army in Operation Desert Storm and left behind by the Americans in their standard practice of leaving equipment rather than shipping it back - defence contracts were worth billions of dollars every year, and cuts were taken by politicians and the higher military echelons to constantly precure new equipment. The practice rather cynically armed the next threat and the cycle of armament naturally continued, feeding the need for arms dealers and contactors and keeping the weapons in perpetuity. Pierre had come by several of the mortars in Sierra Leone after he had been paid to shut down an illegal diamond mine operation using slave labour. He would have liked to think that slave labour was a reason to kill, but in reality it had been sanctioned by one of the five largest diamond companies who wanted to mine in the area. Before the authorities – also paid off by the internationally recognised company - had arrived to secure the work of the mercenaries many weapons had gone missing. The continent was the perfect example of recycling.

Kingmaker

Stewart crouched behind a large rock on the hilltop, surveying the camp below through his binoculars. He could see King in the yard talking to an older man who was waif thin and walked with a limp. The operation had become compromised, and his orders were clear. Stop King from talking. Well, that was an easy order to give, but a difficult order to take, because rescuing King from prison with no time to plan and with no resources on hand, then there was only one realistic way to stop King from talking. But Stewart couldn't shake the feeling of unease that had settled in his stomach. He had trained King, had taught him everything he knew about being an assassin and field agent for MI6. And now he was effectively being told to kill him.

He took a deep breath, trying to steady his nerves. He knew that the operation now relied upon King's silence, but it did not make it any easier. He thought back to the day they had first met, when King was in Princetown, better known as Dartmoor Prison. Stewart had seen potential in him as he researched him during his trial. King had been arrogant, but that arrogance had been knocked out of him when he realised that he was going down for a twenty-stretch and all the bravado, all the face he fought to keep didn't really seem to matter anymore. Life was life. And it gave prisoners more than enough opportunity to reflect, none more so than in those first few months. After King had been 'removed' from prison and the body of an unfortunate homeless man who had died from exposure on the bitter streets had been placed in a peat bog on the moor in a scenario that Stewart had taken straight out of 'Operation Mincemeat' of World War Two, Stewart had taken him under his wing. And now, here he was, about to end the man's life.

He closed his eyes, trying to push the thoughts from his

mind. He couldn't afford to let his emotions get in the way of the mission. He never had before. That was what he was known for, why he was held in such high regard by all the intelligence officers he worked with during a mission.

"He's right there," said Pierre. "I'll use the rifle. It will be quicker for him, and easier for us. One shot and we exfiltrate back through the bush and get the reconnaissance back on track."

"Wait!" Stewart snapped at Pierre, who was already nestling the stock of the SMLE .303 rifle into his shoulder. The rifle was British army surplus from the fifties when the British military had switched to the FN SLR, but with a decent 4x40 scope secured to retro-welded scope rails it had served as an excellent sniper rifle throughout campaigns all over the African continent. The camp was four hundred metres below them, and King was presently five hundred and fifty metres distant. Stewart knew this by counting the fence posts and estimating the height of the men against the height of the posts. For a man of Pierre's experience, it would be like shooting fish in a barrel. "He's making his way inside..."

"I can do it on the move. There's no wind and I have the elevation."

"No!" Stewart snapped. "I owe him a clean death."

"You have your orders," he replied pragmatically. "And I want to be on the winning side of this debacle. We can't wait any longer."

Mercenaries... thought Stewart. Still, he could hardly blame the man. The Burindi authorities were not known for their leniency when they captured enemies of the state, which King would already know. Stewart wondered what they had done to him, but the fact that he was still standing and not limping around with crutches and a clear two-foot of air where his leg once was, told him that they had not yet finished with him, and that they wanted a bargaining chip for the future.

"Stewart, it's time," Pierre reminded him, a hint of urgency in his voice.

Stewart nodded, turning back to the camp below. He took one last look at King, then suddenly lashed out and knocked the rifle aside.

"Shit! I almost had an ND!" Pierre snapped. "A fucking gunshot would give us away, and without the kill!" He paused, sighing deeply. "Look, Stewart, I know this guy means something to you, and I know you don't like the decision made in London, but..."

"Shut up, will you?" Stewart cut him off, focusing the binoculars. "There's a vehicle driving in down there, and I recognise it."

Pierre used the rifle scope to get a better look at the vehicle approaching the camp. The two men watched as it pulled in and parked outside the fence and two guards walked over, their FN rifles aimed at the occupants. Slowly, the driver's door opened, and a man stepped out, his arms raised as he spoke to the two men.

"Fuck me..." Stewart said slowly.

"You know him?"

"I do. He's a Russian I use from time to time. His name is Dimitri."

"A fellow merc?"

"Yes. He got screwed over in Afghanistan and again in Chechnya and had a crisis of political conscience. He doesn't care for Mother Russia any longer and has given me more than a few titbits of information over the years."

"I think I know him," he replied. "What the hell is he doing here, then?"

"Guarding her," Stewart grimaced as the passenger door opened. He knew that it would be Lucinda Davenport before he saw her, but her lithe figure and glossy dark hair cascading around her shoulders confirmed it the moment she stepped out of the car and stood on the dry earth. "You can put a bullet in that one, if you like..." Pierre shouldered the weapon and took aim and Stewart said, "For fuck's sake, man. I was only joking!"

Pierre shrugged and watched Lucinda through the crosshairs of the scope. "Who is she?"

"A bloody reporter. An entitled bitch whose husband is a politician and multi-millionaire with his fingers in many pies. She's nothing but trouble and would sell her grand-mother for a story."

"What the hell is she doing here, then?"

"Stirring up a fucking hornet's nest I suspect..."

Chapter Thirty-Two

Lucinda Davenport wore a determined expression as the man approached. He wore a white shirt and jeans, and his eyes were hidden by a cheap pair of mirrored aviators. He walked with a confidence that bordered on arrogance, and as she watched him, she thought the walk was more of a strut. Lucinda's expression hid the sense of trepidation inside her. She had heard stories of the ruthlessness subjected to the prisoners of the unofficial prisons dotted over Burindi and had heard that the guards had a penchant for violence that the Mustafa regime mirrored from Mugabe's time in power, but she was determined to secure King's release. The irony that her husband's money could secure the release of her one-time lover was not lost on her, and even though Hugo likely suspected something more, he had not voiced it. He was committed to the financial gains in Burindi first and foremost. The awkward questions could come later, and between them, there had been more than enough of those in their marriage.

The man studied her for an uncomfortable minute. His

eyes turned to the large aluminium briefcase in her hand, but behind the mirrored sunglasses, his thoughts were readable. He met her eyes once more and beckoned her to follow him inside. The two guards halted Dimitri's progress and Lucinda regarded him for a moment, then nodded that it would be alright. Neither of them seemed to have any choice in the matter. She was led into the building past several armed guards along the way. Inside, the building smelt fetid, and the heat was almost intolerable. Inside the man's office, the smell and the heat wasn't much better, but a slow-turning ceiling fan managed to take the edge off it.

"You are here to pay for the release of your colleague?" he said, his tone somewhere between menacing and incredulous.

The journalist nodded. "Yes," she replied, holding out the large aluminium briefcase as if to validate her presence. "I have the money."

"You have connections. Not many people know that this place exists."

"I won't lie, my husband is in government," she replied. The man could search her on the internet and find the connection within minutes so there was no point in lying, and no harm in the credibility it gave her. "He knows a lot of things," she added.

The man regarded her, trying to make her out as much as he studied her figure, his focus on her firm breasts underneath the damp shirt. "I see... Tell me, who does your colleague work for?"

"He is a freelance photographer. I have worked with him many times."

"Then who has hired him?"

"Another freelance journalist. I do not know him, but I

know Alex and I have the resources to broker a deal. If you'll allow it."

The man shrugged impassively. "I could just take the money." He paused reflectively, letting the fact sink in. "My guards could kill your bodyguard and after I have finished with you, the guards could share you around the barracks. Nobody outside would ever know."

Lucinda nodded. "You are certainly no fool," she replied. "But you would be if you thought that nobody knew I was here. My editor for one, a Burindi government contact for another," she lied. "And I have political allies and family money. Your life would not be worth living. As we have established, my husband is extremely well-connected. He could wage war on you from behind his desk."

The man snatched the case from her and slammed it down on the desk. "You have a wealthy husband, that is all!" He attempted to open the case, but the two, four-digit combination locks were not going to get him any closer to his money. He stared at her and said, "After you contacted the ministry, I searched online and learned all about you and your wealthy husband. The British government are impotent. They can do nothing. They cannot simply invade Burindi, so they must wait until our government is willing to talk to them about their precious mineral rights." He paused. "But this is not enough money. You left a trail finding this place. And a trail finding me. This is Africa. People need paying off. The three million you promised me is now worth less than half to me."

She had known that the 'ransom' would be steep, but she had not anticipated that it would be so high. Three million was a lot of money in the West, and an unimaginable fortune in a Central African nation like Burindi, but even here the amount had dwindled with payoffs to get to the source. "That's not my problem," she said defensively. "You need to renegotiate with your people. Now, bring him to me."

"You are in no position to..."

"Bring him to me!" she raged. "We have a deal! There is a total of three million pounds in that case, in one-hundred-dollar bills, fifty-pound notes and five-hundred-euro notes. It was drawn in Basel, Switzerland this morning and flown here by private jet. That same jet will take you and your case full of cash anywhere you desire. You have my word. No need for pay-offs, no need to jeopardise your own security waiting for someone to rob you of your new-found wealth. I will make sure that the plane can land and be refuelled before taking off again, so the world is your oyster."

The man contemplated this. He had been visibly irked by her outburst. In Burindi, it was uncommon for a woman to be anything other than subservient, and he really wasn't used to being spoken to in such a manner. But the thought of someone taking his money was food for thought. He looked back at Lucinda his expression full of loathing. However, somewhat pragmatically if not willingly, he shouted something at the guard standing outside the door and his running footsteps echoed down the corridor. Lucinda had not caught the sentence, shouted in a mixture of pidgin English and heavily accented native dialect. She had once holidayed with Hugo in Jamaica and found Jamaican Patois almost impossible to understand. The language was a lyrical mixture of Creole, English and West African (and a good deal of slang), originally developed to stop slave traders and slave owners from understanding them. She had found that Jamaicans all spoke excellent English but resorted to Patois when she and her husband had walked nearby or stepped into a shop. The language that the locals spoke to each other in was just as indecipherable.

"Tell me the combination."

"All in good time," she replied, keeping up the display of dominance. "Do you have your passport," she asked casually, giving the man little time to think and taking another step above him in the hierarchy that she was successfully creating. "The plane can be ready when you are." The man was hesitant. He hadn't thought it through this far. Too many options. Lucinda could see that he was wracking his brains. Many countries required visas; others were a no-go from Burindi. "It has a maximum range of four-thousand miles, so you might want to do it in two stops. Or Switzerland may be a good option. But it is an expensive place. Somewhere on the African continent may be more practical. Morocco, perhaps? Plus, it's the gateway to Europe."

"I haven't given it any thought," he admitted. "How will I get to the aircraft?"

Lucinda reached for a pen and pad on his desk. She scribbled a few lines and handed the paper to him. "That's the registration number of the aircraft. It's at Umfasu International Airport for the next two days. Call that mobile number to speak to the captain."

"Who owns the plane?"

"My husband."

The man nodded sagely. He had the money, and he now had the means to leave Burindi and the payoffs in the chain. But would he have the courage to take it? Lucinda did not care either way. She had asked enough of her husband, and he was putting himself at great risk allowing the use of his private jet to a man from Mustafa's regime, particularly as the British government was backing Lucky

Man Jonathon Mugabe. She would have preferred the man to refuse the offer, but right now it seemed the best bargaining chip she had, and the man's only means of keeping the entire three million pounds for himself.

Lucinda looked up at the sound of footsteps in the corridor. She watched the doorway expectantly, her heart fluttering as King entered behind the guard and another guard pushed him roughly over the threshold. His hands were bound in front of him in heavy-duty cable ties and he did not hide his surprise when he saw her, his eyes soon darting between her and the man who had overseen his torture. "What's going on?" he asked incredulously.

"Your *colleague* has just secured your freedom..." the man said, and by the way he had emphasised the word colleague he had clearly not believed Lucinda's story. But money talked, and never more loudly than in Africa.

King frowned, but he did not waste any time, holding up his hands for the guard to unfasten.

"No, no, no, my friend," the man smiled. "Outside, in the car." He turned to Lucinda and said, "And now, the combination, if you please..."

Lucinda smiled. "Now that's going to be a problem," she replied. "You see, it's a trust issue. Oh, and don't get any ideas about the briefcase. If the combination is not done in sequence, then a compressed air cannister inside the lid activates an indelible ink pouch. Dye, to be precise. The money will be rendered unusable. Swiss banks are so very thorough when it comes to security."

The man considered this. Adding insult to injury, he consulted King's Rolex as he contemplated his next move, going through the timings and options in his head. Decisively, he picked up the case and nodded to one of the guards to free King's restraints. "You will take me to the airport now," he said, then looked at King. "No, how you English say, hard feelings? We all have what we want."

King shrugged. "I just want out of here," he replied earnestly, rubbing his wrists now that the cable ties had been cut off.

The man smiled and led the way, swinging the briefcase and with more spring in his step than before. He dismissed the guards at the gate and ordered the two covering Dimitri to stand down. Dimitri frowned at Lucinda, who nodded towards the vehicle, her eyes telling him quite clearly to hurry before the camp commandant changed his mind. Lucinda got in the front seat giving King and the man no choice but to get in the rear beside each other. Dimitri started the engine and pulled away, the dust road throwing up a cloud behind them.

"Where are we going?" the Russian asked.

"The airport," Lucinda replied.

"Are you leaving?"

"No. But our new friend is borrowing my husband's plane for a while."

She turned to King and smiled thinly. She wanted to do more, wanted to express her joy at getting him out of the camp, and she could see from his expression that he wanted that, too. They looked at one another like two secret lovers at a party, each wanting to be closer and wishing that everyone else would simply fade away. The road soon became rutted with potholes and rain gullies from the wet season, and she turned around in her seat and faced forwards as the vehicle bounced and lurched from side to side as the suspension was put through its paces. Elbows and knees knocked against the doors, and it was an effort to hold on as Dimitri weaved his way as best he could over the rough surface. When the road finally smoothed out once more, she turned around in her seat to see the man slumped in his seat and King fastening his watch bracelet on his wrist.

"Change of plan," he said. "I'll be needing that plane..." He took the man's Makarov pistol and tucked it into the waistband of his shorts.

"Is... is he dead?" she asked, her eyes fixed on the man who looked like he was sleeping soundly but with his eyes fractionally open, and his head at an unnatural angle. The more she looked at him, the more it looked less like sleeping and altogether more permanent.

"I certainly hope so," King replied, then said, "Thank you for getting me out."

"You're welcome," she replied somewhat distantly, her eyes not leaving the corpse within touching distance.

"How much was I worth?"

She smiled. "Three million pounds."

"Christ, if my mother could see me now..." He handed her the case and as she manoeuvred it between Dimitri and herself, the Russian moved his shoulder to allow her room and King leaned forward and snatched the 9mm Sig from the man's shoulder holster. "Sorry mate, but you're a mercenary and three-million quid may be enough to tip the scales."

"Alex!" Lucinda protested.

"Coming from a trained killer?" the Russian sneered.

"What I do, I do for my country," King said coldly. "Not for cash."

"I was there to help you in the Congo," the Russian protested.

"You were there to guard Lucinda. Lucinda got taken and you fought with us to get out of there. Stewart trusts you, which is why you're still driving the car."

Dimitri chuckled. "Well, it sounds like you are learning, my friend." He paused. "And what about when we reach the airport?"

"Lucinda, give this man a hundred grand out of that briefcase when we get there," King ordered her. "I'm grateful for you stumping up such a sum, but I think we can agree that you can afford a hundred thousand bonus for your bodyguard."

"Absolutely," she agreed, as easily as if it was loose change. "Where are we going?"

King sat back and allowed himself to relax for the first time in days. "Someplace where MI6 can't find me," he replied.

Chapter Thirty-Three

"I can't believe what I've just witnessed."

"The guy's got friends," Pierre replied putting the lens caps back on the scope and unloading the rifle. He slipped the rifle back into the canvas gun slip and added, "And not to mention the mother of all luck."

"Money talks," Stewart said bitterly. "That journalist bitch has two things that piss me off..."

"Tenacity and guts?" Pierre interjected. "She did a better job than we did!"

Stewart scowled. "No. A sense of entitlement and a rich husband."

"Well, it seems to work pretty well for her."

Stewart shook his head. "I just hate wealthy politicians who feather their nest at the expense of the British taxpayer. Her husband has a fucking knighthood, too. Sir fucking Hugo fucking Truscott. Eton, Oxford, The Bullingdon Club of fucking Tory tosspots."

"But Sir Hugo is Labour..."

"New fucking Labour," Stewart sneered. "And that makes it fucking worse because he's a Tory who veered left when he saw how far to the right Labour had gone. He saw the writing on the wall for the Tories and knew that the Labour Party would have a safe couple of terms at least. So, he's a fair-weather sailor to boot."

"I have no idea what half those words mean," Pierre replied. "Can't you English talk properly. He's a sailor now?"

"I'm not fucking English, I'm Scottish." Stewart started packing the mortar back inside the wooden crate. They had returned to Pierre's safehouse and were taking everything of value and use or that could identify them. They would consider the place compromised. "It means he doesn't carry on when things get tough. That he'll change his values to suit the times. Sir Hugo Truscott is the epitome of a Tory who self-serves, is entitled and embedded in the aristocracy, but to further his career he changed just enough to get on the radar of government. He saw that the Conservatives were in for a long spell in opposition and hedged his bets."

"I didn't think men in your line of work were supposed to be political," Pierre observed. "It doesn't make for impartiality."

Stewart nodded. "I'm not. Ok, I would like the people to have more and for the NHS to operate effectively and not be constantly on the brink, but I understand matters of defence and security more than most. I can see that all the parties have good and bad points and policies, but I don't like the extremes. I see far-left socialists as a threat to freedom and the economy, and the recklessness with finances and policies of the far-right as just as dangerous. Historically, Britain has always been a better place with centre-left or centre right governments. That's when people had more money in their pockets and a better standard of living. Sir Hugo Truscott is dangerous in that he fits the far-right characterisation, but he has embedded himself on the left. A man like that lacks morals and integrity. A man like that can't be trusted on any level. And when a man like that is in government, then nothing can be discounted. He'd make a fucking deal with the Devil, that one."

Chapter Thirty-Four
Mombasa, Kenya, three days later

King watched Lucinda as the waiter drew near. She sat up on the sun lounger, her black bikini managing to be alluringly minimalist, yet somehow tasteful in what it covered, what it concealed and what was left to the imagination. Maybe it was the body it barely covered that carried it off so well, but King suspected it had as much to do with the designer. It would be a fair assumption that most of Lucinda's wardrobe would not be found in high street chain stores.

He ducked under the water again, the salt stinging at the cuts on his face and his fingertips, but he knew that the ocean would do it good. He started out in a front crawl and got into a good pace. He could see the ridges in the white sand four feet below him, and darting fish of every colour and pattern. Taking a deep breath on his stroke, he dived deep and turned onto his back, blowing an air ring that he watched float all the away to the surface before popping. He enjoyed swimming. It calmed him and enabled him to think, and he reflected as he pushed for the surface, how swim training had helped him through his ordeal in the prison camp back in Burindi. He had been taken to the edge, almost broken, but he had ultimately prevailed. He had killed the man responsible in a moment and would not lose sleep about it. And he was sure that he was done with MI6. It had been a way out for him and had seemed such an exciting way to live. He had enjoyed the training, most of it at least, and he enjoyed the thrill of the work, the anticipation of the planning, the adrenalin of the operation and the feeling of relief when the mission had been completed. However, that had all paled into insignificance once he had been captured. The fear of death, the agony of torture, the sense of failure, the feeling of abandonment – all were too discerning to contemplate experiencing again. The Secret Intelligence Service would hardly let him go – he knew too much about its covert operational wing for that - so secretive that there wasn't even an official name for it committed to paper - and then there was the fact that he had changed his identity. Stewart and his men had faked the death of Mark Jeffries, a man convicted of murder, and shoe-horned him into the identity of Alex King – a loner who had gone missing in the Golden Triangle in Thailand fixing a drug deal. A man whose parents had died in a car accident, and who had no friends since leaving school. A grey man who had provided King with the life and freedom – for what it was – that he now had. The fact that the intelligence services had undertaken such a scheme was not something they would want getting out into the public domain. At any cost.

King floated for a while, his ears under the water so that all he could hear was his own pulse. Above him a few brilliant white clouds scudded on the wind like candy floss. He tried to recall the name of them. Cumulonimbus? Stratus? He gave up, realising that if he was on *Who Wants to be a*

Millionaire? then he would have to phone a friend, but the realisation that he didn't have any friends broke his train of thought and he stood up and walked into the shallows towards Lucinda, who was nursing an icy Mojito and watching him with her Gucci sunglasses on the tip of her nose. It gave her an endearing look and he wondered whether he would see more of her, fall in love with her and grow old with her. He thought he could, but she was from a different world and that world did not involve men who killed for a living or were born on council tower block estates and spent time in and out of care. The story did not fit his legend, but he would bet that if he told her how his mother had sold her body for crack, then it would mean there wouldn't be an invite to the hunt ball. He wondered, as he took in her wonderful body, her tanned and toned legs and her engaging smile, just how a husband could fail to hang onto a woman like her. But then again, the thought occurred that this was part of the problem. A woman like Lucinda Davenport would be pursued by many and flattery really was the start of a slippery slope for many relationships. Perhaps Lucinda was secretly living with low self-esteem and the compliments and attention sparked a need to be validated. King shrugged it off, his phycology skills likely on a par with his meteorological knowledge.

"I got you a mojito, sweetheart!" she called at him as he strode through the shore break. The waves fizzled and receded as quickly and as undramatically as they had broken. The water had been warm, but the sun baking down on his shoulders felt warmer still. "I might get quite squiffy by lunchtime..."

King smiled at her cultured, Home Counties accent. A world away from his own. *Sweetheart* was new, too. He liked it. "Thanks," he replied.

"How was your swim?"

"It stung a bit," he said as he towelled himself down and ignoring the spare sun lounger, sat down crossed-legged on the warm sand. He took the glass from her outstretched hand and took an uncultured gulp of the cocktail. He had never tried one before and the tastes and aromas of white rum, sugar syrup and mint went down well with the crushed ice. A dangerous drink, in that it went down like pop and before he knew it, he would be drunk. King preferred not to get drunk. He never allowed himself to relax and be off his guard. He looked at his fingertips where the nails had been. They had scabbed and had now softened in the sea. His index finger throbbed and ached as he flexed it, but after a few days immobile it was important to get it moving again. Dislocations could freeze the joint if they were not worked. "A few days on the beach should heal things nicely," he added.

"Margot says that we can have the beach bungalow for a week, and if we require more time then she has a room in the main hotel available for another week. She's blocked it out, just in case." She paused. "Of course, the plane has gone back to Biggin Hill, and we'll have to buy tickets to wherever we're going next."

"Next?"

She nodded enthusiastically. "We've got three-million pounds, well, less the hundred thousand we gave Dimitri. That should be enough to last us." She paused. "If we're sensible, that is. But I don't really feel like being sensible. Do you?"

"I suppose not."

He looked back at the sea. The place was paradise found. Margot was an old school friend of Lucinda's and after her husband had made a killing in the city, they had retired young and opened a boutique hotel in five acres of botanic gardens with three-hundred metres of private beach frontage. Margot now ran yoga and well-being retreats, and never a fan of Sir Hugo, she would never whisper of Lucinda's 'indiscretion' with the rough, tough-looking soldier type who had arrived in what she had later described to her husband as a school PE kit, and a batch of rather nasty cuts and bruises all over his body. His hand had not gone unnoticed either and Margot had sent the hotel's chief first-aider to their beach bungalow to patch him up and leave him with some medical supplies.

She put her glass down on the small round table nestled between the two sun loungers and stretched out her arms. "Come here, lover..." King got off the sand and bent down to her and she reached up and kissed him tenderly. He responded, suddenly aware of how aroused he was by her touch, her smell, her entire being. "Give it all up, Alex. Give up the silly games of cowboys and Indians and living in the shadows. Give up the gun and the world of deception. I'm falling for you. And I know you're falling for me, too..."

King hugged her close. "You'd give everything up for me?"

She hugged him even more firmly. "I want to wake up every morning with you beside me. Your hard, warm body against mine. Spooning me as we slowly come round from a peaceful sleep..." She giggled. "I can't think of anything better."

"Nor can I," conceded King. Sometimes the best things in life came out of a clear blue sky. There was no telling what life had in store for you, so you simply had to take the road in front of you and trust your gut instincts. Could he make a life with Lucinda? Hell, he didn't have to think as far ahead as that, merely enjoy the ride. But he could imagine it, and that was enough for him. "I want it, too," he said, raising his head to look into her eyes, but catching the sight of a grizzled, aging Scotsman trudging across the sand towards them instead. "Oh, fuck..." he managed.

"What is it, darling?" Lucinda sat up as King got to his feet, his past, present and future colliding like disrupted atoms. The convergence of irresistible force and immovable object and between the two forces, fading dreams of what might have been. She looked at Stewart approaching, then turned to King her thoughts mirroring his own. "Oh, no..."

"It's easy to track planes," Stewart said coldly as he stood before them. "With a room full of people with a specialist skillset checking friends, family, acquaintances or business interests, it doesn't take long to find someone. It took longer to fly here than to find a link."

"Am I supposed to be impressed?" Lucinda asked icily.

"I don't give a fuck about you, lady. But my agent has a job to do."

"Well, take this as my resignation," said King.

"Funny one, son..." He looked at Lucinda, holding her eye contact and sneered. "Does the lady know about you killing two Royal Marines in a drunken brawl, and giving a third man life-changing injuries? Does she know that you went down for murder? A common council rat who stole and robbed and hurt people, who went to young offender's institutes and had several stints in prison before you inevitably got a life sentence? Does she know that we scrubbed your identity and shoe-horned you into a dead man's life? Does she fuck..." He paused, looking back at King. "Too late now, son. Can't build a relationship on lies. And this one likes her social standing. You're nothing more than a novelty fling. A bit of rough trade. She'll be back with her delightful husband before you've finished rubbing in the after sun."

"I'm a different person now," King explained, looking desperately at Lucinda, but seeing nothing but the doubt in her eyes. It was done. He knew that there and then. He looked back at Stewart and said, "You could have left it. You could have said you couldn't find me."

"Like you did with that safecracker Simon Grant, after that French affair with the IRA?" Stewart shook his head. "There's no room for sentimentality in this game, King. No happy endings, either. You'll learn that if you live long enough."

"And what if I walk away and never look back?"

"Grow up, son."

"I want out."

Stewart smiled, mirthless and menacing. He had a silenced automatic in his hand. King hadn't seen where he had got it from. Only that one second his hands were resting on his hips, challenging, dominant. The next second the tiny .22 Beretta and stumpy four-inch suppressor was resting beside his right leg. The weapon was so small that it looked like a toy, except King had trained with one relentlessly. He knew its capabilities and had learned to place T-shots with it – every shot placed in the centre of a one-inch imaginary line from the cross of a 'T' from temple to temple, and a vertical line from the bridge of the nose to the navel. Every shot placed in either the brain or the spinal column. It made up for the weapon's lack of power, but almost silent delivery. "The Firm haven't had their money's worth out of you yet, son."

"Jesus Christ!" Lucinda stared at the gun. Stewart shrugged. For some reason silenced weapons always elicited more fear in people. A practical solution to the drawbacks of using a gun in public, and thus the person would be more inclined to use it.

"You're going to kill me?" King asked incredulously.

"Not just you. No witnesses, King."

Lucinda gasped and King placed his hand on her shoulder. "Don't worry. He's bluffing. He just wants to use you to get to me." He paused. "And I saved him in the Congo," he added, staring at Stewart and leaving him under no illusion how cold the feelings were towards him behind the even colder eyes. "Even he isn't such a bastard as to kill me just for going AWOL."

Stewart scoffed. "If not me today, then somebody else tomorrow. Or next week. Or next month. They're not going to let you go until you've levelled up the balance sheet and given them something for their investment." He slipped the weapon back into the thigh pocket of his cargoes and stared back at King. "There's a flight out of Mombasa at eleven tomorrow morning." He reached into his other pocket, retrieved a British Airways folder and tossed it onto the sand at King's feet. "Be on it or spend the rest of your lives looking over your shoulders." He turned and walked back across the sand without further word.

Chapter Thirty-Five
London

King saw the headquarters of MI6 looming ahead of them. The taxi driver was a doctor from Uzbekistan. King suspected that the closest the man had come to the medical profession was when they drove past St. Thomas' Hospital a few minutes ago. If the foreign taxi drivers plying their trade in London could be believed, then any NHS staffing crisis could be solved overnight.

Peter Stewart sat next to him, but they had exchanged few words since the incident two days ago on the beach in Mombasa. In fact, once the fasten seatbelts sign had cleared after take-off, King had headed for one of the empty seats a few rows back and settled in for the flight and complete silence for the remainder of the journey. They cleared the luggage carousel, even though King only had a carry-on with him and what clothes he had bought on Lucinda's dollar when they had first arrived at the hotel in Kenya.

As King suspected, they drove right past the River House, crossed Vauxhall Bridge and headed for Whitehall. Non-descript, boxroom offices with little or no refreshments was what he had become used to. Even MI6 distanced themselves from him. Distance. It covered a multitude of sins. He wondered whether he would ever see Lucinda again. News of his past life made him suspect that the woman would be having second thoughts about any reunion and their lovemaking before he left had felt cold and dispassionate and empty, both with minds on other things. The passion was gone. She had cried when he had left in the taxi, but he wondered whether the tears were for him, or for the loss of something new and exciting being snatched prematurely from her. Or whether she now regretted giving thought to leaving her husband, or even cheating on him in the first place.

King left Stewart to pay for the taxi and headed for the east side of the building. He heard Stewart running to catch up but did not slow his pace. A flock of pigeons were scavenging a packet of crisps that someone had dropped, and King walked through the feeding frenzy without slowing.

"Okay, lad, I get it," Stewart said as he walked around the pecking melee of birds. "But you need to be on your game here. This is the first time that you've been requested at a meeting for one of these briefings. Which means they're looking at you more objectively. You need to make a good impression."

"They'll take the impression they get," King snapped. "I'm not putting on any airs and graces."

"Your call..."

"How much do they know?"

"Only what's in my report."

"Trips to Mombasa?"

"No."

"Then how did you explain my release?"

"I didn't. We had a successful reconnaissance. That's all

the seat polishers need to know. They can imagine all sort of heroic shit getting you out, but they don't need to know your girlfriend bought your freedom with the Business Secretary's own money." Stewart shrugged. "Look, we have a difficult job to do, sometimes there's no sense in making it more difficult. As much as I loathe the likes of Sir Hugo fucking Truscott and his wife... yes, King, his *wife*... I don't want the story of an up-and-coming journalist conducting an extra marital affair behind her husband's back with a serving MI6 officer. That would be a bit of a tangled web. Factor in him funding your release, indirectly or not, and his position in government and his role as business secretary with national and personal interests in Burindi and the press will never let this one go. Top it off with our involvement in a *Coup d'état* and too many heads would roll, too many rocks would be lifted to see what lies underneath."

"The big picture?"

"The big picture."

"Shit."

"Can I assume that you're back on the reservation?" King nodded reluctantly. "That's the ticket, son. Plenty more fish in the sea."

King said nothing, but he followed Stewart through the security check where they both showed their passes, then climbed the stairs to the third floor where Armstrong was waiting impatiently for them beside a water cooler. He checked his watch, as did King. The man seemed agitated at their lateness, only they were five minutes early.

"Gentlemen, the fact that you are both here, alive and well can only mean that you've had a successful reconnaissance." He led the way down the corridor without further word or motion and opened the door to a box room without tea or coffee making facilities. Stewart remembered a time when he had been met with a good Scotch and niceties. He'd had more than one dinner at *Simpson's*, *Rules* and *The Ivy* to discuss a mission. It seemed now that every MI6 mandarin wanted distance between themselves and the shadow men on the ground. "Take a seat," he said curtly. There were four plastic chairs around a Formica table. It reminded King of school behaviour meetings with his head-master and his foster parents or social workers as a teen. His mother had never made it to any of those meetings. Soon after, neither had King. "Feasibility," said Armstrong. "Yay or nay?"

Stewart looked thoughtful for a moment. "Yay," he replied. "With six, eight-man SAS teams, two Parachute Regiment battalions, four fire support and artillery units, two light infantry units, and six RAF Tornados flying sorties, then yes. Very much a big, fat yay."

"Preposterous!" Armstrong snapped. "Absolutely out of the question. The UN would be apoplectic. NATO would make things extremely awkward for us, too. There's no way they will allow it, and we'll likely be expelled. The bloody Russians would love that!" He paused, shaking his head incredulously. "You were briefed that it was to be a special operation. Plausible deniability. So, bloody well think again."

Stewart shrugged. "That scenario would give a ninety percent chance of success." He paused. "The other ten percent is the unexpected. Like the Soviet Union and Afghanistan, or the Americans and Vietnam. We haven't had one of those moments, yet. But it could well be coming our way in Afghanistan and Iraq. And certainly, Burindi could well just be it. It's a land-locked country and that means that there is no obvious neighbouring ally for logistics."

"It's completely out of the question!" Armstrong snapped churlishly. "What is the likelihood of removing Mustafa from power, reinstating Lucky Man Jonathan Mugabe without the support of the armed forces."

Stewart shrugged. "Slim to none."

"What about with Mugabe promising to double all government employee's wages, including the police and armed forces for six months before reinstating pay structures at twenty-percent premium over Mustafa's regime?"

"Is that what the government has come up with?" Stewart scoffed. "Typically, I'd wager none of these *thinkers* have been out there. Not many African governments make good on their promises, and the people know that."

Armstrong did not share Stewart's assessment of the scheme. "It is what the best analysts in combined intelligence have come up with. It's what a secret research and development committee have suggested."

"A committee?" Stewart snorted. "A group of people who singularly can do nothing; and collectively get nothing done?"

"It's where we are," Armstrong said quietly. "I want you to make it happen. I want you to do the job you're paid for and not speculate." He stood up. "Our meeting is adjourned. You've got carte blanche, but you keep it low key and deniable. No blow-back on the UK Government, and especially nothing coming back on the Firm."

Stewart watched Armstrong leave and close the door without looking back. He turned to King and said, "Well, that was worth the time and effort. Looks like you got beaten up for nothing."

"Great."

"Well, you got laid and had a couple of days on the

beach." He stood up and slapped King on the shoulder. "Time to go, lad."

"Where?"

"Hereford," Stewart replied. "I know someone there who will be useful. No, vital if we're going to get this thing done..."

Chapter Thirty-Six
Hereford

King swung the Jaguar XJ6 into the carpark of the *Horse & Groom* public house and slotted into the widest available space. There was an array of parked vehicles, but nothing fancy. He could already tell that this was a place for locals who came for the cheap, basic pub-grub and did not ask to see a wine list. The building looked dated and in need of a lick of paint and new guttering. King noticed that there were a few work vans parked – general builders, plumbers and electricians - but assumed that the owners were all on their lunch break and that any refurbishment plans were a long way down the road.

Stewart got out and followed King across the carpark. They had made good time and the luxury saloon had made for a comfortable trip. Seniority gave Stewart the keys to the higher end of the motor pool. As they reached the entrance Stewart pointed to a blackboard and said, "There you go, a pint, pie and chips for five quid. Don't see that in London. My treat."

"That's pretty generous for a Scotsman."

"It'll be a packet of scampi fries and a long wait in the

car in a minute!" Stewart replied gruffly and headed in through the scuffed and worn green door.

At a time when many of London's pubs were being turned into wine bars or gastropubs, the trend was certainly not happening in Hereford, or at least at the *Horse & Groom*. Fruit machines whirled and flashed next to a wood burning stove that had seen better days, with a pair of buffalo horns mounted high above. The carpet was busily patterned, threadbare in places and stained with a thousand gallons of beer over the years. A scribbled sign in felt-tip pen informed patrons that credit or debit cards were not accepted and that there was no such thing as a tab or slate. In a side room the crack of pool balls cannoning into each other was audible over Radio Two playing from a cracking portable set wedged behind the optics.

"Fuck me, Stewart, this is your kind of place," King commented.

Stewart grinned. "I've fallen out of here at two in the morning after a lock-in more than once..." He walked to the bar and leaned against the counter. "A long time ago, now."

King knew that Stewart had served in the SAS, or 22 Special Air Service Regiment as it was officially known, for many years after leaving the Parachute Regiment. King had trained with the SAS on various rotations but had never served. For MI6 it made sense for its highly secretive and deniable special operations agents to undergo training with the best. After its operatives had trained in escape and evasion, survival, weapons handling, close quarter battle techniques and unarmed combat, the clandestine field craft element of the training was taught in Surrey and Norfolk and then honed on the streets of London. Operatives such as King were often sent back to Hereford to join new SAS recruits for a few days or a week to assess and hone their fitness levels. These operatives were known at Stirling Lines as 'grey men', who never socialised in the mess or the local pubs and clubs and disappeared as abruptly as they had arrived. Stewart on the other hand had lived in Hereford for years, married his wife Margaret here and knew the place well.

The barman greeted them without either warmth nor the prospect of conversation and they took their drinks to a corner table next to a fruit machine. Stewart explained that it had always been a locals' tavern, and that he had not been back in more than ten years. By the look of the paint and grime covered overalls of the men drinking, it was also a local workmen's lunchtime hangout. Stewart sipped the double Scotch, appreciating the warmth as it went down. King, drinking just an orange juice, watched the Scotsman's obvious pleasure. He had seen Stewart drink from a hip flask before eight in the morning, but nobody ever said anything. It was clear that Peter Stewart was a high-functioning alcoholic and a veteran MI6 officer had once told King that if he had seen half of what Stewart had in his career, then he may well be taking a drink to forget, too.

There was a scuffing and banging, and a dishevelled looking man of around fifty years of age, wearing a torn and stained anorak wheeled himself into the bar in a wheelchair. The green door was scratched enough to reveal several shades of paint and some bare wood, and King thought the man to be responsible for most of the damage. He wheeled himself to the bar, grunted and was grunted at in return, and then he made his way across the room and paused at the fruit machine. He dropped a pound coin in the slot and pressed the button. There was the rolling, holding and jingling noises that came with such a machine, and he held a cherry, was dealt two oranges and pressed again. He held two, pressed again and three cherries lined up and the machine made all sorts of noise as it paid out ten pounds in one-pound coins. A man stuck his head around the doorway, pausing his game of pool and jeered. The man in the wheelchair ignored him and pocketed the coins before wheeling himself to their table as the barman placed a pint of lager down in front of him and returned to the bar without a word.

"King, meet Ronnie," proffered Stewart. "Ronnie, this is King."

"How 'do..." Ronnie grunted in a broad North Yorkshire accent.

King tried to hide his surprise. They had driven to Hereford to meet a fixer who could provide them with mercenaries and equipment. Ronnie looked like a man who spent all day in a pub nursing a single glass of booze just to save on the heating at home. King sipped his orange juice and nodded at the man, who had started to drain the lager in large gulps.

"What's the job?" Ronnie said quietly, placing his half-empty glass down making another ring on the table.

"Central Africa," Stewart replied.

Ronnie nodded, picked up his lager and drained half of what was left. Stewart caught the barman's eye and indicated another round, but by the way the barman returned his gaze, it was clear that table service was reserved for cripples and locals. Or more specifically, local cripples. Stewart held up two twenty-pound notes and the barman had a sudden change of heart.

"Anywhere in particular?"

"It begins with a B, ends in an I and is due a regime change."

Ronnie nodded sagely. "Jungle, highlands and urban scenarios." He paused. "How many men?"

Stewart waited while the barman put down a tray with another round on it. "One more round in fifteen minutes, then three of the pie and pint specials." He dropped the two twenties on the table and added, "And get yourself a drink before putting the change in the Mars and Minerva charity tin you've got behind the bar."

The man regarded Stewart for a moment, then his demeanour changed, and he said, "Yes, sir," quite amiably before walking back towards the bar. The town had a strong pride for the SAS who had made its headquarters in the village and later the town, and the charity tin for the Special Air Service Regimental Association raised hundreds of thousands of pounds a year for veterans fallen on hard times, widows and orphans and those left with life changing injuries. Mars & Minerva was the association's official magazine. Stewart turned to Ronnie and said, "I reckon thirty men should do it."

"Thirty?" King interrupted somewhat incredulously.

Stewart stared at him and said, "You were at the meeting earlier, weren't you?" He paused. "We don't have the luxury of an army at our disposal."

King shrugged, looked up as the drinks came. The barman managed to grimace a thin smile. Ronnie sipped some of his lager before the rest of the drinks were on the table. King had noticed the cider museum on the way in. Hereford had an altogether more rural feel than he had expected, and he realised the ridiculousness of his life. He had trained with the SAS many times, been driven out to the Brecon Beacons, the Black Hills and the Forest of Dean for exercises, but he had never even set foot on the pavement in Hereford.

"Skills?"

"Ex Regiment boys, of course," replied Stewart. "But paras and Royal Marines with a good record can be considered. I'll let you be the judge of that. Five team leaders, five medics and four snipers." Stewart paused. "And make them mother fuckers. The hardest, nastiest bastards on your books."

Ronnie nodded, combing his lank, greasy hair out of his eyes with his fingertips. King noted that the man still hadn't committed anything to paper. "Weapons?"

"Deniable."

Ronnie nodded. "Russian?"

"That'll do."

"A long and a short each?"

"Yes," Stewart replied. "And a fucking container load of magazines and ammunition."

"Specialist kit?"

"Four sniper rifles with decent scopes. Make them civilian. Sako, Remington, Winchester... I'm not bothered which, but quality pieces. Point three-oh-eight, because we can run seven-point-six-two through them in a pinch. Swedish match-grade ammunition would be favourable. Zeiss, Schmitt and Bender or Leopold scopes. Suppressors, slings and spare magazines, bipods and gun-slips." He paused. "Webbing, camel packs, water canteens... better have knives and machetes as well."

Ronnie nodded. "I can supply US Marine Corps Ka-Bar knives. Pound for pound, about the best knife ever to grace a soldier's hand."

"Agreed," said Stewart. "And then there's fire support. I'd say the good old Gympy, but because we must absolutely leave no clues to British involvement, how about M60 machineguns? But I want seven-point-six-two millimetre in case we have to engage vehicles or material targets."

"That's quite a shopping list," Ronnie remarked. "I can get close, but I might struggle with the civilian rifles. I have good Lee Enfields with scopes already out there. Or near enough, at least. And Gympies are all over the African continent, so nobody is going to point fingers. I won't let you down."

Stewart shrugged. "Alright. And I want a LAW for each man as well," Stewart added. "A rifle, a pistol, a knife and a LAW. That's non-negotiable. But I want ammo to be common and shareable."

King had not used a LAW before, but he knew all about the disposable LAW weapon system. The M72 LAW (light anti-tank weapon) was a portable one-shot 66mm unguided rocket launcher. A simple tube carried easily across the top of a bergen and complete with instructions printed on the frame, with one pull of a pin the weapon was made ready with a drop-down trigger and sighting system.

Ronnie smiled. "It sounds like quite a war you're not getting into."

"A rapid strike that will hopefully meet our objectives."

"And you're going to pay me this time?"

Stewart shrugged. "That was a long time ago, Ronnie. Not my call back then."

"That kit almost bankrupted me."

"Well, you don't pay much in the way of tax or VAT, Ronnie." He paused. "Add a bit of compo on for old times' sake."

"I will, but I'll need the cash up front this time, Peter."

"Done."

"Anything else?"

Stewart looked up and waited as the barman walked out

with a tray. He put down the tray and plonked three plates of pie and chips in front of them, and a pot of cutlery. The three pints of lager had spilt on the tray, and he put them down, adding more rings to the table. When he walked back to the bar Stewart said, "Mortars. And grenades." He paused, swiping a saltshaker from the next table, then liberally covered his chips so that it looked like it had been snowing. "Each man will bring his own personal kit to do with as he pleases. I'll make my own arrangements for ration packs and medi-packs, comms and maps."

"Where and when?" asked Ronnie.

"We're training in Kenya in a week's time. I'll send you separate flight details. We'll aim to get the men out on five flights so as not to arouse suspicion. Tell the men to clear their calendars for a month."

Ronnie still hadn't written anything down and King was starting to wonder how the man did it. "And the bounty?" he asked, before taking a large mouthful of steak and kidney and getting a dollop of gravy on the front of his anorak.

"Experienced team leaders will receive fifty-grand. Specialists get thirty-five and the rest of the men will be paid thirty-thousand-pounds." Stewart paused. "Twenty-percent will be paid to them upon sign-up. The remainder will be paid upon completion. Widows and loved ones will receive the full bounty. Of course, we'll need details to set it all in motion."

"A week will be tight."

"A week is all we have."

Ronnie sipped his lager and placed the glass back down making another ring. "And you'll trust my judgement regarding the men?"

Stewart nodded. "We'll need some right hellcats," he replied. "It will be a shock and awe attack on a nation with a standing army of ten-thousand men. I don't want any boy scouts or union shop stewards."

Ronnie smiled. "Most of the men I have in mind weren't dishonourably discharged from the regiment for failing to show up for work."

"That's what we need." Stewart turned his attention towards his pint while King had almost finished his pie and paid little attention to the chips. Ronnie seemed to be eyeing King's chips and he pushed his plate aside and indicated that the man could help himself. As designated driver he had not bothered with his pint, finishing off his second glass of orange juice instead. He passed the lager across to Ronnie, who now had pints double parked. Stewart slid an envelope across the table and Ronnie took it, slipping it inside his tattered anorak pocket. "Something else that is required, but better left unspoken..."

Chapter Thirty-Seven
Monaco, two days later

S tewart ordered a whisky, while King and Redwood took a cold beer each. The café was typical of Monte Carlo and the French Riviera, with waiters in white shirts and black waistcoats and tables with immaculate white linen tablecloths. Glasses of water and bowls of pistachios were brought over on arrival and each time the waiters brought an order it was carried above their shoulders on large silver trays. The café looked out on the glistening waterfront and the billion-dollar view was full of boats, exotic cars and even more exotic women. Redwood helped himself to another handful of pistachios as he thought about Stewart's question.

"He's been shaken up," he said finally. "That snake in the grass Cilla has had a real grounding, too."

"And the Russian died in the..." King shrugged, searching for the right words. "Boating accident?"

"Yes. I saw the body myself."

"And Lucky Man Jonathon hasn't had any other Russian contact?" asked King.

"No. We've tapped his landline, have frequency scanners picking up every mobile phone conversation within half a square mile. GCHQ are monitoring that, and they'll inform me if there's any traffic from Lucky Man Jonathon or Cilla." He paused, taking a sip of beer from the frosted glass. "So, it's on, then?"

King said nothing, took a sip of his beer and leaned back in his seat. Stewart nodded. "Imminently."

Redwood nodded. "So, I'm babysitting him until it's done?"

Stewart nodded. "You work for the MOD, not me. The SAS were tasked with protecting him."

"And spying on him."

Stewart shrugged. "That's the game we're all in."

"Some of us more than others," Redwood replied.

"Are you looking for a sideways move?" Stewart asked.

"It's a consideration."

Stewart swirled his whisky thoughtfully before draining it in one grateful mouthful. "I've read your file," he said. "I think you would be more suited to the Security Service. I have a contact, well the deputy director. Charles Forrester needs a mix of muscle and brains to aid his fight on Islamic extremism. You would be a good fit."

"Box?" Redwood sounded a little dejected.

"You're not what I need right now," Stewart said matter-of-factly. "You're a good soldier, a proven leader. And there's no doubt that you can kill. But is that what you really want to do? Become like King and me?"

"None taken..." King said icily, before picking up his beer and staring off down the street.

Stewart ignored him and added, "It's a tough thing to live with, the things we're asked to do." He paused. "There's a hell of a difference between putting a mine on a boat and retreating to a safe distance and making a terrorist talk.

Especially when that terrorist has a wife and children in the next room. What we do is up close and personal. Many of the hits we do are on unarmed men and women. In fact, we try to engineer it that way. Work smarter, not harder. It takes a certain type of person. But somebody like you, working with Forrester, well, you'd get great things done. See out your tour, take early retirement in a few years. I'll keep an eye on you and what you're doing, and then set something up."

Redwood seemed to consider this, and by no means took it as a brush off. "So, how far do we go to protect Lucky Man Jonathon?" Redwood asked, then added, "Do we simply escort him to the plane, or into Burindi and the palace itself?"

"You keep him alive long enough to walk inside the Presidential Office and get sworn in. By then, Britain will have the mineral rights and it's job done." Stewart paused. "After that, then he's left to his own devices." Redwood nodded, but he seemed far from keen on the idea. "What's the problem?"

Redwood shrugged. "Well, the man's a dickhead. Are the powers-that-be sure that he's the best man for the job?"

"That's a paygrade issue," Stewart replied. "As in; nobody seated around this table is paid enough to even bother thinking about it." He paused. "We take a guy out; and you put a guy in."

Redwood contemplated this over a mouthful of beer. "We'll need to liaise closely. He'll need to march right up those steps as Mustafa comes out."

"*If* he comes out," King corrected him.

"You're not going to kill him, are you?" Redwood asked incredulously.

"We're orchestrating a coup," replied King. "Mustafa

isn't our concern, just as long as he capitulates. But Mustafa's mistake was leaving Lucky Man Jonathon alive. Hopefully we will have learned from that, so I wouldn't put odds on Mustafa living long enough to draw his pension."

"When will I know it's safe to move him?"

"We'll let you know," replied Stewart. "He won't be arriving coach class... we have a private jet on standby that will take him from the airport in Nice to Kenya, where he waits in situ, and then into Burindi International Airport at Umfasu." He paused. "We'll aim to make it an easy run. You land, our team will sweep in and whisk him, yourself and your close protection team straight to Government House, which was formerly the Palace of King Faizal in the late sixties."

"They do like a good overthrow in these parts, don't they?" King commented flatly. "He had three wives and six mistresses, and they were each decapitated by a guillotine that was a gift from Charles De Gaulle, and their heads were placed on spikes on the steps of the palace before King Faizal was hacked to pieces with machetes and gardening tools in the street."

"That's some stellar research, son," Stewart smiled. He had encouraged King to read more, learn more and it was starting to pay off. "But I'm hoping for a seamless change of leadership, none of that bloodthirsty malarky." Stewart took a mobile phone out of his jacket pocket. "This is the new model Blackberry. It has our numbers saved in the call list and you have your own email account activated. Email addresses you need are in the address book. You can browse the internet when you have enough signal." Stewart slid the phone across to Redwood. "King and I both have one, as does our controller in London if it all goes tits up. I have also programmed my Burindi contact, a man named Pierre, a dependable bloke, if you need help in Burindi."

"Help?"

Stewart nodded. "If it comes down to that, then King and I will be dead, and the coup will have failed." He shrugged. "But hey, let's cross our fingers that it doesn't come to that..."

Chapter Thirty-Eight
Mombasa, Kenya, two days later

King collapsed beside her on the bed, perspiring, spent. Lucinda rolled onto her side and propped her chin up on her elbow as she circled his chest with her index finger. King looked at her, catching her eyes and trying to work out what she was thinking. She seemed a closed book. A different woman from the one he had left just four short days ago. Stewart had killed their future together. Any real future, at least. She had weighed her options and they did not extend to a life with a former assassin, and with heinous crimes in his past. But she found him attractive, and she liked the sex. Well, he was damned if he was going to be titillating entertainment to her and had already decided that he would leave for the training camp in the north of the country a day early.

"I didn't expect to see you so soon," she said softly, her index finger still drawing imaginary spirals on his skin. "What happens now?"

King shrugged. "You shelve plans of leaving your husband and I get on with the task I've been given."

"Which is?"

"You know what it is," he replied, a little irritably. "But I still can't tell you."

"You're swapping a socialist monster for a right-wing monster. Big deal. Another thorn in the side of the African people. Only now, it's Burindi's turn."

"There is a better man," he replied quietly.

"Who?"

"Desmond Lambadi."

"What?" She rolled onto her stomach, propping herself up on her elbows looking down at him. "Desmond Lambadi is alive?"

"He is."

"How do you know?"

King shrugged. "Because I spoke to him in that prison camp..."

"What?" she asked incredulously as she sat bolt upright in bed. "You spoke to Desmond Lambadi and never said? He was right there, just feet away and you didn't think to tell me?"

"I didn't think your rescue plan would stretch to two," he said somewhat flippantly. "Besides, they move him around. Or they certainly will now that they know I've seen him."

"But will they?" Lucinda asked thoughtfully.

"Meaning?"

"Well, I got to you via contacts that my bodyguard Dimitri has built up over time. We took a Hail Mary on bribing the prison governor, and he's... well... dead. He wouldn't have advertised the fact that he was taking a bribe to release a prisoner and leaving the country." She paused. "This is Africa. Those guards would simply keep their heads down to avoid any fallout and it's doubtful that they would volunteer anything to a replacement governor or interim army officer taking charge of the camp. I doubt anyone would even know you were there to start with, let alone gone."

"Maybe."

"Oh Christ, what a story that would be!" She slid out of bed and covered her nakedness with a silk robe, tying the silk cord tightly which accentuated her slim waist and the gentle curve of her hips. "Desmond Lambadi is Burindi's answer to Nelson Mandela. What a fucking coup that would be!" She paused. "And we know where he is!"

"Where he *was*," King interjected. "Where he *could* be."

"But that's more than anybody has known in years!" she exclaimed. "Lucky Man Jonathan denies ever knowing what happened to him, and so did Mugabe when he removed Lucky Man Jonathon from power. The fact that he's alive and imprisoned will show the people that neither man can be trusted. That there could be a *third* way for Burindi..."

"You're crazy," he replied. He rolled onto his side and propped himself up on one elbow. "If you go after this story, you'll be dead within the week. Too many people want Desmond Lambadi to stay disappeared. Mustafa and Lucky Man Jonathon had their reasons, and the British government want a greedy politician in power, *not* a man of the people for the people. Desmond Lambadi would sink the money made from minerals into education, health and social projects. He wants a democratic society with a focus on self-improvement and a solid, steady future. A Switzerland in the middle of the African continent. Does that sound the sort of place to sell off its mineral rights and buy arms from UK plc?" King scoffed. "No, as much as Lambadi's life story would make a great film, and as much as news of him still being alive would provide hope for many, he just doesn't fit into the agenda of..."

"Britain?" she ventured. "Jesus Christ, there's more than ten million people in Burindi! Don't their lives matter? Tell me, if Britain got its arms deals and mineral rights, will the NHS be saved overnight? Would we have a policeman on every street or would potholes in the roads become a thing of the past?" She paused, but only for breath. King sensed that the questions were rhetorical and knew far better than to interject. "Would it, bullshit! Not a single penny made from selling out Burindi would make it into a British pocket."

"With the exception of a handful of politicians and your husband, that is..." There. He'd said it. He could only keep quiet for so long, but as she stared at him, looking like a child and he'd strangled her pet hamster, he wished he had kept his counsel. She turned with enough force to raise the silk robe and flash her thigh as she flounced into the bathroom and slammed the door behind her. King slipped out of bed and pulled on his boxers. He bundled his clothes and left via the sliding French doors to the garden terrace. There was no point having a domestic when she had already made it clear that they would never be in a conventional relationship. Affairs were for fun, not the mundane, and arguing was never going to be fun. She could do that with her husband. He was done.

King traipsed across the neatly trimmed lawn and onto the sand. The beach was deserted, and he walked close to the water's edge and sat on the warm sand. Places like this still blew him away. The white sand, the glistening Indian Ocean, the azure sky dotted with tiny clouds high above the two airliners streaking across the sky. There had been a point in his life when he had thought he'd never travel further than Southampton, where he had once escaped to after failing to take a fall in a boxing match. A time when finance and circumstance held him prisoner, constricting his growth and outlook. And then when the judge had dropped her gavel and he had been facing a life behind bars, the first stretch of which was to be in Princetown, deep on desolate Dartmoor, he had thought his life was over. And then there were days like these. Sat on an equatorial beach on the African continent, still revelling in the afterglow of sex with a beautiful woman, the past behind him and a whole life before him. King glanced around him, stood up and took off his boxer shorts, and waded out into the sea. The water was warm, almost blood temperature – so warm that he could barely feel the depth on his skin as he waded deeper – and when he dived under and opened his eyes, the salt water stung and blurred his vision, and worried his cuts and grazes. Gradually, the wounds stopped stinging and his eyes adjusted to the salt. He set out in a front crawl, breathing every fourth stroke with the beach on his right. The water blocking his ears and the rhythm of his stroke, the concentration upon his breathing was almost meditative. There was a clarity to his thinking. Yet all the time, he knew that there would be a price to pay. Everything had a price, and everything had a consequence.

King dived down and drifted into a somersault. When he had spun one-hundred-and-eighty degrees, he kicked out and rose to the surface, settling into his stroke once more. Half a mile in both directions and he was faced with a choice. What was right. Or what was easy.

He stopped swimming when his toes ploughed through the sand. Wiping his eyes, he looked to the shore and saw Lucinda standing at the water's edge in her silk dressing gown. The beach was otherwise empty, and he watched as she stood before him, unfastened the cord and let the gown drop to the sand. She stepped into the water and waded towards him, and he couldn't help but feel aroused as he watched her wade through the water. The water reached her thighs and what had been tantalisingly on display disappeared before his eyes. The water reached her breasts and then her nipples, and again the water covered her nakedness, but somehow, he found this even more alluring and arousing as she dipped under the surface and glided elegantly and seamlessly towards him. He had cleared his head, knew what he had to do now. But that was for tomorrow because tonight was in front of him, and every moment counted in life and especially in his line of work, because any moment could be the last.

Chapter Thirty-Nine
Mandera County, Kenya, two days later

K ing watched the three old Bedford trucks bounce and weave along the track. The men had removed the canvas coverings, favouring the breeze and the baking sun, rather than the stuffy humidity under the superheated canvas.

"Here we go," Stewart commented.

"Can't wait," King replied. "As DS, do we have to join in?"

"Aye."

"Bugger."

"You've always been the same, lad. Never want to run, cough your guts up in the first mile, then you can go all day." Stewart took out his hip flask, twisted the cap and took a sip. "Well, that's the last of that for a day or two."

"Right."

"Cheeky bugger..." He looked up as Pierre walked up to them carrying an enamel mug of black coffee. "We're on. I want to introduce you before you go."

"Go?" asked King.

Stewart nodded. "Pierre is going to set up camp in

Burindi. But it's important that the men know who's who from the outset."

King nodded, feeling out of the loop. But that was how Stewart operated. If it ever came to being captured, then there was only so much a man could tell. The thought made King shiver and he glanced at the tips of his ruined fingers subconsciously. He had played down the broken finger, and he flexed it, only having around half the movement as normal and he hoped that it would not interfere with loading and handling a weapon.

The trucks pulled into the parade ground and parked nose outwards. The men leapt down onto the hard ground and the trucks drove back out, the last few men still leaping over the side with the vehicle still moving. The Kenyan military had agreed to the use of one of their forward operating bases but wanted nothing to do with the operation. The base was used for patrols along the Somali border, but recent piracy on the coast had shifted the Kenyan government's focus.

"On me!" Stewart shouted and the men walked over. King noted that they did not move 'at the double' and knew that the men were used to the more relaxed environment of the SAS, as well as having been on the mercenary circuit for several years.

"Some of you already know me, but for those who do not, my name is Stewart. You don't need to know if it's my Christian name or surname, if you want to call me something else, then make it Boss." He paused and nodded to one of the men, who stepped out from the crown and stood to Stewart's left side. "For those who don't know, this is Geordie," Stewart announced. "He will be joint two IC." He nodded towards Pierre and said, "Along with Pierre, who some of you already know from the circuit. He's Swiss, but don't worry, he's neither a neatness freak nor a neutral party to this little endeavour..."

King bristled as he listened to Stewart. He watched as the men chuckled at Stewart's comment or murmured and digested the news of who the top brass were in their little private army. These were old hands. Old warriors. Most had ten years on King, some more than twenty. He shifted uncomfortably on the ammunition crate on which he was perched. The last time he had been in Africa it had been in Angola and the Congo, and he had felt very much the novice in the small team that Stewart had assembled. Mercenaries were like dogs in a pack. They all wanted to be top dog and they did not hold back challenging their peers.

Stewart turned to King and said, "This is King. You think of him as me. If he gives you an order, you do it or the pay cheque might not get signed. If something happens to me, King will assume charge and what he says goes." He turned and looked at Geordie and Pierre. "Got that?" The two men nodded, but not emphatically, just enough to let Stewart know they understood. "Stan, Boiler, Keth, Tweed and Bunny, come up here and say hello. You are team leaders. We will pick the teams based on specialist skills." The five men stood up and ambled over. King's stare focused on one of the men wearing an eyepatch. Somewhat fittingly the man looked like a pirate with tousled hair and a gold earring. King wondered whether he had looked like that before the eyepatch. Most of the men here seemed to know at least a couple of others and had either served together or recognised others from the mercenary and bodyguard circuit. Stewart knew that they would make a good team, but the operation depended upon teams working individually, and at different locations. "Team leaders, reconvene here in twenty minutes. The rest of you get some scran and a brew and come back in an hour. And yes, there will be some running, and exercise involved." He checked his watch, looked at King and said, "You and I need a chat, son." He waited while the men filed out of the open-sided tent, then said, "That's quite a force out there. If anything happens to me, then you're in charge of them."

"I appreciate that, Boss."

Stewart chortled. "If it all goes to shit, then you need to get over the border fast." He handed King a sheet of paper. "Read, digest and destroy. There are details there of a cache of money, a weapon and passports in both our names. All points of the compass. Five countries. Take your time learning where each place is, but don't leave the camp with that piece of paper. Don't worry about those blokes, they all know the risks."

"Shit..."

"Not your problem. Every man for himself."

King nodded, then frowned. "What the hell sort of name is Keth, anyway?"

Stewart smiled. "He's a good man. He's the one with the eyepatch. Doesn't seem to affect his work, though."

"But Keth? What was his mother thinking?"

"His eye was shot out in Iraq. After he got the eyepatch, he was hoping for a pirate nickname. But the lads in the regiment being what they were, they changed his name to Keth. His real name is Keith, but now he's Keth. Keith without an I..."

"Oh, for fuck's sake..." King paused. "And Geordie? He's from Newcastle, right?"

"Nope. He's from Sunderland, and everyone knows there's no love lost between those two cities, so naturally he got Geordie." Stewart grinned. "Boiler got his nickname because he lost most of his teeth in fights over the years. Pub brawls mainly. He was left with just one front tooth. The lads called him Central Eating, a wordplay on central heating, so some bright spark got everyone calling him Boiler instead."

"Well, I take it Tweed is the man's real name." King paused, "But Bunny?"

Stewart scoffed. "No, Tweed's real surname is Harris... you know, so now he's Harris Tweed, and Bunny, well his surname is..."

"Warren?" King ventured.

"Correct."

"What's Stan's name, then?"

"Stan."

"Of course."

"Listen King," Stewart said seriously. "I've gone out on a limb and put you in charge if I take a hit. It's a big responsibility."

"I appreciate that, Boss."

Stewart regarded him closely, then said, "Good. I know you're up to the task."

Chapter Forty
Msambweni, Kenya

Redwood watched as Lucky Man Jonathan and Mamadou Cilla swilled their champagne, the women seated around them scantily clad in bikinis and the shortest cut-off denim shorts imaginable. Where did the man find these women? They seemed to migrate towards the man, Redwood reflected. Like flies around shit. Redwood kept the mobile phone beside him, one word from Stewart and they either flew straight into Burindi, or back to Nice, although it looked like Lucky Man Jonathon was fitting right into Kenyan beach life. Maybe the man was feckless, or maybe he just missed the beach in landlocked Burindi. Either way, Redwood saw nothing of a leader in the man. Nor his right-hand man. What the hell was the British Prime Minister thinking? But then, since when did integrity and values overrule money? It never had, and it never would.

Chapter Forty-One
Mandera County, Kenya

S tewart had started off the men with runs, calisthenics and a demanding assault course including high nets, monkey bars, high walls and balance beams to acclimatise them to the heat and test their fitness levels. As one would expect from career soldiers who when first joining special forces had all been told that personal fitness was now their responsibility. No more five AM runs or parade ground marching drills. Since plying their trade privately, the men had kept well-disciplined in physical fitness. Regular water breaks were given for the men to hydrate, each ordered to down a litre of water on the hour. Once the men had been put through their paces, he gathered half the men to organise the weapons and the other half were tasked with filling sandbags and humping them into piles to make a series of ranges for the initial weapon testing.

King, drenched in sweat from the runs and dripping with the water he had poured over his head, organised the men into setting out the groundsheets before unpacking the weapons from the single shipping container in the middle of the parade ground. Pistols and the magazines to go with them were placed in neat rows. The same was done with the AK-74 assault rifles and a few FN SLRs. Ronnie had failed to secure civilian hunting rifles, instead sending .303 Lee Enfield rifles with scopes already fitted. King suspected the man had wanted to shift them like a grocer tries to sell their old stock. The rifles looked at odds with the expensive Schmitt & Bender optics. Like fibreglass spoilers on a classic car. The men all saw what needed to be done and before long the entire arsenal was out and being counted. At the rear of the container, the mortar shells remained in wooden crates. They would check them later, once there was space and all the weaponry had been removed. King stepped inside the container and checked the crates. He frowned and bent down to inspect the lower crates in the stack.

"Leave that," Stewart said from behind him. "You won't be on mortar detail, anyway."

King stood up and turned around. "What's in the lower crates?"

"Different strokes for different folks," he replied. "It's a mixed bag. Ronnie has struggled to get us enough ordinance. We've got sixty-mil, sixty-six-mil and eighty-eight-millimetre mortars to feed. Some of this is Chinese, Russian and American as well as British." He paused. "I want you to go to Burindi and do a thorough reconnaissance on your own."

"On my own?"

Stewart nodded. "Solo and covert. If you're caught, then it's over."

"What do you want done?"

"We've got to hit this thing like a street fight," Stewart told him. "A street fight where we're outnumbered and there's nobody coming to help. So, we fight hard, and we fight dirty."

"Naturally," King replied, but he had never seen Stewart like this before. The man never beat about the bush, never called a spade anything other than a spade. "So, what do you want me to do?"

"I want you to find out the feasibility of kidnapping Mustafa's wife and children..."

Chapter Forty-Two
Burindi, three days later

King had entered the country through a gap in the Tanzania border that Pierre had told him about. No visa, no passport, no trace. He had used one of the stash bags that Stewart had spoken of to replenish his funds and arm himself with a weapon, and the passport with his photograph and an assumed name would get him out of Burindi without a red flag. However, he did not plan on leaving Burindi until the job was done, and his travel arrangements would be altogether more typical once Lucky Man Jonathon was back in power.

King had used the intelligence reports from MI6 and GCHQ, including satellite photographs of Mustafa's personal residence. But photographs were one thing; seeing the property and watching it thoroughly was quite another. King had built a hide on the hillside at night. He had used the foliage in the area, cutting fronds and branches to cover the fox hole he had dug out by hand to lie deep in on his stomach, using the powerful field glasses to survey the property below. Beside him he made notes on a notepad using a thick pencil. The field glasses were equipped with a view finder, and he jotted down the distances in the notepad. He was under hard routine, which meant cold food and water and relieving himself in a plastic bag which he would take with him to leave no trace. He had a blanket with him in case of a night chill, but he had not needed it last night. In addition to the satellite photographs he would use he had taken pictures with a powerful digital Canon camera that he had purchased in Mombasa.

King watched the security detail return from the city on the municipal road. They veered right onto the track without slowing and the gates ahead of them opened seamlessly for them to drive through. They favoured large American made SUVs. King did not know the model but recognised the gold cross emblem on the grille as Chevrolet. They appeared far larger than the Land Rover Discovery - to his mind one of the largest vehicles of its type on British roads – and the security detail had three of them. He watched as the middle vehicle turned towards the villa and the other two vehicles headed for a smaller building that he assumed was staff accommodation. Sure enough, a tall, slender black woman got out of the vehicle and sauntered up the steps, a large gold handbag nestling in the crook of her elbow. To King, it looked like opulence without any real class. But more importantly, he was left questioning the security detail's skills. Contrary to popular belief, it was standard operating procedure (SOP) with diplomatic protection to place the VIP in the lead vehicle. In the event of an ambush, the middle vehicle would overtake and shield the VIP's vehicle, allowing for a smooth J turn to get out of trouble. The middle vehicle acted as a buffer from behind, able to ease out across the road to stop anyone from overtaking, and if the VIP vehicle was attacked, then neither escort vehicle was left separated. It was only a small detail, but

King wondered what other operation practices were being ignored, or indeed unknown. There was no gate security, although the gate operated automatically. This could have been controlled via a security guard monitoring a CCTV system and radio or mobile phone, or it could have been opened via remote control from the lead vehicle. Either way, King had to assume that any CCTV system installed was highly effective. And it must be, because he hadn't spotted any yet.

King zoomed in on the security detail. The men were all dressed casually in either jeans or cargoes and T-shirts or white dress shirts left open. They wore gold jewellery in abundance and carried UZI 9mm submachine guns or had pistols tucked in their waistbands. They reminded King of Lucky Man Jonathon's entourage in Monaco. Undisciplined and full of ego. They looked more like LA rappers than bodyguards. Weapon discipline was poor, too. Several men were holding their UZI submachine guns as they smoked and talked outside what King had now named the guesthouse. They did not regard muzzle or trigger discipline, and King knew that sloppy weapon handling meant sloppy fighters. He doubted that this rabble would operate effectively, but it was almost certain that the men had all proven themselves in one way or another, and he was in no doubt that all the men were killers.

King put down the field glasses to rest his eyes. He rolled onto his side and stretched out his back, before unwrapping a filled roll. It had sweated inside the clingfilm in the heat, and the meat – a variety of cured sausage - had leached oily fat in copious quantities. The day was only going to get hotter, and he wrapped it back up and put it back in his pack, pulling out some fruit instead. He ate a banana, then tackled something spikey and orange with black dots on it. King had never heard of, nor seen a kiwano before, and once he had tackled the skin with the blade of his Leatherman and taken a taste, he hoped he never would again. Like a cross between a cucumber, a passionfruit and a banana. Not one of nature's better efforts. He washed it down with some water, which he had added a little salt and sugar to, to help with countering dehydration. Not one of his best meals, but certainly not one of the worst.

He rolled back onto his stomach and picked up the field glasses once more. A teenaged boy and a younger girl were playing tennis on a hard-surface court. A hundred metres to his left, a large woman wearing a gingham dress and white pinny watched over a young girl splashing about in a wonderfully azure blue swimming pool. King watched the water, tantalizingly cool and inviting. What he wouldn't give to have a swim in it right now. Instead, he was drenched in his own sweat and covered in leaf litter and debris, and tiny insects had worked their way into his trousers.

Mustafa spent a great deal of time away from his family at Government House. With a country where revolution and insurrection were commonplace, and with whispers of Lucky Man Jonathon Mugabe's intentions to make a comeback, Mustafa had sent his family to their villa and put them under, what King had now estimated as, a guard of at least twenty men. This was a sizeable force, but what King had noticed was that the perimeter fence around the ten-acre property was deemed security enough. Mustafa's wife had gone into the villa on her own, the two teens playing tennis did so alone, and the child in the pool was being watched by either a maid or a nanny because the child was young, and children should never swim unsupervised. There was not, however, security guards at every turn. In the distance, a guard patrolled the fence, another did so directly opposite. Like two hands of a clock moving clockwise, only in unison. It was SOP for roving patrols, and these men were sticking to it religiously. King photographed the entire camp in various magnifications. He paid particular attention to the single strand of mesh wire and the solid stone wall around the entire property. The mesh wire was topped with razor wire, but the inner stone wall was higher, so the residents would not look out and feel that they were inside a prison camp. Royal palms were dotted around the perimeter and the two guards had managed to find one each and were now smoking in the shade afforded by the giant palm trees. They would have to have comms running for each man to know when to stop. King made another note in his notebook, building a more detailed overview of the property. His main worry, though, was having not found evidence of a CCTV system. The property would undoubtedly have one. The only thing he could do now was get closer.

Chapter Forty-Three
Mandera County, Kenya

S tewart sat back and watched as the sun kissed the horizon. The colours of African sunsets could seldom be replicated in this world, and he had begun to realise why so many Victorian era explorers and prospectors had found Africa too alluring to return home. For a wealthy young man with adventuring pretentions, leaving the smog of Industrial Revolution London and hitting the expansive plains of wild and unchartered Africa must have outdone all expectations. One sunset like this, and the thought of stuffy afternoon tea and piano recitals with the vicar's daughter and the dowager as chaperone would seem torturous.

Geordie sat down heavily beside him, holding two opened bottles of beer for him to take one. Stewart took up the man's offer, reasoning to himself that it wasn't whisky, and they hadn't technically started the mission. "The boys have performed well," he said, crossing his ankles on the ammunition crate in front of him.

"Aye," Stewart replied. "They know what they're doing."

"I'm happy with the mortar placements," said Geordie.

Stewart nodded. They had used dummy chalk rounds and the mortar teams had struck the centre of the target several times. On the day, Stewart would be happy for the men to get within ten feet. They would not be firing upon their targets with different colour chalk, but something altogether more deadly. "Any concerns with the ordinance?"

Geordie shrugged. "It is what it is. The guys have been chosen accordingly."

Stewart looked at the Chinese writing on the side of the crate. He sipped his beer and savoured its coolness, the numbing effect on his mind as it went down. "I don't want King to know," he said eventually.

Geordie frowned. "He's a big boy..."

"He has morals," Stewart replied. "Don't get me wrong, he'd put a bullet in you as soon as look at you, but he has a sort of... I suppose the term would be... a code."

"A code?"

"He's not a soldier by any means. Not deep down. Orders only go so far with him, he needs some gentle coaxing for some things, a kick up the arse for others. But there's lines he doesn't want to cross. He'll find an alternative way to arrive at the required result."

"Sounds like a liability."

"No. He's sound. But he's a bit of a thinker. That usually doesn't go hand in hand with soldiering."

"None taken..."

Stewart shrugged. "He's got a hell of an IQ. Way more than my own. He doesn't know that, though. He has an iron fist, but it's inside a silk glove. He can do more than one thing, have more than one purpose." He patted the crate beside him and said, "Trust me, I just want him kept in the dark about this. Understand?"

Chapter Forty-Four
Burindi

Two hours behind Kenya, Burindi was starting to glow in the evening sunset. The shadows across the grounds were long markers to the west, as accurate as compass points, and the ground around the shadows was dull, fading with the light. Far to the east, King could just about make out stars in the dark blue sky. To the west, the sky was a spectrum of reds, oranges and yellows, as if the horizon was on fire.

King had moved from his elevated position, five-hundred metres from the property, which he would now refer to in his notes as the compound. He had concealed himself in long grass, ever mindful of the venomous snakes that may be lurking there hunting rats and other rodents, but there was little he could do except place his hands carefully as he crawled and hope that he made enough sound for the snakes to feel the vibrations yet remain quiet enough to avoid any roving patrol. This, however, was where he had found the weakness. The compound was a luxury residence and as such, had remained that way for the occupants. Conventional security measures had been added as a matter of course. King had no way of knowing which had come first - the fence or the wall - but while the fence provided a visual deterrent to would-be invaders, the wall made that threat difficult to see from inside. The security guards patrolled the grounds, but any threat they encountered would already be inside the compound. In providing the occupants with privacy and aesthetic design, security had been compromised. The roving patrols needed to be inside the fence, yet outside the wall. So far, King had only spotted security cameras on the gate and three sides of the villa, but that wasn't to say there weren't more of them. In the last dozen rotations – each one taking thirty-five minutes - a guard had taken a route between the wall and the fence just once.

The light all but gone now, just a sliver of dark orange on the distant horizon. King eased out of the grass and crawled across the open ground on his belly, using his toes and elbows to propel himself in what he had been taught was a 'sniper's crawl' to the perimeter fence. He took a long length of grass and held it firmly against the wire mesh and waited. If it was electrified then he would feel anything from a mild tingle to a thumping jolt depending on the volt-age, but certainly measurably less than if he had touched it with his bare hand. Nothing. Not a trace of an electrical current. He rolled onto his back and looked up at the razor wire on top. He already had an idea about how to tackle that, but the fence was high, and the task seemed daunting now that he was so close. He estimated the height at ten feet which meant if they could scale the fence and get over the razor wire then the drop would be considerable, but not undoable. Except that a clean drop from the razor wire would be nigh on impossible. Now that he knew that the fence was not electrified, he was confident of cutting through with wire cutters. But in the attitude of belt and braces, he would prepare for both eventualities. But that still left the sheer stone wall to scale, which was even higher than the fence, and although King could not see the top of the wall, he wouldn't bet against it being spiked with shards of broken glass, something he had noticed was common practice in Africa and Eastern Europe. Again, the idea he had for the razor wire should work, but it would take time and slow their progress.

King took a stick he had sharpened to a point and pressed it into the earth. He wrapped a piece of cotton cloth around the top of it and tied it tightly with the loose strands of cotton. He then crawled back across the open ground, disappearing in the long grass and the risk of vipers and scorpions hunting in the dark. He saw it as a lottery. If he thought about the odds, the chances of getting bit were slim. He estimated the distance from the marker he had placed and made a mental note of it. When he reached the road, he walked slowly and calmly across. Sudden movements are easily noticed, but he was sure that the chances of being spotted by Mustafa's security detail was up there with the odds of a snake bite. Once across, he climbed the incline, the foliage thick and unyielding, and he took a leaf out of Pierre's book and went with the path of least resistance. All the while, he estimated his progress in metres. Once he was back inside his hide, he noted down his estimates and totalled them up before taking a long drink of water to rehydrate. He then tried some more unidentifiable fruit that was yellow and firm but tasted like strawberries and vanilla ice cream. Not the worst to have in your five a day and he now regretted not finding out its name.

Hot and soaked through in perspiration, King settled back onto his stomach and used the field glasses and the night-vision mode to study the compound once more. Another two guards kept up their repetitive counter-clock-wise sweep and he finally got to see the CCTV cameras emitting a single red dot that was their passive infrared vision. A dozen in all. But he had not been spotted on his approach, and he had not been spotted crossing the open ground to the wire, and as he settled his focus on the electric junction box outside the property on the road, it gave him an idea.

Chapter Forty-Five
The Burindi Highlands

"I t's a bit close to the military base, isn't it?"

"Twenty miles. Perfectly safe."

"Right," King replied. "I seem to remember being told that there was no chance of meeting a patrol and look how that turned out."

Pierre shrugged, but the movement caused him to grimace. The man had been lucky, but he still had stitches and massive bruising to contend with. "Shit happens. Tell me, how did you get out of that place?" he asked incredulously. "The woman, she paid for your release?"

"How did you know?" King asked suspiciously.

The mercenary frowned as he negotiated a particularly rough section of potholed road. "We saw the whole thing, my young friend. Did Stewart not tell you?"

"You saw?"

Pierre nodded, but he already looked as if he did not want the conversation to go any further. "On our reconnaissance."

King did not take his eyes off the road ahead. Stewart had not told him that he had seen Lucinda Davenport at the prison camp. King had simply assumed that Stewart had found him in Kenya, because that was what Stewart did. The fact that Lucinda was with King would have made his search so much easier. But why, if Stewart and Pierre had been there, had Stewart not mentioned it? The answer came out of the blue, pounding King like a sledgehammer. Pierre and Stewart had not been there to rescue him; they had been there to kill him. To silence him before he succumbed to torture. The nape of King's neck tickled as a shiver tingled up his spine. His heart started to pound against his chest, and he wondered if he could not count on the people that he worked with having his back, then who could he ever hope to count on?

King said nothing. He knew from the uncomfortable silence that Pierre knew he had said too much, and that King had worked out the connection. Thankfully, they pulled into a clearing and King could see that the man had been busy. Olive green eight-man army tents had been erected in neat rows with guy ropes as tight as guitar strings, with neatly placed tent pegs. However, it was the camouflage netting draped over them that was most impressive. The camp would be almost invisible from the air, but as if to account for the chance of detection, a sandbagged fire position had been erected with twin swivel mounted .50 calibre Browning machineguns, the barrels resting at a forty-five-degree angle ready to engage helicopters and prying eyes.

"You've worked hard," said King.

"Thanks," Pierre replied, almost thankful that they had moved on from the sensitive subject he had not meant to broach. "What further training has Stewart in mind?"

"Just equipment readiness, further conditioning and acclimatisation. It's far more humid here than in Kenya." King paused. "I suppose we'll put the weapons through another test fire and zero, then each team will be given their objective."

"And what's yours?"

"Can you keep a secret," King replied.

"Of course!"

He smiled. "So can I..." King opened his door and stepped out of the vehicle as soon as it stopped moving. Pierre had constructed a safari shower surrounded by outstretched tarpaulin for walls and another that he assumed was a toilet trench. Buckets and water containers were piled high beside the makeshift en-suite facilities, and a large, open-sided tent housed folding tables and chairs and a safari kitchen. "Quite a set-up," he commented, genuinely impressed.

"Oh, I had a lot of help," said Pierre as he strode up to him.

"Help?" King asked incredulously. Help meant people knowing things and people knowing things generally talked about things. "Who?"

"There are people here loyal to..." He paused, searching for the words. "Well, not so much loyal to Lucky Man Jonathon Mugabe, but certainly wanting a change from Mustafa."

"Really?"

"This is Africa, my friend. Sometimes the need to change something takes precedence over what is good for them." He paused. "Let's face it, they have a socialist dictator and they're going to swap him for a capitalist dictator, and in the end, nothing will change for them."

"Can I meet these..." King thought about what they were, then said, "... rebels?"

"Why?" Pierre asked, not hiding his curiosity.

"Intel," King replied. "Local knowledge can prove to be

invaluable."

Pierre nodded. "I suppose it would be a missed opportunity not to."

King headed for the machinegun post and said over his shoulder, "Get a meeting set up for me. I'll go alone." He did not wait for a reply, simply studied the twin machinegun setup. He had never fired the Browning .50, but he could see that the principle was the same as some of the other weapons he had used. Feed from belt, locking and cocking mechanism, charging handle and ejection port. Sights were the same principle with every weapon, whether it was a Vee and pin, circular peep sights, rings or cross hairs. He knew that the .50 calibre bullet was good for three-thousand metres and easily accurate enough with the addition of spaced tracer rounds to draw the bullets in. The underbelly or rotor blades of a helicopter wouldn't stand a chance if it came snooping overhead. King looked at the green, metal ammunition boxes of .50 calibre bullets which were stacked high. Pierre wasn't messing around. He had done a thorough job of setting up their forward operating base. Stewart had compartmentalised the operation like a 'cell system' and King wasn't even sure whether there was another man like Pierre somewhere in Burindi, with another man like King inspecting their efforts. It certainly would not have surprised him of the Scotsman.

King looked up as a minibus drove in. He glanced at Pierre and said, "We need a warning system ASAP. The next vehicle in here could be a fucking APC with a point fifty on the turret..."

"Noted."

"Well, get it done..."

Pierre stared at him, but the stare which met his own was cold and unnerving. "I didn't realise that you were in charge." He couldn't hold King's stare, his eyes darting at the minibus and the men climbing out onto the dusty ground. "Stewart gave me tasks, but he didn't say anything about taking orders from someone else."

"He told everyone back in Kenya. I seem to remember you being there."

"I was under the impression he said that if anything happened to him. Well, nothing has happened to him yet and I'm joint 2 I/C. You being in charge is someone to pin all this shit to if it all hits the fan."

King shrugged. "Well, I didn't get the detailed memo, either. But I'll say it like I see it. You're a mercenary hired by a clandestine wing of the Secret Intelligence Service, to aid in an operation. I work for that wing, and I'm not going to stand here and embarrass you in a dick-measuring competition."

"You weren't so indispensable back at that prison camp." Pierre paused. "I should know."

"Well, I'm still standing," King replied with a shrug. "So, if you're ever caught and become a threat to the success of the operation, then I'll know how it is and won't hesitate to extend you the same courtesy. Let's just hope you have an escape plan or a guardian angel like I did." He paused, watching the men gather their bags together as they looked around the camp, then started to head towards them. "I want to get on, Pierre. I want to trust the men I work with. So, would you please install a warning system for the last section of that road? You've been embedded here for a while, so you should know how to get it done quickly."

Pierre considered this for a moment, then nodded. "OK, I will get it sorted."

"Great," King replied. "Now, let's go and show these buggers who's in charge."

Chapter Forty-Six

I t was pin in map stuff. The spin of the roulette table, the flip of a coin. Stewart had arrived and inspected the camp, approving of King's insistence for a pressure-plate alarm system that Pierre had buried in the track a hundred metres further down the road. He had pulled King aside, not asked about his recon and given him his instructions. Take four men he had barely met and devise a plan to kidnap a woman and her three children. Stewart had handed King the file on Mustafa – a compilation of intercepted CIA emails showing open dialogue with the Russian government, as well as intel gathered by MI6 and GCHQ.

King had relayed Pierre's use of the locals, and he could tell that the Scotsman was less than impressed. When King suggested a meeting for the purpose of intelligence gathering, Stewart had been adamant that they would not make contact, explaining to King that the locals were all loyal to Desmond Lambadi, and that Pierre had been foolhardy to trust them. He had decided then and there to move the operation forward. There would be no more testing or acclimatisation. He had formulated attacks on two fronts, it was now up to King to oversee the third. If one failed, they would all fail.

There were to be three simultaneous states of readiness, with carefully timed attacks in an order that Stewart was confident would give Mustafa no choice but to capitulate. The coup relied upon momentum and shock and awe. The men had been divided into their strike groups and ordered not to talk to anyone about their objective. As a precaution, the men were to sleep in their strike groups and meals were on a rota basis. Showers and latrines were separate. King had wanted to know more about the other operations, especially as Stewart had afforded him such seniority, but it wasn't to be. The Scotsman was adamant that King should focus solely on how he was going to 'lift' the family. Pierre had given King an address that his team could use on the outskirts of the capital. The Swiss mercenary had left soon after to check on the property – a villa that had once belonged to the former foreign minister under Lucky Man Jonathan's presidency. The house was now abandoned, but none of the locals had been brave enough to lay claim to it. Africa tended to revolve instead of move forwards. Revolution was the way Africa worked, and things that revolved eventually turned full circle. Nobody wanted to be squatting in a government minister's property when a troop of undisciplined soldiers came calling.

King had secured three Jeep Grand Cherokees and almost at once they had picked up a government tail. Using their mobile phones, they had aborted going to the safehouse and split into three different directions until they could lose the secret police. It had fallen to King and a former Royal Marine and SBS commando called Clive to lose the car now behind them. As Clive drove, King kept the compact AKS-74U rifle beside him, his hand on the pistol grip and the muzzle resting against the rubber floormat. Clive had made his Makarov pistol ready and slipped it underneath his right leg, sandwiching it to the seat.

"We're fucked if they pull us over," commented Clive, his eyes darting almost constantly between all three mirrors. "We can't explain all the kit in the back. What do white people visiting Burindi want with half of that lot? And the other half are bloody weapons!"

"Calm down," King replied, not taking his eyes off the vanity mirror through which he constantly surveyed their tail. "Take the next road on the right. Towards Viga. By the look of it from the map, it cuts through the mountains and runs parallel with the highway out of Umfasu."

"On it." Clive swung the wheel and they bounced over potholes; the road less well maintained than the roads of Casu.

"There's three of them," said King. He checked his watch. They still had to devise a plan and execute the damn thing in under thirty-six hours. "We need somewhere quiet to deal with this."

"What's your plan?"

King wished he had something better, but it came down to either losing them, or killing them. They did not have time for this, and either way he knew that they needed to get rid of their vehicle or find some new numberplates for it. He surveyed the road ahead looking for a turn off where they could act. The land was terraced sugar cane plantations and what he guessed were pineapples, looking like miniature palms. His phone vibrated in his pocket, and he was tempted to ignore it, but he answered it tersely.

"Yes?"

"King, it's Ollie, where are you?"

"On the road to Viga."

"Great, keep heading straight until you see the signal."

"What's the signal?"

"You'll know..."

King frowned and hung up. He looked at Clive and said, "Just keep going, something's going down..."

"What?"

"Your guess is as good as mine. But Ollie says he has something in mind." King checked his mirror again and the white Toyota Corolla was still on their tail, far enough back to be constant and intimidating, close enough to show that the secret police did not care if they were seen. In the distance, a red truck was rapidly gaining on them. He watched for a few seconds, the truck getting steadily closer. As it grew larger in his mirror, King could see that it was a large open bed lorry with wooden sides and laden high with pineapples. It pulled out into the crown of the road to over-take without the use of signals and drew close enough to make out a large white man at the wheel. "Shit. That's Ollie..."

Clive checked his rear-view mirror, his expression saying it all. "Oh crap, this doesn't look good!"

King saw that Ollie's plan was going to be simple, yet effective. Hopefully. He had no idea how the former body-guard had got hold of the lorry, but the man had used his initiative and was now looming down on the car behind and barrelling along the rutted road in kamikaze fashion. "You might want to speed up, mate."

Clive floored the accelerator and the powerful diesel engine roared, the exhaust billowing out smoke in their wake. The vehicle was old and well past its service date, but it surged forward and left the Toyota behind as the lorry swerved into the vehicle's off-side rear panel travelling twenty miles-per-hour faster than the car. The resulting noise sounded like distant thunder and the car spun one-hundred-and-eight degrees before a wheel clipped the grass verge and sent it high into the air. When it came down, it rolled roof over chassis then remained on its roof and spun around in the road. Ollie kept the accelerator mashed into the rusted footwell and the truck smashed into the rear of the Toyota and pushed it forwards. Sparks ignited the petrol vapour escaping the ruptured fuel tank and the car caught fire and made a terrific 'whump' sound that Ollie could almost feel as well as hear. The lorry was listing badly but thankfully came bouncing back down on six wheels, but the engine started to make a whining sound as steam and smoke wafted out from the bonnet like a thick fog. He slammed on the brakes and when the vehicle juddered to a halt, he leapt out and sprinted across the road into a pineapple field without looking back. Behind him, the tyres of the truck had already caught fire after driving through the burning fuel.

"Bloody hell!" Clive exclaimed. "That was fucking hardcore!"

"Well, it certainly solved the problem," King replied, watching Ollie sprinting through the field. He picked up the map and flipped over the well-folded page. "Next right," he said. "A track goes behind these fields and runs back to the main road. We can pick that nutter up there."

Chapter Forty-Seven

"I don't think this is a wise thing to do."

Lucinda laughed hollowly. "This is Burindi, it's probably not that wise being here in the first place!"

Dimitri nodded. He had often thought the same. The work he did was fringed by madness, shadowed by insanity. He either protected people in some of the most dangerous regions on earth, or he went to war in those same regions for the highest bidder. "But we've already been there. You used your contacts and instincts to find the place, but the people at the prison camp will know that the commandant left with you, and a prisoner. The commandant has disappeared, his absence will make for awkward questions when you return. I expect we're both wanted for questioning by now. We should be getting out of Burindi, not going deeper."

Lucinda Davenport seemed characteristically unperturbed. "It's not like they are going to find him in a hurry. King saw to that. And the flight manifest showed me leaving the country with his name, not King's. It will look like he just hitched a ride, and I'll say that the last I saw of him was at Mombasa airport in Kenya."

"What about passport control?"

Lucinda scoffed. "This is Africa. Money talks. We dispensed with the services of customs and immigration."

Dimitri shrugged. "We can't just turn up there wanting to do a story on a man they have sought to hide for almost a decade." He paused. "They will want to silence us both."

"Did you not hear what I said?" she smiled. "This is Africa. Money talks..."

Chapter Forty-Eight

"Are they dead?"

"You could say that."

"I don't want speculation," King said coldly. "Just confirmation."

"They're not going anywhere," Ollie replied. He was a big man, as tall as King and a sight broader with a tremendous chest that anchored a pair of arms as thick as most people's legs. He stood opposite King. Calm and undaunted, although he couldn't quite hold King's stare. Not many could, his eyes being cold and glacier blue and leaning towards animalistic. Wolf-like. "Trust me, they're dead. The car caught fire, and nobody was in a rush to get out. Accidents happen. It will look like a hit and run. By the time they trace the pineapple truck, we'll be long gone."

King nodded. "Okay. And thanks, by the way. You solved a problem and kept us on track."

"Don't mention it."

King liked the man. He knew that he had an extremely brief army career straight from school but had ended up working security and from there had entered the murky world of investigations and close protection. Normally mercenaries were former career soldiers, but Ollie had seemed to navigate this dangerous world and be highly recommended by Stewart's fixer. King was no solider either and he drew some comparisons with the man's background. While King was a boxer, Ollie was a martial arts expert in Judo, karate and Brazilian Ju-Jitsu. But whatever skills the man had to offer, quick thinking and initiative had just saved their day. He would make it a point to keep Ollie near him and was sure that the man could pick up the slack if anything happened to King and the mission stalled.

King looked at the other men in turn and said, "The Burindi secret police know that we're here. Thankfully..." He looked at Ollie. "We got away from them."

"They'll be on the lookout more than ever now," Clive commented flatly.

"Too many white faces," said Phil. "Think about it, how many other whites have you seen out here? And now there's a load of white, physically fit, fighting-aged men poking about. We're hiring cars, buying motorcycles, coming in over the various land borders, flying in... It doesn't look good if the Burindi government are hearing whispers of an overthrow. And those secret police guys saw us coming out of the hardware store. That's why they were so curious. What the hell were a bunch of whites doing with that stuff?"

"It is what it is," King said firmly. "We can't black up our faces like *The Two Ronnies* in a sketch. We now have the equipment we need and the intel, so we have to make it work for us."

"The family will have a large protection detail," said Ollie. "I'm guessing twenty at least."

"Approximately twenty-five," King informed him. "So,

as a career bodyguard, what's the most effective way to snatch a VIP?"

Ollie shrugged. "Kill the bodyguards." He paused. "There's nothing else for it. Anything else will quickly escalate. They will be armed and dangerous, whether they're highly trained or not won't matter when they have access to automatic weapons. And we know that most of these people are off their heads on cannabis or khat most of the time, anyway."

King nodded in agreement as he pinned several pictures to the wall. "My thoughts exactly. These are the personnel tasked with shepherding Mustafa's family. The family are not to be harmed..." He then pinned the photographs of a woman and three children aged between nine and thirteen on the wall. "I will reiterate, *not* to be harmed. There is a maid or nanny in the house. I wasn't quick enough to photograph her, but she's a hefty lass in her fifties. And black, obviously. Everybody inside that compound is black. Likewise, there were two gardeners in the grounds. Scrawny, dressed in overalls. You will have to use your judgement there, but we don't want civilians harmed."

"Shit happens when you play rough," David said quietly. He was a quiet and reserved individual who seemed instantly forgettable, which was why he had been a great asset to the DET, or detachment of intelligence officers operating in Northern Ireland. He was a grey man. Ideal for blending in and disappearing. He shrugged, looking at King. "Just saying it like it is. These scenarios get tricky."

"Just see that they don't get hurt," replied King. "If that means roughing them up to make them compliant, then so be it. I'm not worried about cuts and bruises, just stray bullets."

The men nodded. They knew the score. With the exception of Ollie, they had all trained in hostage rescue. But Ollie had been around the block and Stewart had told King that when his VIP had been snatched in Mexico, Ollie had taken the man back leaving several cartel members dead and a substantial price on his head if he ever returned to the country.

King pinned up a satellite image of the compound. There was a large colonial house, a guest house, swimming pool and extensive gardens. Outside what appeared to be a row of garages a red convertible Ferrari and a garish yellow Range Rover were parked next to three black SUVs, that were so large that they could only be American. King had been able to confirm this and had noted he thought them to be Chevrolets. Two gardeners could be seen tending to an array of well-established plants, and a woman was receiving lessons on a tennis court using a tennis ball machine. "Welcome to socialism the Burindi way," said King. "This is Mustafa's private residence, although he spends most of his time at Government House, or the Presidential Palace depending upon who is in power... the name changes as much as the leaders... but this is where his family live when they're not holidaying at their beachfront home in Zanzibar."

"Twenty-five bodyguards for just four people?" Clive asked incredulously.

"They'll have shifts and downtime. We may be lucky and find some are off site when we go in," Ollie commented. He pointed at the photograph on the wall. "I take it the guest house is for the security detail?"

King nodded. "It is."

"Right, well there will be at least two personnel in the main house while they sleep, and by the looks of the two men at each end of the grounds, two on a roving patrol during the day. There's no reason why that won't be a constant. But it's habit forming and predictable."

"Agreed." King paused. "So, hitting them at night will make the most sense. Two in the grounds, two in the house, the rest in the guest house."

"But it won't be as simple as that," said Phil. He was a tall, smartly turned-out individual who had an air of superiority about him. Stewart had told King that he had once been a captain in the Household Calvary, but when he had returned to his unit after a four-year tour with the SAS, had been dishonourably discharged for dereliction of duty, although Stewart had maintained that loyalty and bravery were not lacking in the man's character, and it was likely he had fallen on the proverbial sword for the regiment's honour. "It's all guesswork."

King nodded and pointed at the image. "Two ideal observation points here and here..."

Clive looked at his watch. "We can get those OPs covered today. A change of watch and we'll have a better idea twenty-four hours from now."

"We have night-vision and field glasses," King replied. "You and David can take first watch, Ollie and Phil, you take second watch. Six hours on, six hours off."

"What will you be doing?" David asked drolly.

"Don't worry about me," King replied without looking at him. "Tool up with the Makarovs and keep the longs in the vehicles. This is a surveillance operation and we've had enough interest today already." He paused. "And if you get seen, then don't bother coming back here and you can kiss goodbye to the rest of your bounty..."

Chapter Forty-Nine

Lucinda Davenport had the story mapped out in her head. She had already written the introduction and two summaries, depending on the outcome of her visit. What she needed now was the man's own words. She had left Dimitri behind. The man was being paid handsomely by her husband to be her bodyguard, but in a country where money could buy anything, it wasn't enough for the Russian. Unconvinced that she would be allowed access to interview Desmond Lambadi, he had got out of the vehicle and given her a choice. She had made her decision and driven off in the Land Rover, leaving Dimitri at the side of the road. The man had left his Sig 9mm pistol in the glovebox for her and wished her good luck. The fact that the man tasked with her security thought it too dangerous to proceed was not lost on her. But if she could bribe her way inside, with the camp commandant now gone, then perhaps she would get lucky. The thought of what could happen to her did not outweigh the possibility of such a monumental story, and she knew that she was being reckless and optimistic at best, suicidal at worse.

Dimitri had left her with few words, but haunting, none-theless. *No story is worth your life, and too often in Africa, lives are worthless. Especially that of a young, attractive Western woman...*

Lucinda, meanwhile, could see Nobel and Pulitzer Prizes ahead of her, if she could deliver the man and his story to the world.

Chapter Fifty
Umfasu Parish, 24 hours later

The night-sight turned everything green. Shade upon shade, but all green as he swept the scope across the compound. Compound. The name did not do the place justice. A Garden of Eden on the outskirts of the hub of commotion, poverty and bustle of Umfasu. The property's boundary was a tall wire fence with razor wire on top. Inside the fence tall palms hid the razor wire, while a ten-foot stone wall with climbing plants on the inside fooled the occupants into forgetting the wire security fence and the world outside. In total, the compound occupied ten acres of prime Burindi real estate.

Phil could see the entirety of the grounds from his vantage point – King's initial surveillance hide which had been hidden by cut fronds and easily reconstructed - but was on the cusp of his marksman abilities and the vintage .303 rifle's range at eight-hundred metres, so he would have to hope that the furthest sentry was at the three, six and nine positions of his imaginary clock face, rather than twelve. He centred the crosshairs on the furthest sentry, who was now at the six-hundred metre mark. Each line of the crosshairs was marked with a line which gave him markings for distance, windage and elevation. He had placed markers with material tied to the top of pegs that told him the direction of the wind, and the marker that King had placed on the boundary fence during his reconnaissance gave him the distance from which he could make further calculations. King had assured the man that the marker was exactly one foot in height, and that allowed Phil to calculate using it as a scale.

He moved the rifle to his right and could pick out David and Clive making their way through the wire fence. They had been equipped with wire and connectors to divert any electrical current – although King had assured them that it was not electrified, the men had elected to take precautions just in case - and heavy-duty wire cutters to slice cleanly through the fence. Both teams carried light-weight extendable ladders that they had purchased from a hardware store in the capital, to make easy work of the stone wall, and as he swept the sight over the compound, he could see both King and Ollie scaling the stone wall and covering one another with their rifles. King laid the thick folded builder's membrane over the top of the wall, covering the shards of glass, then hauled up the ladder and spun it around, sliding it down the other side and waited for Ollie to climb down. After two long minutes, Phil checked both teams and could see that they were ready. All four men were crouched low, using the palms as cover, weapons shouldered and facing their objectives. As planned, they had maintained radio silence. Phil moved the rifle slowly and steadily, bringing the crosshairs onto the electric junction box on the road. He fired once, worked the bolt and fired again. The PIR lights dotted around the grounds went out, and he immediately turned the sights to the chest of the furthest sentry. The man, who had been walking slowly some six-hundred metres distant stopped at the sound of the gunshot echoing across the valley. Phil took a deep, steadying breath and kept the sights fixed on him then inhaled, slowly exhaled and when he had no breath left inside him, he gently squeezed the trigger. The rifle recoiled harshly, and he lost sight of the man in his reticule, resighting urgently to see the man's body lying motionless on the neat lawn. Phil brought the crosshairs back across the lawns and to where he had last seen the second sentry. Panic rose within him as he realised that he had lost his second target, but the man stepped out from some flowering bushes, the lit cigarette in his mouth glowing red, as he craned his neck to listen. Phil wasted no more time. Four-hundred metres. He used the line directly above the centre cross and aimed just below the man's neckline. The gunshot rang out as he squeezed the trigger and he caught sight of a spray of mist as the man slumped to the ground.

"Electricity and targets are down..." he said into his throat mic. "Go! Go! Go!"

* * *

Upon Phil's confirmation King sprinted out across the lawn and made his way to the main house. He heard two more gunshots, both as loud as before and knew that if Phil wasn't giving follow-up shots, then he was already working on the engine blocks and front tyres of the escort vehicles. By the time he had crossed the lawn and the large patio area surrounding the swimming pool, four more shots had thundered across the compound and if all had gone well, Phil would be packing up his rifle and kit and heading for his vehicle. King checked for Ollie, who for a big man was faster and more agile than he expected but was slowing pace as he reached the patio. King held back to aid Ollie with breaching the doors, but the man-mountain pounded past him and launched a leaping front kick at the centre of the two doors, splintering them inwards. He flicked on his headtorch, and King followed him through the doors, his own head torch illuminating the gloom. Both men switched on the Maglites taped to the fore-ends of their Kalashnikovs and swept the area inside. King took the lead and checked the open living area, his torch beams casting deep shadows across the whitewashed walls, occasionally silhouetting a mounted animal head, or tall skinny pieces of African art.

"Clear!" shouted King. He turned and headed out through the large kitchen which was furnished and equipped with everything in the brochure. Standing in the corner with their hands raised in the air and a shattered bottle of milk at her feet was a stout woman who King took to be the maid he had seen on his earlier reconnaissance chaperoning the child who had been swimming. She certainly wasn't a member of Mustafa's family. With a dressing gown pulled tightly over her she stood frozen in fear, and yet as King's light illuminated her, she started to babble angrily at him in pidgin English. King glanced at her bare feet surrounded by shards of glass and figured she wasn't going anywhere in a hurry. He yelled at her to stay where she was and headed out through into the grand-looking hall which was packed full of African wood carvings with tribal weapons and artefacts adorning the walls.

"Heading upstairs!" Ollie shouted and proceeded to take the stairs one at a time, his weapon shouldered and everything he surveyed passing through the open sights and beam of terrific white light. King followed and had no sooner stepped on the first stair tread when gunshots rang out from above and Ollie went down.

"Shit! Man down! Man down!" King shouted into his throat mic as he fired a short burst up the stairwell and was met with return fire. Ollie grimaced and jerked on the stairs as whoever was firing at King sent a few more bullets into him for good measure. "Man down! Man down!"

King emptied his magazine up the stairwell and changed seamlessly to a new magazine as he charged up the stairs, caught hold of Ollie's ankle and hurled him back down the stairs and out of the line of fire. It was the best he could do for the man, and he threw himself onto the next flight of stairs and fired at a movement on the landing. He pushed himself up the next four treads on his belly and caught another movement as someone ducked behind the corner of the wall. King fired a foot or two inside the plaster-work and a man stumbled out and fell onto his knees clutching his stomach. King fired again and the man slumped and lay still. He changed magazines again, the awkward tilt and snap of the Kalashnikov's magazine so much slower to make ready than his favoured M4, Sig 516 or Heckler and Koch G3 assault rifles. By contrast the weapon was tinny and crude. He worked the bolt and dropped the selector down all the way to 'single fire'. He was closer to the family now, and he needed precision shots. He had taken down the guard, but his lack of discipline firing through the wall had put the family at risk and he knew that he could not risk another shot like that and had to maintain calm in the heat of battle. He pressed onwards. Briefly thinking about Ollie lying injured downstairs, but he wasn't going to risk the success of the mission for a man he had only just met. Every man knew the risks involved and for the entire overthrow to succeed, Stewart had insisted that they needed this vital bargaining chip with Mustafa. Given the breadth of the operation, King had been miffed and felt side-lined considering the size of the task ahead of Stewart and the other team, but here he was, and he was not going to fail at any cost. He tried to steady his breathing, but his adrenaline levels were off the scale. He dried the palm of his right hand on his trousers, then gripped the pistol grip of the rifle once more and eased out around the corner of the wall and played the torch beam down the corridor. Gunshots echoed across the compound as David and Clive engaged the bodyguards at the guest house. He could hear chatter on the net between them, and he tore the earpiece out of his right ear to tune into his surroundings and listen for any tell-tale sign that would give him the edge. He could hear hushed whispers and knew that panic was panic in any language. A girl was crying further down the corridor, and he held his breath to hear more, but all he could hear now was the thudding of his own heart and his pulse hammering away in his ears. His hand was wet with perspiration again, but he dare not take his finger away from where it was hovering just millimetres from the trigger. Somewhere ahead of him a door creaked open. He played the light of the torch strapped to the rifle down the walls, his headtorch illuminating the other side of the corridor. The thought that if someone fired at the light then they would hit his fore-head dead centre plagued him, and he snatched at the band and ripped it off his head, just as a door opened and a man stood before him with a machine pistol raised. The man was frozen to the spot, but then again, so was King until a split second later he tossed the headtorch at the man's feet, and it illuminated him like the spotlights on the plinth of a statue. The man was temporarily dazzled, but he fired the machine pistol as King dropped to one knee and emptied the Kalashnikov into him. The man fell as King continued to fire, then the weapon went quiet, and King heard the 'dead man's click' as the bolt struck a final time on the empty chamber. The feel of the trigger was loose without the firing pin being cocked on the last bullet's gas recoil, and King tossed the weapon aside knowing that he was out of magazines, and he drew the tiny Makarov pistol instead. He carried on down the corridor, snatched up the headtorch and held it in his left hand as he kept the pistol raised in his right. He opened the first door he reached and checked inside. Empty. He dropped onto his stomach and swept the torch underneath the bed. Nothing. Outside, the gunfire had died down and had been replaced by the occasional single shot. King thought at first that the men had been mopping up stragglers, but he felt a chill down his spine as he wondered whether the two experienced ex-soldiers were negating the taking of prisoners. For a moment he pictured men on their knees, hands on heads and the two men using their pistols as they stood behind the surrendering bodyguards. He shook the thought from his mind and headed for the next door. He had barely placed his hand on the handle when the door flung wide, and a man pushed a large revolver into King's face. King batted the weapon aside with his left hand and dropped the torch. The man countered with a parry and a punch and at once King could tell that the man was strong. He had King's right wrist in his clasp and clamped his other hand on King's elbow to hold the arm like a vice. King kicked at the man's shins, his military boots smashing against the bone like a mallet. The man started to pull on King's arm, using his hip to place King off balance. King was familiar with the basic judo move, but even with it happening by brute strength and in slow motion, he knew that he would be off his feet in a matter of seconds, and he reached his left hand for the KA-Bar knife on his belt, drew it from its leather sheath and buried the seven-inch blade deep into the man's side. The knife went in and out effortlessly, aided by the blood-groove pressed into the blade, and King followed up with three more thrusts and the man released his grip and fell back on the floor. Blood pooled around him, and King could see that he had stabbed the man's liver. He sheathed the knife and was about to leave, when he thought about the dying bodyguard and his effort to fend him off so desperately. He found a light switch and flicked it on, forgetting that the power was out. He cursed his own stupidity as the two cut-crystal chandeliers which would have brightly lit the room did nothing. He picked up the headtorch and played it across the room, his eyes fixed on a fitted mahogany wardrobe that filled the far wall ten feet high and twenty-five feet wide. He'd given up trying to hear anything – his pulse still thudding in his ears – and kept the pistol trained on the doors of the wardrobe. It was an exquisite French design, installed a hundred years previous, but King did not take in the rich colours and patterns in the wood, nor the carved roses and leaves at the edges. He could hear movement inside and stood to one side as he tried the nearest door. The gunshot sounded like a cannon and a hole the size of a cricket ball appeared in the centre of one of six doors. Another hole appeared almost immediately, and the room filled with the noise and echo of the shotgun and smoke wafted out of the second hole. King caught hold of the doorhandle and wrenched the door open, grabbing the scorching barrels of a double-barrelled shotgun. Knowing it was empty after its two shots, he snatched it out of the teenaged boy's hand and to his credit, the boy rushed at King, but he had too much to control with the other three sets of eyes peering out from the gloom of the closet and King brought the butt of the pistol down sharply on the boy's head and kicked his legs out from under him. He stepped back, the pistol aimed at the boy as he shouted for the two girls and their mother to get out and kneel on the floor. They screamed and howled and cried, but they stepped out one-by-one and King stepped back further to prevent the chances of somebody else being a hero. He looked down at the boy. Part of him was feeling guilt at having hit him, another part of him was angry at being put in that position, but he knew that the boy had only been trying to protect his family. If the situation was reversed, King would have done the same. Anyone would have.

With the family located, King put his earpiece back in and tried the throat mic. "This is King, sit-rep, over..."

"Security personnel neutralised," David drawled into King's ear. *"Clive's taken a bullet in the calf, but he's walking wounded."*

King grimaced. Another complication. "Ollie's down at the foot of the stairs," he reported. "Family located, three tangoes down. Rendezvous on me in the master bedroom." He looked at the woman and said, "Do you speak English?"

"Of course," she replied hatefully.

"Good. Do what I say, and you and your family will be OK."

"But not my husband," she sneered. "Just kill us now, you *baturai* pig and go about your day!"

"Nobody is going to kill you," King assured her, but he was shocked by what she had said, and he knew deep down that Mustafa would be lucky to survive the overthrow. Britain had no allegiances or business deals to do with the socialist dictator. He simply had no value and would be perceived as a threat by Lucky Man Jonathan Mugabe. The woman knew this too, and in that moment, King understood the futility of the operation. When this was over, he couldn't tell himself he'd done the right thing and installed a leader who had his peoples' interests at heart, or that Burindi would be a better place for all the bloodshed. He was no better than Mugabe or Mustafa. But at least those men had some skin in the game. King, like so many warriors fighting on the continent before him had merely taken the 'King's Shilling' and blindly followed orders.

"Ollie's gone," David said quite casually as he entered the room.

King was startled by the man's silent arrival. He looked around and said, "Gone?"

"Dead."

"Right," King replied, trying to make sense of it all. "There's two more rooms I haven't checked." The man nodded and stepped back out into the corridor. King pushed his thoughts aside and set about clamping the woman's hands with the heavy-duty cable ties he had brought along for the task. The woman did not resist. There was a fatalistic acceptance to her demeanour that King found altogether unnerving. He fastened the teenaged boy's wrists next, checking his skull as he did so. There was a lump the size of an egg, but no blood, so at least he felt better about that. The girls were frozen, and he made short work binding their wrists behind their backs. He looked back at the woman. "You and your children will not be harmed in any way," he assured her. "You have my word."

"Your word means nothing to me, you *baturai* animal!"

King said nothing. He knew his words would be worthless. This time he heard David approaching. The ringing in his ears from the gunfire was subsiding and the pounding of his pulse had eased.

"Clear," David said. He made his way across the room

and manhandled the two girls ahead of him. "Come on, what's the hold up?"

"Nothing," King replied irritably. He pulled the boy to his feet and pushed him forwards. The woman followed and King hesitated beside a framed photograph of Mustafa, his wife and their three children. They seemed happy, there was a lake in the background and a mountain in the distance. He snatched the picture frame and tucked it inside his jacket, then followed with his weapon ready and his head back in the game.

Chapter Fifty-One

Mick had the sentry in his sights. One hundred metres. No wind. He double tapped his throat mic and waited. A double tap came back almost immediately. Ten seconds later, a second double tap squawked in his ear. All three men were in position, and now had five seconds to take the shot. Not one second before, not a second after. His finger tightened on the two-stage trigger taking up all slack. He held his breath, kept the crosshairs centred. Three... two... one... He squeezed the trigger and the compound crossbow made a sound no louder than the thud of a shoe being dropped on a carpeted floor. He caught the flash of the bolt and then the sentry slumped in the tower. He could not see, but at the same moment the other two sentries had met the same fate. The broad-headed arrow tips, sharpened to a razor's edge and coated in potassium cyanide had done their job. Mick couldn't vouch for the others, but his bolt had struck the sentry in the centre of his chest, and it was unlikely that the man would have needed the addition of cyanide, but it had been a matter of belt and braces.

Stewart put down the field glasses and nodded at Stan. "Okay, you're up."

The veteran soldier nodded. There was no hint of guilt nor anticipation for what he would do next. The man had been taking orders his entire adult life and he had got over the emotion in killing people years ago. He had a handsome payday on the horizon and the fact that he was working indirectly for the British government motivated him past financial gain. Stewart had selected each man for their task, based on their military records and Stan was the man for this job.

Stewart watched as Stan led the team of eight down the hill, the gas canisters and spray pumps weighing them down. Stewart activated his mic and said, "Bravo Team, go…" He brought the field glasses up to his eyes and surveyed the scene before him. Keth and his eight-man team were armed with silenced Makarovs and were tasked with leading Stan and his team silently to their objective. Stewart could see all eight men donning gas masks, while Stan's team were wearing full NBC suits and breathers. The Scotsman took a deep breath. This was about the worse thing he had ever done, and he closed his eyes as he watched the men file off into three lines and cross the camp. He was still an agnostic, and this mission wasn't going to find him the light of right and truth any time soon, but he prayed for forgiveness, nonetheless. Had he gone too far this time? Undoubtedly. Had he been played by the higher echelons of MI6 who knew he was the type of man who couldn't bear to lose? Possibly. Or perhaps they were simply too attuned to assign seemingly impossible tasks and people like Stewart had created their own *res ex necessitas, sui facere*. For as long as men like Stewart found a way, expectations would always be unreasonably high.

Stewart watched as one of the lines of men reached the barracks block and another stood outside the armoury. He checked with his laminated plan of the camp. The darkness made it difficult to see, the high intensity field glasses picking out too many shadows now that the men had successfully crossed open ground, but he could see single muzzle flashes in the gloom, and thankfully no return fire. They were taking down the guards one-by-one and from his position some three-hundred-metres distant, Stewart couldn't hear a thing. It was all going to plan. For now, at least.

Stan pressed his back up against the wall as Keth neutralised a guard with a single headshot from the silenced Makarov. Despite being cut loose from the SAS and honourably discharged from the army on medical grounds after losing his eye in a gun battle in Iraq, the Brummie was a superb pistol shot, primarily because he had only his right eye and there was no struggle for eye dominance. He had worked as a mercenary ever since and was highly regarded on the circuit. He nodded to Stan and stepped to the side of the door while the rest of the team caught up with them. Keth eased the door open then holstered his pistol and unslung his Kalashnikov. The other men followed suit and they crept forward, the sound of men taking in some down-time ahead of them. Voices, laughter, music and the drone of a television set. Keth stepped in past the stacks of muddy army boots and tatty and worn M-65 field jackets hanging off pegs and peered in through the second door. He held up a hand and beckoned the others inside. He counted off quietly. "Three... two... one... go!" He kicked the door open and swung inside, his Kalashnikov aimed at the mass of men who looked up in an air of confusion. Three more men held their weapons on the room, while Stan walked confidently through the hut to the other end. The second man with the gas canister upon his back and the spray pump in his right hand, his pistol in his left. Before the men could protest both men sprayed their way down the hut, meeting briefly in the middle before turning around and spraying the men perched on the beds on the other side. There were coughs and eye rubbing, then choking. But it was over quickly and by the time Stan and the other soldier switched off the battery powered pumps, forty men lay dead or dying before them. One of the team was filming the scene on a digital camera. He held the frame on the last dying man, then followed the rest of the men out into the night.

* * *

Stewart watched the men mopping up guards with the silenced pistols. They had fanned out through the camp, and only one Republican Guard soldier had returned fire. He had been cut down after a minute-long firefight. Nobody stirred within the huts. The cyanide gas had been absolute. When he saw the men take three separate paths back towards his position, he put down the field glasses and took out his battered silver hip flask and took a large pull on the twenty-year-old Macallan inside. He had tried and failed to remain dry on this mission, and now he frankly didn't care. He closed his eyes, savouring the burn and the calm the whisky brought to him. He had done some terrible things in his past, things he would have to live with, but this really was the pinnacle. And he was no less responsible than the unfortunate men he had tasked with using the pumps. More so, even.

Chapter Fifty-Two

Phil was at the wheel of the Jeep Grand Cherokee, its engine running and its headlights illuminating the bodies of the security detail lying lifelessly on the ground. The rear of the vehicle was dented and had lost its bumper from where he had used it as a battering ram and reversed multiple times into the gates to gain access. The glass of the rear window was smashed, and the tailgate was twisted. When he saw Clive limping behind the four family members, his pistol in his left hand and using his assault rifle as a makeshift crutch, he got out, opened the rear door and started to shove the children inside. He looked up as King and David came out carrying Ollie's body between them.

"Forget it, there's no room," he snapped at them, his military seniority and experience coming out. "There's no playbook for this. We can't take him home." He pulled King away and David struggled with the weight on his own and dropped the body on the ground. "Get in the Jeep!" he shouted, then bent down and checked Ollie's pockets. They had all been told to leave wallets, ID and personal effects at the house, but he made sure, none-theless.

King made room for Clive in the front and the man grimaced as he got in. "Is it bad?" he asked, looking at the blood-soaked white bandage wrapped over his combat trousers around his calf.

Clive shook his head. "Technically, no. Through and through the meat. But it hurts like fuck..."

King nodded. "Do you want morphine?"

"No. I want my senses intact until we're in the clear," he replied through clenched teeth, the pain obviously challenging his resolve.

King thought it made sense for him not to hit the morphine yet, and he closed the door and watched as Phil pulled the pin on a soviet era phosphorus grenade and placed it underneath Ollie's body. He walked calmly back to the vehicle as the grenade popped and fizzed and started burning white-hot, green smoke billowing into the air. He got back behind the wheel as King and David stepped onto the step bars on either side of the Jeep and hung on tightly to the roof rails as Phil set off down the driveway. King looked back and regretted it. Now he knew why soldiers never looked back. Ollie's body was burning fiercely in the centre of a white, green and orange fire and the spare ammunition he had been carrying was cooking off in the heat, gunshots ringing out in the night. By the time they had driven out of the smashed gates and a mile down the road, only faint 'pops' were audible behind them, a faint glow in the distance as the white phosphorus burned fiercely at 800°C.

They reached the parked SUVs, hidden from the road on a plantation track, and King unloaded the woman into his Jeep and the boy into another. The girls were placed in the third with Clive still in the front and David now behind the wheel. There were screams and a lot of yelling as the family were separated, but King knew that he could not afford to have all their eggs in one basket and separating them was essential. In the distance blue and red flashing lights were accompanied by sirens as the police and emergency services arrived at the compound. Their escape route had been meticulously planned to avoid the roads leading to Umfasu and as they now started out on three different routes to their safehouse, King thought their chance of success to be more than fifty-fifty now they were clear of the compound, and that was a hell of a lot more than he thought when the five of them had first stood around an outspread map and started to plan this madness.

"What are you going to do to my children?" the woman asked from the rear seat. Her hands were bound with cable ties behind her back, and she rested awkwardly in the seat, the seatbelt stopping her from slumping forwards. "Is it money you want?" King said nothing, but the woman persisted. "Tell me!" she snapped. "I can get you money. A lot of money!"

"I don't want money," King replied quietly, reflecting the irony that a socialist leader would have such a fortune. But that was Africa. Hell, that was politics the world over. "And your children will be fine. I said that they would not be harmed. I gave you my word."

"Your word!" the woman scoffed. "The word of a mercenary?" She laughed bitterly. "Why should I believe you, a *baturai* pig?"

King did not appreciate the racist slur. His family had been a mixed bag, and he had a mixed-race brother. The boy had been fostered after their mother had died and King had never seen him again, but he had loved him, missed him dearly and despised racism of any kind. "Listen, I'm trying to put you at ease. I have said your children will not be harmed, and I mean it. You will be with them within the hour."

"You're lying..." she said, but King did not reply. "Murderous scum! I hate you! I hate your kind! Murderer!"

"Coming from the wife of an unelected dictator," he sneered at her in the rear-view mirror. "Living a life of luxury in a protected compound while men, women and children starve in your slums and have their rights taken away without anyone being held to account. And don't talk to me about murder. Your husband has thousands of deaths on his hands!"

"This is Africa," she replied hostilely. "What leader hasn't? Certainly not that playboy Lucky Man Jonathon Mugabe." She laughed contemptuously. "Even the self-righteous Mandela killed people and advocated violence and torture! He wasn't always a fucking choir boy!"

It was true that Nelson Mandela rose to greatness. Freed after twenty-seven years in a South African jail, the anti-apartheid fighter emerged not bent on vengeance but healing the political system. He negotiated a peaceful end to apartheid, and as the first president of democratic South Africa, preached - and practised - reconciliation. In this he was great. A healer. An inspiration. For many whites abroad, he seemed even Christ-like - someone who'd suffered for the sins of white guilt and absolved those who believed in him of the sin of racism. But Mandela was no Christ nor even Gandhi nor Martin Luther King. He was for decades a man of violence. In 1961, he broke with African National Congress colleagues who preached non-violence, creating a terrorist wing. He later pleaded guilty in court to acts of public violence, and behind bars sanctioned many more, including the 1983 Church St car bomb that killed nineteen people. Mandela even suggested cutting off the noses of blacks deemed collaborators. His then wife Winnie advocated 'necklacing' instead - a burning tyre around the neck. Mandela's support for other leaders of violence was even less forgivable. He maintained close ties to Cuban dictator Fidel Castro and backed Palestinian terrorist leader Yasser Arafat. As president in 1997, he gave his country's highest award for a foreigner to Libya's dictator, Colonel Muammar Gaddafi, who had donated $10 million to the ANC. He gave the same award to the corrupt Indonesian president Suharto, who was said to have donated $60 million. He supported Nigerian coup leader Sani Abacha, refusing to say a word publicly to stop the 1995 hanging of writer, television presenter and environmental activist Ken Saro-Wiwa. It was true that Mandela did many great things. But many of his more radical supporters in the West used that greatness to wash clean his record of political violence - and his support for dictators who'd used it. Perhaps the woman had a point. Even great leaders with Nobel peace prizes had blood on their hands.

"There's Desmond Lambadi," King ventured.

The woman was hesitant, but after a few seconds' silence she said, "Well, that man was a dreamer. Yes, he had many great ideas, but it was Lucky Man Jonathon Mugabe who cut short his presidency."

"As indeed did your husband with him."

"Lucky Man Jonathon is a worthless playboy. He needed to go." She paused. "He killed Desmond Lambadi. Just as he will kill my husband. That was my husband's mistake, leaving Lucky Man Jonathon Mugabe alive."

"Not for want of trying. He escaped to South Africa ahead of a death squad. And your husband has sent men to try and kill him in Switzerland, and then again in Monaco." King paused, realising he had said too much, but the woman's arrogance had infuriated him. "Anyway, Desmond Lambadi was not killed. I have seen him. Spoken to him, even."

"I do not believe you."

"Your husband knows that Lambadi is alive. He is in one of your government's unmoderated prison camps." King paused. "No better than a concentration camp for anyone who speaks out against the Burindi government."

"A British invention, you will find. Concentration camps were created by the British for the Boers in South Africa and Rhodesia." She stared at him somewhat defiantly in the rear-view mirror. "Anyway, like I said, I don't believe you. Desmond Lambadi is dead."

"I don't care what you believe." The headlights swept across the plantation as King took the rutted track to the house. Once tarmacked, the rains had washed much of the road away and after Mustafa's overthrow of Mugabe's government, nobody had been around to mend the driveway. King swung the car around and parked nose outwards as a precaution. He always liked the option of a fast getaway. "Time to get out," he said, and he watched as she tensed in her seat. He got out, opened the rear door and unfastened her seatbelt. She was reluctant to move, her eyes on the house which was shrouded in darkness.

"You are going to rape me, kill me..."

"Just get out of the damned car." He reached inside and pulled her out. She was unsteady on her feet, and he helped her up the path and the seven marble steps to the imposing front door. Inside, the house smelled damp and unused. They had not opened the windows to improve the smell but had taped cardboard to the windowpanes instead. King closed the door and switched on the light. Nobody outside would see that the building was occupied, as having been empty for so long it would have created suspicion. He led the woman to a seat and told her to sit. Outside, he could hear a vehicle and he walked to the door and picked up the FN SLR rifle that had been made ready and left in an umbrella stand. He switched off the light and eased open a slit he had made earlier in the cardboard. He relaxed when he saw David getting Clive unsteadily out of the passenger seat of the Jeep, and a set of headlights in the distance which he hoped would be Phil.

King got the door and Clive struggled through the doorway while David shepherded the two girls inside. King closed the door and switched on the lights. The girls saw their mother and rushed over amid tears and hushed words that King found difficult to understand. Once again reminded of Patois spoken in Jamaica with its English and Creole influences.

"Lights again," he said and switched them off, peering outside. Phil was already walking towards the house with the teenaged boy gripped tightly around the collar. King opened the door for them, then closed it once more and switched on the lights. The boy saw his family and went to walk towards them but hesitated, looking at Phil. The man nodded and the boy ran over and dropped onto his knees in front of his mother.

King took out a digital camera and took a series of photographs of the family. He checked the display for the results, then nodded to Phil, who pulled the boy to his feet and walked him towards a closed door.

"No!" the woman yelled. "Where are you taking him?" The girls started to sob, and the boy looked back at his mother, fear in his eyes.

"Everyone, please relax," King said quietly. He walked over and helped the woman out of the chair. "We have a room for you all."

Once inside the cavernous open-plan living area, King cut the woman's cable ties with the folding scissors on his Leatherman. The woman rubbed her wrists, looking at King dubiously. The ties were cut on all three children, and they all ran to their mother and embraced one another tightly. They had prepared the room by screwing planks to both the inside and the outside of the window frames and had placed a chemical camping toilet in the corner along with toilet rolls and hand sanitiser. On the large oak table, long enough to seat twenty people, there were stacks of bottled water, tins of fizzy drinks and packets of crisps and biscuits. Four camp beds had been laid out with pillows and sheets, and on the floor a bowl, bags of toiletries and more bottled water acted as a makeshift bathroom.

The other men backed out of the room leaving King standing in the doorway. "You stay quiet, don't give us any trouble, and you'll get out of this situation." He reached into his jacket and retrieved the framed photograph of Mustafa and his family and placed it on the table. "I'm sorry this has happened to you..." he said, then backed out and closed and bolted the door.

Chapter Fifty-Three

Pierre surveyed the ground below through his field glasses. His mortar was in place, as were the three-man team who would rain down cyanide and high explosive shells on the ten-thousand souls below. Or would they? The three 60mm mortars and four 66mm mortars had been set up on the south, east and west sides of the valley. The two 88mm motors were set and ready to fire from the north side, with a mile of open ground between the mortar positions and the camp. Snipers were in place with .303 Lee Enfields from a by-gone era, though lethally effective. The snipers had set targets of the guard towers, fuel dump, telephone junction boxes and electric transformers. After these priority targets had been acquired, then the snipers would work on guards, retaliatory weapons such as heavy machinegun and artillery crews. Four two-man teams were dotted along the hillside with a stack of LAW rocket launchers, their priority being the twenty-seven helicopters parked up in neat rows on the north side of the camp.

"We're ready to go," Boiler said gruffly. "Just give us the word and we'll obliterate the fucking lot of them..."

Pierre nodded. The man seemed to want a fight, but that would be the last resort. Could thirty men really take on ten thousand? Unlikely. But the cyanide mortar rounds could be the game changer. But at what cost? Pierre had served in the Foreign Legion and spent the last ten years on the mercenary and security circuit. But not after this job. He would have to lie low. They all would. The Hague would indict them all for war crimes if they went ahead.

Pierre used the digital camera to photograph the camp below them, then turned his attention to the crates of mortar rounds resting a few feet away from the Soviet-era mortars. He made sure to get a close-up of the chemical and biological symbol, and the cyanide wording alongside the Russian and Chinese translations. He scrolled through the other photographs, satisfied that the pictures showed other firing positions with the 66mm and 88mm mortars, but all with the same deadly ammunition. He checked his watch and then the mobile phone. Nothing from Stewart, but he knew that the man would not contact him until after his own operation. He just hoped to God that the man would succeed in bargaining and that he would not be forced to take the next step.

Chapter Fifty-Four

King had left soon after they had all worked together to treat Clive's wound. Phil had administered some morphine while David stripped the bandages and cleaned the wound on both sides with plenty of iodine. King had used coagulant powder before suturing four stitches on the entrance wound and a dozen or more on the exit wound, which had left a flap of skin needing to be reattached. King could not see any fragments in the wound, and thankfully the bullet had been a 9mm and standard full metal jacketed, which meant it had punched in and out of the flesh and luckily missed the bone. More iodine, some more coagulant powder and a sterile adhesive dressing patch was placed on both sides before bandaging. A cup of sugary tea and some chocolate biscuits and the man had nodded off in a chair with his leg elevated while Phil had checked their ammunition supply and reloaded the magazines and David had sent the pictures of the family to Stewart's email account using a laptop and a military satellite phone.

King drove northwards, the route still mapped out in his

head. The other men had not questioned where he was going, or what he was doing. That privilege came with seniority and Stewart had effectively given King a free rein. He had brought with him the FN SLR battle rifle, two AK-74 rifles, two silenced Makarovs and plenty of ammunition for both. Grenades came in the form of stun, smoke (white phosphorus) and high explosive, and each was denoted by different coloured tape holding the release handle as an extra safety measure. King also preferred to spread the split pin further thus requiring a strong pull to make it ready. He did not like carrying grenades, but they were vital equipment and could change the course of a battle, especially when the numbers were not in your favour.

The call had come shortly after they had tended to Clive's injury. He had slipped outside for privacy, but that was par for the course in this kind of work and the mercenaries had not batted an eyelid. Again, when he loaded the weapons, his kit and most of their combined ammunition into the Jeep, the men had not asked any questions. For their part, the job was done. They were babysitting the family until further notice, and Clive was out of action anyway. King had told him to get out of Burindi and wait for his pay cheque. Stewart had what he wanted, a solid bargaining chip to rock Mustafa. It was now down to Stewart and Pierre to add further pressure. All the way to breaking point.

Chapter Fifty-Five

Stewart knew that it would not take long. He suspected that the secret police would be attempting to trace the call, but he was using an encrypted satellite phone that piggybacked various networks and even military satellites within NATO. He had used the system all around the world and it had never yet let him down. He looked at the display, the incoming call showing no number. But that was to be expected.

"To whom am I speaking?" asked Mustafa.

"You don't need to know my name, pal. But you do need to listen."

"You have my attention."

"Have you seen the photographs and footage?"

"Indeed..."

"And you take the situation seriously?"

"Yes."

"If my men get wind of anything, they will rain down terror on what we estimate to be seventy-percent of your armed forces. Such as they are."

"My country is small, but my men are fierce fighters."

"Your men can't tie their own boot laces, Mustafa. Trust me, we have the means to disable your helicopters and kill all of your men." Stewart paused. "The first mortars will be high-explosive and take out the armoury. The next salvo will take out the equipment block. So, if your army have NBC suits and breathers, well, they'll be incinerated before your men can even get a leg in a suit. The next mortars will be..."

"I understand. What do you want?"

"We'll get to that," said Stewart. "Now, I'm sending you some more video footage and photographs. Call me back when you've seen them. But don't wait too long, eh?"

Stewart hung up and sent the email. He wondered whether Mustafa was seated alone at his desk deciding his fate, or whether he was surrounded by intelligence and police officers and receiving all sorts of advice that would get men killed.

Chapter Fifty-Six

The dawn light, as Africa does so well, was a hue of red and orange and gold, and cast a brilliant glow on the eastern horizon, while to the west the gradual blue of the new day transcended to black. Like death and birth, on a continent where there was always plenty of both. King thought the transition to dawn, like the coup d'état, to be a metaphor for new beginnings.

King pulled the vehicle into the side of the road at the road marker and waited. He did not have to wait long as Dimitri stepped out from the brush and walked straight to the passenger door.

"How long has she been missing?"

"She went in yesterday. I made my way there by *borrowing* a motorcycle and watched her approach the guards. She wasn't negotiating for long; some senior soldier came out and the guards pulled her inside."

"What the hell was she thinking?"

"She's tenacious at best," Dimitri said. "Downright stubborn and a pain in the ass the rest of the time."

King knew what the Russian meant. He pulled back out

onto the road while Dimitri reached around and looked through the kit resting on the back seat. He turned around with a Makarov and a suppressor and he quickly checked the breech and safety, then screwed the suppressor into the adapted muzzle thread. He slotted the weapon under his seat and checked his mobile phone.

"There's a tracker on her phone," he said. "Her husband insisted that I fit it." He shrugged. "He's the one who signs my pay cheques."

"So, he always knows where she is?" King asked incredulously, thinking about the time they had spent together in Kenya.

"Yes," Dimitri replied, still checking his phone. "Here, her phone signal is still at the prison camp. Doesn't mean she's there, of course. But her phone is, and it's switched on and sending out a signal."

King shook his head. "And she thought money would simply talk?"

"It did with you," he pointed out. "I suppose she thought that it would work again."

"Right. But the man who took the bribe is dead. His replacement is now likely to be a stoic government type, who is loyal to Mustafa's regime. They would view the previous commandant dimly and do everything to avoid a repeat performance." King did not say it, but he thought Lambadi's days would soon be numbered if Lucinda had gone in right off the bat and mentioned the man's name. She wanted her story, but she had unwittingly signed not only her own death warrant, but Desmond Lambadi's as well.

"What's the plan?" Dimitri asked. "Bearing in mind I have a hundred thousand pounds sitting in a locker at the airport and intend on living long enough to spend it."

"Silent and violent," King replied. He checked his

watch and dipped his head underneath the sun visor as he studied the horizon. "We have an hour until daylight, and another hour until we get there."

"And the plan?"

King shrugged and told him what he could remember of the camp.

Chapter Fifty-Seven

"You are a butcher..."

"I haven't even got started yet."

"This is Africa, we see cruelty every day."

Stewart knew that the footage of the man's elite Republican Guard being gassed to death had struck a nerve. The man had witnessed his elite protection unit decimated and had now realised the threat posed to his main body of armed forces, and what would happen to them if he did not cooperate. He pressed send for what he hoped would be the sickener. He had learnt of the value of 'sickeners' and implemented it in the training of his recruits as well as the men and women he came up against in his duties. There were many types of sickener. When recruits were into their final mile or eleventh-hour during training, the instruction to do it all over again could drop people to their knees and weed out the men from the boys, the winners from the losers. It might be the bribing of a foreign asset or double agent. The final layer of evidence that got them to turn double agent. In this case, for Mustafa, he was about to open an email that would change the course of his power. His life, even. Would he go for it? Stewart hoped so, would bet all he owned that he would. "You should have mail, Mustafa. And know this... we are deadly serious." He listened as he could hear the man tapping on the keys of a computer. He heard the gasp, felt the anguished silence.

"Animals..."

"Your family will remain unharmed... for now."

"I... I... can't do it..."

"You can and you will. You will announce your resignation and a caretaker leader that will take your place. You will sell this as an interim period with elections that will take place in six months' time."

"Who?"

"Lucky Man Jonathon Mugabe."

Mustafa scoffed. *"He will be no mere caretaker president! He will never allow elections!"*

"I don't care," Stewart replied coldly. "With you out and him in, that's job done for me. And I avoid cutting your wife and children's throats on camera."

"You ask the impossible."

"You are a wealthy man. If you make the announcement and endorse a caretaker leader, then you can leave the country freely. I will send your family to you, but only when you have announced an end to your leadership."

"But Lucky Man Jonathon..."

"I understand it's a crush to your ego, but it is what it is."

"He will send a death squad for me!"

"As you did to him in Switzerland and again in Monaco."

"I can't," Mustafa said quietly, the anguish in his voice easy to hear.

"Perhaps you need some more encouragement?"

Stewart ended his call and slammed his fist down on the table, narrowly missing his open laptop.

He stared at the wall, seeing nothing, his heart pounding. Ten-thousand lives, or just one? He drummed his fingers, weighing up both the act and the potential outcome. A bullet through a child's head, or the slaughter of countless men? Stewart picked up the phone and started to dial.

Chapter Fifty-Eight
Msambweni, Kenya

"How much longer?"

"You'll know when I know," Redwood replied.

"This is ridiculous!" Lucky Man Jonathon raged.

"Utterly ridiculous!" Mamadou Cilla concurred. Redwood supposed that when one was a sycophant to an unstable man who had never hesitated to have his opposition killed, then one tended to concur regularly and with much enthusiasm. "What is the hold up?"

Redwood sighed, putting his phone back in his pocket. "Would you like to fly to Umfasu and get off the plane with Mustafa still in power and his troops ready to form a firing squad?" He paused, watching their expression. "No? I thought not..."

"Then when?" Mustafa glared, trying to keep face.

"When I get the word, we'll board the plane. When a caretaker leader has been announced, and Mustafa is on a plane of his own, then we will land. Not before."

"Caretaker?" Mustafa raged. "I am no caretaker!"

"What you sell the electorate down the line is your

concern." Redwood paused. "But I imagine you will not have any qualms about delaying an election for the foreseeable future."

Lucky Man Jonathon stared at Redwood long and hard. He turned to his personal secretary, then his expression mellowed, and he looked back at Redwood, beaming a large, toothy white smile. "Do you see? This is Africa! This is Burindi!" He laughed raucously. "Mister Redwood were you not so pale, you could fit right in with my new government!"

"Thanks. I won't take that as a compliment," he said getting out of his chair and ignoring the annoyance in Mugabe's eyes. "Stay around the hotel. Don't get drunk, and don't leave the protection of my men. We will leave for the airport the moment we receive word from Stewart, and not before."

Chapter Fifty-Nine

King pulled off the road half a mile from the camp and drove into the brush. After they had unloaded their kit, King sliced off some fronds with his machete and covered the vehicle quite convincingly. He doubted anyone travelling down the track would notice, and he turned to see Dimitri cutting and dropping foliage on their tyre tracks for good measure. After walking fifty metres into the brush, they were in dense jungle and King used his button compass to keep on a northerly heading. Dimitri carried the explosive charges that King had prepared in a bergen, and a LAW rocket launcher held in place by the top flap of the bergen. He had slung his AK-74 over his shoulder on its sling leaving his hands free to pull at vines and branches and hack his way through with his machete. King had learned from Pierre and twisted and ducked through, only using his machete on stubborn thorns crossing his path. The thorns were the length of his fingers, and as thin as hypodermic needles at their tips. They were irritants as well, mildly poisonous and although not harmful, they made any scratches or puncture itch, and that was when the most damage could be done as dirt and bacteria got into the bloodstream.

Both men carried silenced Makarovs and Kalashnikov AK-74 assault rifles. These rifles were remodelled AK-47 rifles in the smaller, but more lethal calibre of 5.45x39mm. Lethal only because the light bullets tumbled upon penetration and caused more tissue damage. They had a more effective range and made for a lighter package. As the name suggested, it was designed and produced in 1974 by a man named Kalashnikov, whereas the AK-47, designed by the same man, went into production in 1947. The Soviets had been anything but imaginative in naming their weapons, but there were ten times more AK-47s in the world than any other firearm, so they had to have done something right in their design. King also carried an FN SLR on a shoulder sling. This rifle had been known as 'The Right Arm of the Free World' and was a tried and tested rifle of immense ability in the powerful 7.62x51mm cartridge. One shot, one kill was another name for it. It was only replaced by the British army when NATO called for a smaller calibre that would wound and take more people out of the battlefield, thus tying up medics, pilots, doctors, nurses and admin staff. Dead soldiers needed a letter to relatives. Injured soldiers needed thirty people to save them. He too, carried a LAW rocket launcher and both men were laden with ammunition and hand grenades. He didn't really have a plan, but they had the element of surprise and King had a mental map of the camp. It wasn't much, but he wasn't leaving Burindi without trying.

Chapter Sixty

Pierre hung up and put the phone back in his pocket. He felt numb, his limbs feeling like they were weighed down, or that he was walking in syrup. He turned to Boiler and the man looked back at him with a glint in his eye.

"Fuck yeah! We're on!" he growled, his single tooth in what should have been his top row snagging on his lip. "I don't even need paying for this!"

"Wait," Pierre said with little emotion. He opened his mic and said, "All call signs, we are a go. A barrage on the helos, the equipment stores and the arsenal." Pierre paused, his voice shaky. "Then ten cyanide shells on the admin block. Repeat Hi-Ex on the helicopters, the equipment stores and the arsenal. Ten, that's one-zero, cyanide on the admin block." He closed his eyes, crossed his chest in the sign of the cross and whispered, "Forgive me, Lord..." Pierre then opened his eyes, then shouted, "Fire! Fire! Fire!"

The hollow thump of the mortars filled the air and with it, the ominous pause before their terror rained down on the camp below. Pierre filmed the barrage turning the helicopters into burning hulks of scrap, then panned across the barracks and settled the camera on the stores and armoury. Flames roared and smoke billowed into the air. He watched the direction of the smoke as an indicator of where the cyanide was likely to drift but being an invisible gas that was considerably heavier than air it would lay close to the ground, trapping its gasping victims further. He felt a chill as the first of the cyanide mortar rounds found its target and crashed through the roof of the admin block. More rounds followed. Men exited the various huts and ran around the compound, first towards the armoury, but that was now ablaze with hundreds of rounds of ammunition cooking off and firing in all directions – tracer rounds looking like a fireworks display - and the equipment stores was already an inferno as various flammable products combusted. But Pierre noted that nobody was leaving the admin block. The poor souls hadn't stood a chance. Some men reached the gas and simply fell onto their stomachs, writhing for an agonising ten seconds or so, that to the Swiss mercenary felt like an hour.

Pierre stopped filming, turned his back on the ghastly scene and uploaded the film to his laptop, then sent the encrypted file via the satellite phone. He called ceasefire through his voice-activated throat mic and gradually the mortar rounds subsided. Boiler continued to drop rounds into the mortar tube and Pierre hollered for him to stop, but the man was in the zone and the team he was working with looked to Pierre with concern.

"Cease fire! Cease fire!" Pierre raged, but Boiler continued to rain mortars down on the compound and Pierre was forced to watch as cyanide rounds landed in the centre of the camp with no explosion, just a puff of dust as the ordinance hit the dusty ground, and men within a twenty-metre radius started to fall to the ground. "Boiler! Cease fire!"

One of the team rushed forward and shoved Boiler away from the mortar tube as he fired another round, but the man merely got back to his feet and ran to his kit, taking a LAW rocket launcher and pulling the pin so the tube extended. "Fucking have some!" he shouted, then turned and fired down on the camp, the heat exhaust flaring out of the back of the tube as the rocket launched. Pierre could not move out of the way in time, and the flare engulfed his face, igniting his hair and catching his left eye, and melting his cheek. He screamed and fell onto the ground and already one of the men was standing over him dousing him with water from his canteen and another was ripping open a medical pack. His screams were sickening and as the man tore open the medical pack, another man arrived on the scene and poured his own water bottle into Pierre's eyes.

Boiler had picked up another LAW and the men scattered as he sent another rocket into the compound. He searched frantically for a suitable weapon, his eyes wide and set in almost a trance like tunnel vision. Something had triggered within him, perhaps a manifestation from a life pushing down post traumatic stress disorder. He settled on a L7A2 GPMG – affectionally called the 'Gympy' in the British army - and started to pick the men off below with bursts of ten or fifteen shots from the belt fed weapon, screaming and laughing as the machinegun rattled off and men in the compound below started to fall.

"Stop him!" Pierre shouted, but his voice was nothing more than a creek, the skin around his mouth pulled tight and blistered. "Fucking stop him!"

The men looked at Boiler, indecision on their faces, torn between helping Pierre and stopping a madman in his tracks. Pierre rolled over onto his stomach, dragged himself forwards and drew his pistol. His hand shook terribly, and he gasped for breath as he aimed and fired four rounds in quick succession. Boiler fell forwards, the weapon dropping out of his hands and Pierre rolled onto his back, dropping the pistol beside him as he gasped for air.

Chapter Sixty-One

King watched Dimitri through the binoculars as he laid an explosive charge on the fuel tank. He had already watched the ex-Spetsnaz soldier dispatch a guard using his knife and place a charge underneath an armoured personnel carrier, with a 7.62mm GPMG fixed between a split steel shield atop the turret. King placed the binoculars on the ground and swapped between the two rifles, choosing to use the SLR first because it was a heavy weapon and he only had three, twenty-round magazines for it. The ammunition was heavy as well, and he would ditch the weapon when he was out and swap to the lighter 5.45mm Kalashnikov with its thirty round magazines.

King accessed the compound from the same slit that Dimitri had cut through the fence. From the rear the camp had one line of mesh wire twenty feet high and topped with razor wire. It was to secure the admin block, fuel dump and vehicles, as well as the guards' accommodation in the form of portacabins. The prison yard was double lined with wire and part of the main building protruded into the prison yard, acting as the prisoners' entrance and exit. From the rear, the compound's security was lax in comparison, and had been their choice of entry. King moved silently and kept to the dawn shadows, using the edges of huts and portacabins for cover as he made progress towards the main building. He stopped and placed an explosive charge underneath a portacabin. He had no idea what was inside, but the charges were all linked to the same receiver and would detonate in unison and the more chaos they could create, the better.

King had brought a pair of voice-activated throat mics with him. They were a simple two-way radio design, and the radio was clipped inside their jackets with the earpiece trailing through their collars and the collar activating and opening the net when they spoke to one another. King gave Dimitri the heads up as he approached. "On you..." he said quietly.

"Received."

King rounded the corner of the building and saw Dimitri aiming his rifle at him. The Russian lowered it and made a chopping motion with his hand, indicating where the perceived threat was with his fingertips. King saw a guard smoking between two portacabins. He nodded to Dimitri, who took out his silenced pistol and aimed, squeezing off a single shot that sounded like a champagne cork popping. The guard made more sound when he fell than the gunshot had made, his body hitting the dirt with a hollow 'thud' and the wind rushing from his lungs. King darted down the gap, caught hold of the man's left ankle and dragged him back with him, dropping his leg to the ground when he reached the Russian. Between them, they rolled the body underneath the portacabin, flies already pitching on the blood at the man's neck.

King took out his own silenced pistol and said, "Use these until we no longer can."

"Okay..."

King led the way, but they only progressed a few paces before running right into three armed guards. King dropped to one knee and picked off the first two men, feeling and hearing Dimitri's shots over his head as the Russian took down the third. Both men reloaded. The used magazines still had a few rounds in them, which they slipped into their pockets and hoped they would never need, because when you were down to scrapping for a few loose rounds, you were inevitably in big trouble.

There was no time to hide the bodies, but as they passed, King whipped a magazine out of one of the guard's SLRs and tucked it into his bandolier. He heard Dimitri take something and assumed it was the other guard's AK-74 magazine. The Burindi military used a mixed bag of weapons, sold to the country at different times in its political history. From Britain under Lucky Man Jonathon Mugabe, and from Russia under Mustafa's dictatorship. He had seen some soldiers carrying Lee Enfield .303 rifles which he assumed were sold off by Britain in the fifties after they joined NATO and upgraded to the SLR.

King knew that the prisoners would be released soon. They would brave the swarms of flies and use the outside latrines and eat bowls of tasteless posho from the field kitchen, those same flies now pitching on their food. He could smell the pungent damp wood burning on the smoky fire and the aroma of boiling maize, and his guts clenched as he recalled the taste and feel of it in his mouth. He wiped the sweat from the palm of his hands on his jacket and gripped the pistol firmly as he waited for Dimitri to catch up. He had described the inside of the building, the route to the commandant's office and the corridor of cells. He had no way of knowing which was the right cell, but he imagined he would find the answer in the commandant's office, where he had noted the names and respective cell numbers on the chart behind the man's desk.

A bell sounded and King checked his watch. Dawn in the exercise yard. Ablutions, strong black tea and a bowl of posho. The sound of the bell was followed by bolts unlocking and voices grumbling as the prisoners made their way out into the yard that was separated from the admin block by a fence, although King knew that the west wing protruded into the yard, with great heavy steel doors inside.

There were two guards on the admin block and Dimitri took both down as he edged around the corners and fired a single shot into their foreheads. King swiped a key fob from around the neck of one of the bodies and slid it through the lock, which opened with a satisfying 'click'. Once inside, King led the way to the commandant's office, and immediately heard a shout behind them. He spun around, but Dimitri was in his arc of fire and the guard fired a burst from his Kalashnikov as the Russian fired. The noise of the rifles filled the corridor, clouds of smoke from the muzzle flashes wafting over the dead man's body and around both King and Dimitri. The Russian checked himself over and smiled somewhat nervously back at King, the relief visible on his face.

"I don't know how he missed..."

King nodded but said nothing. He reached across his stomach and felt his left side, then looked at his fingers. They were all covered with blood. For a moment, he turned his hand over, saw the scabs where his fingernails once were and thought how silly this profession of his truly was. He touched the wound again, this time feeling its sting. There was no hole, just a deep gash that was bleeding heavily. He was in it now, there was no time to triage himself. He holstered the pistol and took hold of the SLR. Things had gone way past the point of silenced pistols now, and outside he could hear shouts and movement. He reached the commandant's office and tried the door. It was locked, so he stood back and put two rounds through the lock, then kicked as hard as he could with his right foot. The door splintered at the lock and swung inwards. Guards rushed past outside the window, oblivious that the two men were inside the building. King looked on the wall and saw the list of cells with names written beside them. Some cells had a single name, others as many as five. King had seen the list when Lucinda had bartered with the commandant for his release, and he was filled with relief that it was still here.

"They're getting closer," said Dimitri, his voice giving way to some concern. "Find her and hurry up!"

"Cell forty-two. East wing," he replied. He looked at the bank of master keys and selected the key for cells thirty through fifty. He tossed it to the Russian and said, "Go and get her."

"We need to cover each other. What will you be doing?"

King checked the chart along with the bank of keys. He found the one he wanted and said, "I'm going for Desmond Lambadi..."

"But we came for Lucinda Davenport!"

King did not argue. He never told the Russian that was what he had intended on doing all along, but he had doubted the man would have come if he had told him his plan. Especially with his new-found nest egg curtesy of Lucinda. "Meet me back at the wire in ten minutes."

"We won't last ten fucking minutes!" Dimitri protested.

King took out the control unit and nodded as he armed it with a single red switch. "Then let's give them something to think about..."

Chapter Sixty-Two
Ugandan airspace

"I will take Burindi, and with it the people of Africa's most promising nation, to new heights of expectation and achievement. No longer will we look towards outdated socialism and misguided allegiances. We are a brave and noble people, resourceful and resilient. We have resisted attacks on all borders, and escaped the famines of Sudan, the criminal piracy of the Congo and Somalia. We will look towards independence, become less dependent on African nations and foreign aid..."

"But we still need foreign investment, whether it is in the form of aid, or investment," Mamadou Cilla interjected. "We don't want it to look like you are going back on your pledge when we apply for foreign aid."

Lucky Man Jonathon nodded and scrubbed out the last sentence with a red pen, then continued, "...towards independence and while we accept foreign aid from our friends, we will endeavour to rise above the necessity for this in the future, and look to attract investment in our resources, rather than charity for our people. Jobs instead of handouts..."

"Good, I like that..." Cilla nodded enthusiastically. "Extremely *presidential*..."

Redwood got up from his seat and walked back to the close protection team at the rear of the plane. A bevy of scantily clad beauties had tagged along and were enjoying the British government's champagne and selection of canapes freshly made and supplied by special guest services at Moi International Airport, Mombasa. The young women wore lots of animal print and leatherette and the tops were minimal and the skirts short. From the glister, the abundance of tasteless chains and jewellery was gold plate. Maybe things would change for them later. If they were still around. Redwood ignored their flirtatious comments and seductive glances as he squeezed past them. He sat down heavily in the leather swivel seat and picked up a bottle of mineral water from the cooler beside him.

"Alright, Boss?" Mitchell asked.

"Right enough," he replied. "He's writing a bloody sermon down there. I expect he's dreaming about a Nobel Prize."

"Well, he ain't no Nelson Mandela," Mitchell scoffed. He checked his watch and said, "What time do we touch down?"

"It's still fluid," Redwood replied. "Imminent, but we're still waiting for the word. The pilot will tell me when he gets the call."

"Can't wait. The sooner we're shot of this dickhead, the better."

"I couldn't agree more," Redwood replied, thinking about his conversation with Stewart and the man's recommendation to work with Forrester at MI5. He shook the idea from his head and added, "I can't wait to get back to some proper soldiering."

Chapter Sixty-Three

King charged down the corridor engaging the guards one by one. The prisoners had been released into the exercise yard from the outermost cells and now the process had stalled because of the explosions outside, and the chaos that had ensured. King had to be mindful of hitting bewildered prisoners in the crossfire. The large rifle was proving unwieldy in the confines of the corridor, and with just a few rounds remaining, he dropped it to the floor and switched to the Kalashnikov, flicking the selector from safe to automatic. He gave a short squeeze on the trigger each time he engaged the enemy, sending three or four rounds into them. There was a time and a place for well-aimed single shots, but not here. Not today. The last thing he needed was an injured man going for broke – his fear and care used up and giving him nothing to lose. The advance was a process. Aim, fire and move on. But he did not step around or over anyone still alive. He could give no quarter, and he did not expect it in return.

Darting into a cell when the corridor ahead of him

yielded too many men, he took out a stun grenade, pulled the pin and tossed it towards them. He wasted no time taking a high-explosive grenade out, pulled the pin and sent it after the first. The stun grenade thudded and flashed, rendering the men disorientated, and in the confines of the corridor the second grenade blew them to kingdom come. King advanced, drawing a deep breath as he stepped over torn limbs, twisted weapons and slabs of scorched, burning flesh. An injured guard was crawling towards an open cell, his uniform scorched and smoking. King shot the man as he pressed onwards without breaking his stride. There were no more guards between the cells to Desmond Lambadi's cell, and he judged by the closed cell doors that this wing had not yet been released into the yard. He checked the numbers off, then paused outside Lambadi's cell, his heart sinking as he saw the door open. The imprisoned leader must have been the last man released into the yard. King changed to a new magazine and continued down the corridor. He hadn't even taken three steps when a guard appeared from an open cell doorway and King fired. The man went down, and King squatted on his haunches and swiped a spare magazine from the guard's ammunition pouch. Another guard appeared and King threw himself forwards onto his stomach and fired, the guard's own volley of bullets sailing over King's head, scattering guards who had now started to gather tentatively at the other end of the corridor. King wasted no time tossing a grenade behind him, and a stun grenade ahead of him as he ducked into an open cell and waited for the concussive blasts and flash of brilliant white light from the stun grenade. A pair of huge steel doors now blocked his path, and he knew from his brief time here that when he passed through them, he would be in the exercise yard, its entrance another fifty metres ahead of him.

He placed one of his 350g explosive charges against the bottom of the door, directly in the middle where the two doors met. The charges were Semtex, more volatile and powerful than the regular PE4 or C4 he had used before, so it really was an unknown entity. He armed the switch and stepped back into an open cell and got down onto his stomach, closing his eyes and pressing his left ear into his shoulder to save his hearing, as he placed a cupped hand over his right ear – never a finger in the ear as it increased the vibration and could shatter the eardrum – and flicked the switch with his left hand. The blast was significant, and he felt the concussive blast deep inside his chest. His ears rang and his heart seemed to skip a beat, and as the smoke and debris dust cleared, he got back to his feet and stepped out into the corridor, neither fearing guards behind or ahead of him, such was the ferocity of the blast. The doors were blown inwards, and part of the ceiling had fallen in, the sun shining brightly through having emerged from dusk in the short time since they had stepped inside. King trudged through the debris, sidestepping the remains of more than one guard who had been holding position behind the doors, and as he emerged into the light fresh air of the exercise yard, he kicked the rifle away from an injured guard and deemed him no longer a threat. The gesture was short lived, however, as a prisoner rushed forwards, snatched up the rifle and shot the man a dozen times where he lay. The prisoner held the rifle to the sky with one hand, firing and chanting, his legs stamping and throwing up dust in what King could only assimilate as a tribal dance. The man was soon joined by two more men, both having taken up arms, joining in the dance. King held up a hand to show he was no threat to them, but they seemed to have worked that out already and were soon heading off to a crowd of other prisoners who all had the same idea. The mob started to run back towards King, and he stepped aside as they headed for the corridor, which without the double reinforced steel doors, would lead them directly to freedom.

Desmond Lambadi walked unhurriedly towards King. Gunshots echoed from all around the camp, and King could see unarmed uniformed men running for the brush on the other side of the fence. Mob rule had taken over and King could hear the screams of men being put through a painful end.

"What have you done?" Lambadi asked incredulously. "Violence and death are not the way! Look at all this death and destruction!"

King caught hold of the man by his worn and filthy T-shirt. "Well, that's fucking gratitude for you!"

"Where are we going?" Lambadi asked, panic upon his face, and his legs barely working. "We are just creating trouble for the other prisoners; they will execute them for this!" King pulled the man until his T-shirt ripped, then he pushed him ahead of him. The gunfire was increasing, and King watched as a tyre from the destroyed armoured vehicle was put around a guard's neck and over his body clamping his arms to his side. Fuel had been found and the tyre had been doused, and was then set on fire, the mob dancing around and chanting as the man went up in flames, hollering and writhing on the ground. "Look at what your actions have created!"

"That's on you lot," King said. "Nobody forced upon you the culture of setting poor bastards on fire!" He pushed Lambadi past the huts and the stench of burning flesh and rubber and towards the slit in the wire fence. "This regime created this response," King said, pushing the man through the wire and ducking down behind him. "And now, Mister

Lambadi, you may just get to practice what you preach so bloody well from the advantage of inopportunity and learned critique." He pushed the terrified man through the fringe of trees and into the jungle, where Dimitri stood with his weapon trained on them both, with Lucinda crouched behind him. King gave Lambadi another shove and said, "In other words, my old son, it's time to shit or get off the pot..."

Lambadi stumbled forwards as Lucinda got up and lunged at King, hugging him closely. When she pulled away, she was staring at the blood on her right hand. She pulled at his jacket and looked up at him, her face ashen. "Oh my God! You've been shot!"

King nodded. Now that the adrenalin was subsiding, he could feel the sting and pulsing of the wound. Lucinda tore at his jacket and shirt, tearing the buttons from the shirt. The bullet had skimmed his side but had left a four-inch gash that was a quarter of an inch deep. It was still bleeding but had slowed considerably, although it looked like raw liver in a butcher's counter. "Later," he told her. "When we get back to the vehicle."

Dimitri nodded. "Just a flesh wound," he concurred, then added, "He'll live."

Chapter Sixty-Four
London

Armstrong enjoyed the moment. Seated at a low coffee table in front of the Prime Minister and Sir Hugo Truscott, the three men forming a triangle and taking away the hierarchy normally associated with the Prime Minister and such a prominent cabinet member, Armstrong had the men feeding out of his hand. He imagined that he would be shoe-horned into the Director General's chair before long, the head of MI6. If he wasn't, then he had recordings of his meetings with Sir Hugo Truscott, a paper trail to offshore accounts for his share dividends and would claim his own involvement to be part of an elaborate operation to uncover political corruption. He also had the backing of Felicity Willmott and if he did not need the evidence to push his promotion home, then he would tell her that there was no further action to be taken in the interest of either the public, or MI6. He had not only played the Business Secretary, the Prime Minister and his own number two in the service.

"Gentlemen, I have received word that Mustafa has confirmed his resignation," Armstrong announced, unable to hide either his smugness at devising the overthrow, nor his own brilliance at playing the men before him.

"Yes!" Sir Hugo Truscott punched the air, then seemed to deflate as he caught the Prime Minister's eye. "That is... great news," he added, a little more graciously.

"Indeed," the Prime Minister agreed somewhat more pragmatic and far less emotionally. He knew that Sir Hugo had almost his entire fortune speculated on the United Kingdom getting the lithium and various other mineral contracts, but until now he did not realise just how much it meant to the man. "And his replacement?"

"Should be landing as we speak. The military and police have agreed to support Mustafa's choice in caretaker leader, on the proviso that national elections are held within six months."

"I'm not sure this is what was agreed," Sir Hugo said incredulously.

Armstrong nodded. "About the only way this could be sold, and to avoid a civil war or our involvement on a military level was to agree to elections in the next six months."

"Well that certainly *wasn't* mentioned," the Prime Minister said emphatically. "What the bloody hell was the point if Lucky Man Jonathon could be out before the ink is dry on the contracts?"

"Prime Minister, let me remind you that this is Africa, and more importantly, the land-locked little scrub of land we know as Burindi. They only know despots. They have no idea what democracy is. Six months down the line and Lucky Man Jonathon Mugabe will be ruling with an iron fist, his military will be bought off and the police will be too scared of military reprisal to remind him that there's an election due. The people of Burindi will know which side of their bread is buttered, and Great Britain PLC will be riding high in the lithium market. Mobile phones, laptops, game consoles all need lithium, and if electric cars are ever going to develop, then they need lithium as well, and plenty of it. Cobalt as well, and Burindi has tons of the stuff."

The Prime Minister smiled and stood up. He walked over to his drinks cabinet and returned with a silver tray on top of which sat a decanter of brandy and three tumblers. "Then I do believe that a toast is in order," he said, placing the tray on the low table and sitting back down. "Early in the day, I know..." He poured three large measures and picked up his own glass. "Gentlemen, we have served our country well today. We are now in the lithium business in a big way." He raised his glass and the other two men chinked theirs together with his own. "Cheers! To Burindi!"

"To Burindi!" the men all said in unison, and without any sense of irony that they had not one iota of compassion nor care for that distant land.

Chapter Sixty-Five
Umfasu, Burindi

Mustafa had accepted Stewart's terms. Not that he had been in a position not to. He had seen what the cyanide could do to his elite Republican Guard, and again at the military barracks before the attack had been called off. He knew that Stewart's only hand left to play was the total annihilation of the bulk of his forces, and inevitably that of his family. He had capitulated upon seeing Pierre's footage. Neither Stewart nor Mustafa had been aware just how long the attack had continued afterwards. Pierre had handed over control to Keth, who had withdrawn the men and equipment, and given Boiler the phosphorous grenade treatment as a swift cremation short on ceremony. Pierre had left the country via Rwanda accompanied by two of the men to seek urgent medical attention for his burns in Kenya. The man's mercenary days may not have been over, but he now had a face only a mother could love.

Mustafa had made his announcement on both television and radio, and crowds had started to gather on the streets, with a curious absence of both police and military who had been stood down. The remainder of Stewart's mercenaries had reconvened on the steps of Government House, small arms and heavy belt-fed general-purpose machineguns covering the crowd as government employees handed out hastily printed 'Terms of Political Change' leaflets or relayed the event to people who could not read.

Stewart had escorted Mustafa and his family to the airport along with three of his men as bodyguards until they were safely landed in another country, and the deposed leader was flown out in a private jet courtesy of the UK taxpayer. Mustafa had left the country with considerable assets held in Swiss and Cayman Island bank accounts, as well as several million in bearer bonds. His wife clutched a framed photograph of them as a family enjoying a holiday, the only possession that had made it with them. As part of his deal, Mustafa would be afforded haven in a dozen coun-tries and the British government would take no part in the retrieval of Burindi money in Mustafa's keeping. As deals went, it was better than what he had afforded to Lucky Man Jonathon Mugabe, although what action the playboy dictator would now take remained to be seen. One thing was for certain, Mustafa would be looking over his shoulder for the rest of his days.

Stewart watched as Lucinda Davenport and her Russian bodyguard pulled up in a new rented Toyota Land Cruiser. She snapped pictures of the crowd, the building - that was called palace or house depending on which way the political wind was blowing – and the mercenaries on the steps. She lowered the camera when she saw Stewart and climbed the steps, with Dimitri staying the bodyguard's regulatory metre behind and to the side.

"You've got your exclusive story," Stewart said gruffly when she reached the top. He nodded to the motorcade rounding the corner into view. The vehicles were all black SUVs that had been paid for, once again, by the UK taxpayer. "Not many journalists get the chance to report on a coup d'état as it's actually happening. Even Kate Adie is usually two days behind or writing her script in her hotel room at the time," he said. She turned around to photograph the vehicles which were driving quickly and with purpose. "Helps if your husband is behind it all, I suppose."

She did not look around as she photographed. "Trust me, Stewart, nobody knows what's happening for sure out here. Not even you."

Stewart shrugged and watched as Redwood opened the rear door of the vehicle and Lucky Man Jonathon Mugabe got out waving both hands victoriously to the crowd, which were fast becoming agitated and then angry as it sunk in who was back in power. Stewart really did wonder if it was better the devil you know. Burindi had its supporters of both men, but ideally the majority would want both democratic elections and a president worth voting for. A vote within six months had been sold to the citizens of Burindi, but Stewart quietly knew that it would never materialise. Besides, it wasn't in Britain's interest any more than it was in Lucky Man Jonathon's.

"Ah! It is the crazy Scotsman, come to watch me take my rightful place as President and Supreme Leader of Burindi!" Lucky Man Jonathon greeted Stewart overtly, but with no genuine warmth. This time tomorrow he would have forgotten who had put him in power. He turned to Lucinda Davenport and beamed a large, white mouthful of teeth. It was certainly quite a smile. "A reporter! To capture this wonderful day for Burindi!" He smoothed a hand over her shoulder and said, "Come, my dear. You will photograph me behind the desk of the President. Maybe later, I can give you a guided tour of the palace? Maybe the bedrooms, if you wish. It will be a great honour for you, I am sure."

Lucinda smiled with little warmth and said, "I would certainly like to capture this moment." She paused. "Lead on, and I will record it for posterity."

"Yes! Posterity!" Lucky Man Jonathon ignored Stewart and turned to wave at the crowd but was now being met largely with jeers and boos. "Ignorant fools," he muttered. "But they can be trained. Either by sanctions, or handouts. Or by a bullet or the tip of a bayonet if necessary!"

Lucinda smiled at the comment, her hidden tape recorder picking up everything she would later need to write her story. Stewart followed Redwood, who dutifully shadowed the man. He had been briefed to see the man safely inside. From there on, it was down to Mugabe's own men and his wallet to keep the man safe. Britain would be off the payroll.

"I have spoken with General Filosi, and he has assured me that the army will recognise you as caretaker president," Mamadou Cilla said as they walked, their shoes clipping on the marble flooring. "But he was adamant that the elections should take place six months from today, and no more. He recognises that Mustafa leaned to the left, a communist more than a socialist, and he agrees that Burindi's politics should align to the West."

"We shall see," Mugabe grinned. "We shall see..." He stopped walking and turned to Stewart. "Does Britain want elections in six months? Does Britain want Mustafa to breeze back in with new backers and promises? The lithium and cobalt deals that we have made will go to Russia and this will have all been a waste of time and money." He smiled. "No, Britain wants me to rule Burindi, and they want me to make them players in the lithium market. What is the alternative?"

They reached the grand hall, lined with civil servants who had declared an interest in Lucky Man Jonathon Mugabe's new government - or simply knew to bend with the breeze and adapt to the political landscape – and who all applauded as he entered. Some applauded a little too enthusiastically to be sincere, but they'd been here before, some with Mugabe before Mustafa, and things often went full circle in Africa. Loyalty was bought and disloyalty was punished, so Mugabe was in no shortage of clerical and administrative staff to get his new government off the ground.

Lucky Man Jonathon Mugabe stopped and surveyed the grand oak doors to the Presidential Office. The Burindi flags were placed either side, and the doors were twenty-feet high and eight-feet wide each. Huge solid gold handles shaped into perfectly formed lion heads gleamed brightly, and Cilla stepped forwards and pulled them both open with a well-practised swing. Lucinda stepped around them, photographing the man's entrance and Redwood and his men stepped aside, mindful not to appear in any photographs and satisfied that their role was over. Two of Mugabe's bodyguards, each over six-foot-six and eighteen stone took their place, one either side of the president.

Lucky Man Jonathon walked forwards proudly, caught up in the moment, back where he thought was so rightfully his, his days of exile and looking over his shoulder for Mustafa's hit teams finally over. He strode deliberately into the office, then stopped in his tracks as he stared at the man seated at the great ornate gold and marble desk.

Desmond Lambadi stood up and stared at Lucky Man Jonathon. He had washed and changed into a smart dark blue suit with a crisp, white shirt and a red tie.

"What is the meaning of this?!" Mugabe raged, then turned to Stewart. "What is going on?"

Stewart was speechless and he stared back at Lucky Man Jonathon as King, who until now had been seated twenty feet to the side on an ornate gilded chaise-lounge, stood up and walked over. He held a silenced Makarov pistol in his right hand and didn't falter as he approached. Both bodyguards stared at Desmond Lambadi, then back at King, unable to comprehend. Both men had started to reach for their pistols but had frozen as they took in the situation and in a fraction of a second, with King's weapon aimed at one of them, both men relaxed and walked away in unison.

"Now, lad. Don't do anything silly..." Stewart started but trailed off as King raised the weapon and shot Lucky Man Jonathon in the forehead. "Oh, fuck...!" Stewart gasped as King turned the pistol on Mamadou Cilla and fired once more. "Oh, shit, you've bloody gone and done it now, son..."

"President Desmond Lambadi has assumed charge of Burindi," announced King. "He will announce his manifesto tomorrow at mid-day and will hold free and democratic elections six months from today, and welcome legitimate opposition to government." He looked at Stewart and said, "He is willing to negotiate percentages and royalties in Burindi's mineral rights with the UK government, but quite rightfully, also welcomes tenders from other nations." King slipped the pistol into his waistband and walked over to Lucinda. "You've got a hell of a story here," he said. "Sell it right and Britain will be on the man's side."

"How do I do that?"

"You have a government source, don't you?" King smiled. "Just allude to it being in Britain's best interest, maybe even part of the plan all along. Britain doing the right thing for the people of Burindi."

"And that will take the heat off you, too."

"Couldn't hurt," King replied. He leaned in and kissed her cheek, savouring the softness of her skin, the warmth of her breath on his cheek. Then he pulled away and turned to Stewart who was still staring at the two bodies on the floor and trying to comprehend what had just transpired under his watch. "Come on, Boss. It's time to get the hell out of here."

"You kept me in the dark..." Stewart said quietly, still looking at the hole in Mugabe's forehead. The man's head was tilted awkwardly, his lifeless eyes fixed on the desk he so wanted to sit behind.

"Call it payback for the cyanide," King replied coldly. "This is the better way, and you know it."

"What made you do it?"

"Conscience. Living with my actions." King shrugged. "When I thought about it, I was left with two options. What was right, and what was easy. The easy path is nearly always the one not to take."

Stewart watched King walk out past the confused civil servants, the bodyguards unsure what to do and looking to Redwood and his team for guidance, not that any was forthcoming. Stewart followed, ignoring Lucinda Davenport, who had finished photographing the two corpses and was now focusing her attentions on Desmond Lambadi behind the expansive desk where he had once promised great things. He hoped for King's sake that the man would fulfil his once revered political manifesto and grant Britain a similar mineral deal to that of Mugabe's. The alternative did not bear thinking about. King would either return to the UK an anonymous hero, or the next target on Stewart's books. Only time would tell.

Author's Note

Hi - thanks for reading and the fact you made it this far hopefully means you enjoyed my story! If you did, then a review or rating on Amazon would be really appreciated.

I'm hard at work on another book but you can catch up with me on Facebook or on my Website.

I hope to entertain you again soon!

A P Bateman

Printed in Great Britain
by Amazon

21761188R00179